WHY ODIN DRINKS

BJØRN LARSSEN

JOSEPHTAILOR

ISBN:
978-90-829985-8-0 (e-book edition)
978-90-832304-0-5 (paperback edition)
978-90-832304-1-2 (hardcover edition)

Cover illustration: Ragrfisk
Cover and type design: Ray Grant for josephtailor

FIRST EDITION

For my boyfriend of ten years and counting.

CREATION

In the beginning, a God opened his eyes and sat up, utterly confused.

He tried to recall the evening before, which *must* have been a memorable occasion, but there was nothing. In fact, there didn't even seem to have been any evening. Or anything else. He couldn't have partied so hard that he had simply forgotten all the events preceding *now*. Especially as parties had not been invented yet. As baffling as it was, he seemed to only have just started existing.

The God blinked a few times, then rubbed his eyes. It didn't help. He was still seeing two reflections, one to his left, one to his right. Strangely, they looked different, although the bewildered expressions on their faces were so similar they could as well be brothers.

"Vili," said one.

"Vé," said the other.

"Oooh," said Odin, then cleared his throat. "Odin."

He had only just started existing and so many exciting

discoveries had already been made. His mouth, which was the hole between the moustache and the beard, could produce "words," and the word "Odin" was his "name". And "name" meant a sound one God produced to address another. There were, in fact, many words inside his mind, only they hadn't fallen out of his mouth as sounds. Those were called "thoughts". Odin, too stunned for *words*, needed to give some *thought* to having "thoughts".

The other Gods lifted themselves to their feet. Odin did as well. *Feet.*

"Vili."

"Vé."

Vili and Vé looked at him questioningly.

"Odin."

"Vili."

"Vé."

Odin ground his teeth. "Are you a bit stupid? Are we just going to stand here repeating our names?"

Vili and Vé looked at each other and shrugged. "What else is there to do?" asked Vili.

"Well…" Odin looked around. He did not understand what he was seeing with his "eyes." Above him was… something and they were surrounded by…things, between the things were…spaces, and those spaces led to…other spaces.

"Yes, 'well'?" urged Vé.

Odin's mind, unused to having thoughts, was temporarily blank.

"I'm bored," Vili complained. "Let's go and see what else there is."

"Where do we go?" Vé asked.

Vili looked at Odin. "Well?"

"There," said Odin, pointing in a random direction.

"Why not there?" Vé immediately countered, pointing behind Odin's back.

"Why do you ask if you know better?"

"No, Vé, let's go his way," Vili said, "and then everything will be his fault."

This, Odin's mind informed him, *was called "foreshadowing."*

His brothers were already marching in the direction Odin had chosen as he still grappled with the diverse meanings of "regret," "apprehension," and "ugh." He would never stop wondering about what would have happened had he pointed in any other random direction. This one "well," followed by the accompanying gesture, decided the fate of, well, everything. Right now though, he didn't even know how much of everything there was.

Once they'd reached some of it, it proved to be rather disappointing.

"This is all black," Vé, gesturing around, glared at Odin as if Odin had personally chosen this as exterior decor.

"Not all," said Vili, "because there is the blue and the yellow light that... ugh, don't look at it. It hurts."

"Sounds nice," Vé muttered.

"The black is land," Vili continued, undaunted. "The blue is sky. The yellow is sun."

Odin, puzzled, said nothing. If his brothers asked him to name the three things, he would have called them the same – land, sky, and sun. So, they knew, too. His mind was full of words waiting to be let out, but it seemed that things needed to exist first before he knew what word was connected to them. For instance, the black, slightly damp thing under his feet was...

Soil.

And what surrounded him were...

Possibilities.

The land consisted of soil, but it didn't have to. They could create so many things. Such as... Odin's mind was the opposite of empty, bursting with words that yelled at him, demanding to become – things. Mountain. Goat. Pancake. Peanut butter. Algebra. Centipede. Ship. Sheep. Grass.

"Oooh," said Vili. "I created grass! Isn't it nice?"

Grass, it turned out, consisted of many soft, green... grass-bits that stuck out of the soil. Odin bent to sniff it. It smelled of grass.

Vé picked some, chewed on it, then spat it out. "Wonderful," he said, his tone a perfect match for his grimace. "I have never seen anything more useful. I can't wait to see what you'll come up with next."

His words allowed Odin to discover the meaning of "the strong urge to punch someone in the throat."

"You can do things, too, Odin," encouraged Vili. "Create."

I have never *seen anything more useful.* If Vé was as old as Odin, that was a low bar to clear. Still... Odin frowned. Sofa. Cockroach. Porcupine. Chaise-longue. Wine... his mind sort of longingly hesitated, then sighed and moved on to "fire."

Fire would have some use, he could tell. But *what was it?*

"Look," Vili said, splashing water all around as he jumped in, then back out. "A stream!"

Odin let out a little surprised gasp. Now that the

stream began to be, Odin knew what it was. How come Vili came up with things and he didn't?

Vé put his finger in the stream, then licked it. "It's water," he announced. "It's moving. Where is it going, Vili?"

"Oh... I haven't thought about that yet. I think it goes somewhere, and then turns around and comes back..."

"Ha," said Vé. He flashed a grin Odin didn't like, then he pointed at the place where the stream seemed to come from and slowly raised his hand. The soil trembled under the brothers' feet as some of the land rose together with the gesture. Odin and Vili, open-mouthed, watched the soil and grass slip off grey, sharp edges. The beginning of the stream, lifted by the jagged rocks, headed up, up...

"Stop!" cried Odin. "You'll make a hole in the sun!"

"I'm not stupid," huffed Vé. "I know that." He pulled the middle of the "mountain" down, turning one "peak" into two, creating a gap for the sun to squeeze through. His forehead wrinkled in concentration as he added some smaller mountains around them, then took a sharp intake of breath. "That's not mine! Vili! What are you doing to my mountain? Stop ruining it!"

The grey rocks were now covered with soft green moss, which was like grass, only not at all. There was *also* actual grass, but orange instead of green. As the stream cascaded down, it no longer ran straight, but took several turns, foaming.

"Wait..."

The mountain reshaped itself somewhat, creating a waterfall.

"Vili!"

"Almost done," Vili said, then sprinkled the peaks of

5

the mountains with something white. Odin, trying to keep track of everything, felt something move between his toes. "Flowers," which were bits of colour that wasn't green, were sprouting around them as Vili's fingers moved behind his back.

"What is it that you think you're doing, young man?" Vé's face was a whole new colour – red, and, sure enough, a few red flowers popped up before Vili's head finally hung down.

"It just looked a bit grey," he said. "I thought I'd add some aesthetics."

"Do you know where you can shove your aesthetics?!"

"Stop quarrelling!" Odin boomed. "We have a lot of soil. Let's not ruin it all with…aesthetics. We can do a lot of other things with it. Use your imagination!" He didn't seem to have any, but they didn't need to know that.

"But I like flowers," Vili muttered.

"And I like mountains," said Vé.

"And I like truffles," Odin said. *Please don't ask.* "That doesn't mean we should just turn around and cover everything with them."

"Why not? We're Gods," reminded Vili.

"Imagine that one day someone will ask 'what did the Gods do when they first appeared on…'" Odin looked around, expecting a word to appear in his mind. It didn't. "On here. And we'll say, oh, you know, we created mountains, flowers, and aesthetics. Then we ran out of ideas. Who's going to take us seriously? Think about what's important."

"I don't know what's important," Vili said.

"Neither do I," Odin said reluctantly, "but I'm pretty sure it's not flowers…"

"This," said Vé, pointing. "We came from it and we're important. So it must be even more important."

The brothers' eyes wandered up, up, up... Odin took a few steps back. He still couldn't see the top of the...

"I think it's a tree," he said, his voice a bit shaky. "We have to make it smaller, or the sun will be in trouble."

Vé gestured.

Nothing happened.

"See," Odin said, "it's not a mountain. You have to do it differently. I'm going to show you." Somehow, although he wouldn't have been able to explain, Odin simply knew how to make things smaller. He raised his hands, then lowered them, demonstrating.

His brow furrowed. His hands moved up, down, to the sides, folded into fists.

"Yes?" Vé asked sweetly.

"Shrink!" Odin boomed, taking another step back. He still couldn't see the tip of the tree and they couldn't afford to lose the sun just like that. They had responsibilities. "Shrink, you, you...tree! I command you!"

"I don't like it," said Vili, shaking his head. He too took a few steps back, then tripped on the tree's... foot... tentacle... root. He fell back with a yelp and hit his head on another root. "My head is broken!" he cried. "I have a pain!"

Odin and Vé dropped to their knees. Odin didn't know what he was supposed to do, so he settled for inventing soothing noises, then absentmindedly producing them. *Pain.* There was something strangely alluring about it. He didn't know what pain was, not yet, though Vili's groans and grimaces suggested that he shouldn't hurry to find out. But there was more!

Blood.

7

Inside Vili's head, and therefore possibly inside all of their heads, was blood. It was a red, thick liquid that now stained Vili's hair. Odin couldn't resist touching it and Vili cried out in protest, then again, when Vé did the same. Odin made a few more soothing noises, then sniffed his fingers, wishing he could lick them without his brothers noticing. In silent hope he allowed his gaze to wander towards Vé so slowly that it would have remained unnoticed, had Vé's gaze not been moving towards Odin so slowly it would have remained unnoticed if their eyes hadn't met.

"Pain hurts," Vili complained. His brothers ignored him.

Odin didn't need to ask Vé to know that both of them felt the same way. They wanted to understand more about pain and blood. Obviously not by harming Vili further, especially not on purpose, which they would absolutely never do, just... say... in some other, theoretical way... Odin moved the corners of his mouth up in what he felt was a reassuring smile. He slightly winced when Vé bared his teeth before rapidly refolding his face into a slightly ashamed, friendly expression.

"We can't have been created by a tree," said Vili, massaging the back of his head. The pain didn't seem to last long. "Trees don't create Gods."

How do you know? Odin wanted to ask, but... he also knew it was true. Indeed, trees didn't create much at all. It simply wasn't their forte. They were also not supposed to be this tall. Yet here it was, the tree that proved that he didn't know all that much about trees. *What are trees for?* he asked his mind. *Ladybug,* his mind answered, *baguette, laptop.*

He tried to break a bit off and failed. Vé bit one of

the roots and grimaced. Vili licked another, then spat, muttering something. That, Odin's mind informed him, would become "cursing" soon, once they had found out how to do it properly.

The expressions on the brothers' faces were identical. All three equally disliked the tree, feared it, and wanted it to explain itself. It didn't listen to them, which was both irritating and somewhat impressive. They were, after all, *Gods*. Their powers were so immense they didn't even know how very immense they were yet. The idea that they, and the soil and sky and whatnot, had been created by some stupid tree was laughable. If, theoretically, there happened to be a giant named Ymir, whose blood created the springs, flesh – the soil, bones – mountains, and Gods' ancestors had strolled out of his armpits... now, *that* would have made sense. An enormous tree that wouldn't follow their orders didn't.

"It's a very ugly tree," said Vili. "Very un-aesthetic."

"Absolutely," agreed Odin, consumed by curiosity. He couldn't wait to investigate the tree once his brothers had stopped paying attention. "And useless, I tell you, useless."

"What an awful place," muttered Vé. "I wouldn't want to be here even if there was nowhere else to be." A little sigh escaped his lips.

Huffing in disgust, they strolled away towards nothing in particular, since they hadn't created more interesting vistas to admire yet. As grass unfolded in front of them, Vili absentmindedly waved his hand, distributing flowers here and there. Even the flowers seemed slightly discouraged, though. Vé sighed, his shoulders sloped as they walked. From the distance, the useless if powerful tree seemed much smaller. Now that they could finally see all of it at once, an idea lit up Odin's mind.

"Stop walking," he uttered, "and remain at a safe distance. There is no need to panic. You don't need to be afraid of my powers. I'm going to create something…"

Both his brothers inhaled sharply when another tree popped up in front of them. It was an exact copy of the unsettling one, only so much smaller that they could see all of it without needing to step back. It also responded to Odin's commands, shrinking and growing as he moved his hands up and down. "This," Odin said, puffing up his chest in preparation for admiration, "is a proper tree. It's called 'ash.'"

"It's as useless as that one there," shrugged Vé. A somewhat different one appeared next to the ash. "Mine is called 'elm.'"

"It's like you don't think about aesthetics at all," sighed Vili. His tree was thinner, the trunk and branches white. Odin's mouth opened in surprise and, he had to reluctantly admit, respect. An extra tree was his idea, but Vé and Vili were changing things.

As Vili pranced around producing trees of all varieties, Odin's gaze moved between the elm and the ash. Vé's elm was somewhat taller than the ash and Odin had to restrain his urge to stretch the ash further. They already had one tree threatening to scratch the sun. It wasn't as if the trees were even useful for anything. Size was of no importance and Vé could have a bigger one if he wanted. Odin had only created the obedient ash to show off. He was immediately outdone and his mood kept worsening with each new tree.

"This is called birch," Vili pointed. "And this one is an oak. And this is a chestnut. You can make them any colour, shape, and size you want! And this – that's not mine!"

Vé grinned. "Mine will attack you. Roar."

"Why would it do that, and how? It doesn't even have leaves, only those... needles?"

"Exactly. They will prick you. And there are also cones that will fall on your head."

"But why?" Vili groaned.

Vé's smirk was his only answer.

Vili's lower lip quivered. Odin's didn't. He turned away, ashamed and slightly afraid of how tempted he was to produce some more blood by using pain on the creator of attacking needles. Turning away from Vé's cone-throwing needle-trees, Odin waved his hand seemingly at random, creating stunning flowers that overshadowed all of Vili's creations. (Partly, although he'd never admit it since size wasn't important, by being taller.) They also had thorns that could draw blood. Vé's, for instance, especially if his face continued to look like that.

"Who do you think created the soil and the sky and the sun?" Vili asked.

"Nobody," Vé said. "They were just here."

"But before they were here?"

Vé sighed. "Before they were here, they weren't here."

"But now they are and we are, too, even though we weren't. I was just thinking that maybe someone created us and that tree and the sky and..."

"Stop thinking and add some streams," interrupted Odin. "Or flowers." Vili's thoughts led to a place Odin wasn't ready to visit, one that might have contained a God of Gods, and the stubborn tree was bad enough.

Vili sighed. The group of trees and flowers of

11

different provenances parted. A stream appeared, pretty and clear, until it widened and deepened. Rocks appeared on its sides, interspersed with taller grass. The water moved faster, louder, foaming. It seemed angry.

"That's all wrong," Vili groaned. "I'm losing my powers!"

"You're not, don't worry. I'm simply helping you, like you've helped me with *my* mountains. This, brothers, is a 'river'," said Vé.

"But it's not pretty," said Vili. "My streams..."

"You think small, Vili, I think big." Vé gestured around the empty blackness of the soil that seemed to stretch endlessly in all directions. "Look at all that. Size matters," he added, demonstratively looking first at the ash, then the elm. Then at Odin.

The elm was *just* a bit taller than the ash. Vé was *just* a bit taller than Odin. The word "technique," which tried to pop up, had no chance.

Odin's first instinct was to create an even bigger river, one that would make Vé's look like a particularly small stream. Which would cause Vé to produce another, *even* bigger one. If Odin were to create a terrier, Vé would create a pit bull terrier. Which Odin could counter with a wolf. After which... what was bigger than wolves? This must have been how the enormous tree happened. Some other Gods walked around, creating trees bigger and bigger, until one turned out to be so big that... that...

That nothing could have been bigger.

Odin simply needed to create the biggest *everything* in order to win. First, though, he had to distract his brothers for as long as it took to come up with a way to do that. And to figure out what a pit bull terrier even was.

A revelation knocked rather than struck. It was, indeed, very distracting. For Odin.

"I'm hungry," he said.

"I'm thirsty," said Vili. He looked surprised.

"I'm cold." Vé's smug grin fell off his face, replaced with a scowl. "What do we do now?"

Odin was not happy. Now that his brothers had so generously shared two new words with him, he was forced to understand their meanings. He would have preferred to learn them at some other time. Preferably when he was not cold, not hungry, and not thirsty.

"My stream," said Vili and pointed towards his earlier creation. "You can stop being thirsty with it. Not like with your...*river.*" He dropped to his knees and dunked his face in the cold water. "*Bllrbpl,*" he judged, water pouring from his hair and beard. "I'm even more cold now, but not thirsty. It works."

As Odin attempted to hold his hair and beard out of the water with both hands, regretting he didn't have a third one to lean on, Vé muttered something that ended with a triumphant "ha!"

"What is that?" Vili asked. "It looks awful."

"Who cares what it looks like? It's useful. It's good for you. It's celery. When you put it in your mouth, you stop being hungry." To demonstrate, Vé bit of a chunk of the soil-stained, misshapen thing. His eyes popped out and jaw stopped moving, face turning red. Odin and Vili took a careful step away when Vé attempted to hand them the remaining part. "It's gweat," he mumbled, swallowed loudly, and dropped to his knees to drink some water. "Wonderful," he added when he'd finished spitting. "You *must* try it." And, just like that, the first threat had been uttered, the first meal as vile as everything else Vé created.

He'd eat rocks before celery, Odin decided, then sighed quietly. As difficult as it was to believe, the rocks were *even* more inedible. Which meant remaining hungry.

Vili, his face slightly green, turned the celery in his hands. His eyes rose and met Odin's. Vé stared as well; Vili's gaze – pleading, Vé's – challenging. Odin had to come up with something better than a larger celery. Something that would show his brothers their place. A smash hit that would change everything. One that would satisfy the cold, the thirst, and the hunger all at once. Combining food, drink, attire…

The creation produced a questioning sound. Odin didn't, but only because he'd temporarily forgotten how to breathe.

"What's this?" Vili asked.

The creature seemed half-resigned to its fate of existing, half-curious as to the answer.

Odin's baffled mind feverishly searched for the right word. "It's a…cow," he said, snapping his fingers, relieved. "You can drink from it."

The cow seemed alarmed.

"Does it have a name?" asked Vé.

"Audhumla," said Vili. "It looks like an Audhumla to me."

"Oh, does it? Who created it? Hint, it was I! I declare it 'Odin's Cow.'"

"Then this is 'Vé's River.'" Vé's hands were already folding into fists. "And you can't use it."

"It's useless anyway!"

"Do you know what else is useless? Hint, it is—"

"Stop fighting," pleaded Vili. "Let's just share everything."

Odin's eyes met Vé's. *Over your dead body*, they seemed to say. Odin filed "dead body" onto his list of things to figure out, right after a "pit bull terrier." "Fine, then," he sighed. "Audhumla."

"So...what exactly is it, brother?" Vili asked. "Tell us more about our cow Audhumla. How does it make us not cold?"

"Well," Odin said, "well. I say. Well."

Predictably, Vé sneered.

"She makes a drink called milk, so we're not thirsty. Then you take her skin and wrap yourself in it, and what falls from the inside is meat, which we eat."

Audhumla's eyes widened. She took a careful step back, clumsy on her four legs, pulled down by something like a giant growth with fingers sticking out of it.

"We don't do it all at once," Odin quickly added. "In fact, not anytime soon at all. Ha, ha."

Audhumla shook her head and produced a sound best described as "moo," which made the brothers wince.

"Does she have blood inside?" Vé asked. Audhumla attempted to raise an eyebrow. Vili succeeded in doing it. Odin bit his lip.

Under the weight of both his brothers' and Audhumla's stares, he already began to feel warmer, to the point where he felt himself sweat a bit. This was not the warmth he was searching for, though. Something had gone wrong.

Odin had requested food, drink, and warmth, and knew he got all he asked for, but it wasn't supposed to have eyes and make sounds. Audhumla was definitely

15

more impressive than celery, but that wasn't a difficult feat. She didn't look excited about having her skin taken off to spill edible pieces all over the place. Vé's question was good as well. If she did have blood inside, would they swim in it in search for the meaty bits he couldn't even imagine?

Odin abruptly discovered nausea.

"So?" Vé urged. "What happens now?"

The nausea intensified. "Now we drink the milk," Odin croaked, then cleared his throat. "We leave the foo – *the meat* inside the skin, of course, not to upset poor Audhumla." He smiled pleasantly at the cow, who responded with a glare with a hint of curiosity to it.

"Aha?" said Vili.

"Milk is warm and tastes much better than *celery*." Expressing "disdain" was great fun.

"Ready when you are," said Vé and it turned out that disdain was only fun when Odin was the one expressing it.

Even Audhumla seemed carefully ready. Odin, however, wasn't.

He had to think fast. She had skin – so did Odin. Once he took the skin off – the cow's, not his own – and the pieces of food fell away, there would be no more milk to be had, because Audhumla would definitely be too upset to give them any. The only difference between the cow and his brothers, apart from all the other differences, was that the small dispensers between their legs looked useless. At least for milk production. Also, each of them only had one. Audhumla's massive growth had a *lot* of dispensers. Once he'd had time to invent numbers, he'd count them. What was important for now was that Audhumla clearly carried milk inside

16

the growth and it would soon pour out of the dispensers.

Or not.

Odin half-relaxed. The cow was very large and looked as apprehensive as he felt. If he got it wrong, there might not be a second attempt. Ever. Wishing he knew how to pray, he glanced at Vé. There was no way his bloodthirsty, rather than milk-thirsty, brother would fall for this one. "Lie down, Vili," Odin said. "You're going to drink milk."

"Why me? Why do I lie down?"

"Because you said you were thirsty."

"No, not at all anymore, I drank from the stream. I think Vé should do it."

"Why don't you do it, brother?" Vé's tone was simultaneously sweet, mocking, and threatening.

"Ah," said Odin, "because I will be – helping."

"Moo," said Audhumla.

"So, Vili, lie down under the cow."

"I really don't feel thirsty at all…"

"Oh, but you are," Odin said. "You are *so* thirsty you might fall on the tree again and your head will be in pain if you don't do what I tell you to…" He bit his tongue a blink too late. Both of his brothers took a sharp intake of breath. Odin just stopped breathing altogether. That… that was a Vé thing to say.

He couldn't explain where those words had come from. There was some sort of different heat inside him, slight aching or maybe pressure in his stomach, hairs on his skin – he hadn't noticed they existed – seemed to itch. *Anger.* Wide-eyed, silent, Vili placed himself under Audhumla as directed. Now the dispensers hung right over his face.

17

BJØRN LARSSEN

Vé crossed his arms over his chest and watched. The cow looked as if she'd like to do the same.

"Open your mouth," said Odin. "You, Vili, not you, Audhumla."

Vili opened his mouth.

Nothing happened.

"Whenever you're ready, Audhumla," said Odin. He was feeling very warm by now.

Some more nothing happened.

"Let it out! Let it out!" he cried.

"I think I don't want milk," said Vili, scrambling to stand up.

"Oh, but you *do*," Odin assured him, squatting on the other side of Audhumla, forcibly pushing Vili's head down. There was no protest. And no milk.

"Moo," the cow summarised.

Odin examined the dispensers closely. They just *hung* there. There seemed to be nothing to turn or push. Perhaps he needed to squeeze the whole growth at once, wrap his arms around it? He couldn't do it without falling on Vili. There must have been a way... Odin bit his lip in both fear and concentration, then poked one of the dispensers with his finger.

Nothing.

"Please," Odin whispered.

Vé snorted. Just once. Enough for Odin to see red. Since Audhumla wouldn't cooperate, he'd help her. If she continued to resist, he'd remove her skin and see how she'd like *that*.

With one hand, Odin held Vili down. Reminding himself he had a spare brother in case something didn't work, he grabbed at one of the dispensers and did it all at once – pulled, squeezed, pushed back, pulled again. Hard.

A few things happened simultaneously. The cow let out a sound that was both a low rumble and a high-pitched squeak. Vili rolled away with a "*grrgll!*" as white, thick liquid erupted into his mouth, nose, and eyes. Odin, shocked by his own success, fell on his backside. Vé grunted when Audhumla head-butted him before running away, Vili barely avoiding her hooves. The cow didn't go far though, and when Odin lifted himself up and his eyes met Audhumla's, both seemed to feel the same. Wary, but relieved.

The cow's milk container looked very swollen and heavy. If Odin had a heavy milk container hanging off his belly, he'd want to empty it as fast as possible. He thanked the Gods for only having a small, dangly dispenser of nothing, then remembered they were the Gods and Audhumla was "just" a cow.

"It's not that difficult," he said modestly, his voice shaking only a bit. "You just have to find the right technique. Wasn't it much better than celery, Vili?"

Vili, trying to rub the milk out of his eyes, sneezed and some of it came out of his nose. "It's very good," he said, then coughed. "But I'm completely full now. Couldn't stomach another drop."

"Vé?" Odin asked. "Some milk for you?"

"She attacked me," groaned his brother, massaging his belly. "She's dangerous. We need to defend ourselves."

"I guess that means you'll eat some more celery."

"And your cow will eat what? Gods?"

"It's destroying my flowers!" cried Vili. "And my grass! It's eating it!"

19

"Oh yes," Odin said triumphantly. "That's what I was going to say. As you can see, cows eat grass. They are completely, entirely..."

"When do we eat *her*?" Vé asked.

Audhumla stopped chewing.

"Right now," Odin said, slightly choking, the pleasant feeling gone, "she's only for drinking."

"I understand," said Vé, and glanced towards Audhumla, then positioned himself so that Odin stood between him and the cow. "But we do eat her eventually, right? Are there some bits we start with? Ones she wouldn't mind parting with? Because, brother, celery is right here, right now, and all bits of it are..." He swallowed. "Exactly as good."

Audhumla seemed to clear her throat. The whole everything, including Odin, stopped in wait to find out more. The milk container was out of the question. Horns and tail were out of the question. In fact... all of the cow was out of the question as long as she was listening, while also being so large.

"I can't think suddenly, I don't know," Odin said and dropped down rather than sat, massaging his temples. "I must be too hungry."

Slightly choking on celery – he now understood both "texture" and "taste," and celery combined the worst of both – Odin pondered over the nature of life and not-life. It seemed that things which were alive moved and ate other things. Except ones that didn't.

They *would* eventually eat the cow, once she briefly stopped paying attention, by simply removing her skin and catching everything that would fall out. For now, Audhumla was eating the grass, which didn't protest. The cow moved, so did his brothers and Odin himself, but then the stream moved as well, and the grass didn't. Neither, thankfully, did the celery. Were they alive or not? Was it possible to eat things that were still alive? Would the bits inside Audhumla continue to be alive once they started eating them? That seemed disturbing even before he began to wonder why, and how, milk existed in the first place. He'd created the cow but didn't understand her.

What *exactly* was the difference between being alive or not? The stream didn't seem to eat anything, at least not when Odin was watching. He assumed grass ate the soil, but maybe it was just standing on it the same way his brothers did? For support? But then, the three of them *were* alive... although, if celery was the only food available to him, Odin would starve to death very soon.

He threw away the object and decided to brave Audhumla. If Vili could do it, so could Odin. Probably.

"Good cow," he said. "I'm just here to drink some milk. Not going to eat any of you. I promise. Please don't stand on me." *Stop giving her ideas*, he berated himself.

Audhumla glared at him perfunctorily, then seemed to shrug. *Oh well*, he almost heard. *If you must.*

Telling himself that he was not afraid of getting killed, since he was very brave and knew no fear, Odin placed himself under Audhumla's dispensers. They were a bit too close to the cow's hind legs. And to his face. He'd have to invent something for that. Quickly. Otherwise Vili would come up with something pretty and Vé would make it bite.

Odin squeezed and pulled, much more gently than before, until some of the milk came out. The cow seemed to sigh in relief. Odin made a plan to also sigh with relief once he was done drinking the milk and no longer risked drowning, then his hands stopped moving. Starve to *death*? *Drowning*? Getting *killed* by the cow? He had discovered something again, but what was it? Those words shared some sort of power, or un-power. There was not being alive at all, being alive, and...

Suddenly afraid that Audhumla could hear his thoughts, Odin let go of the dispensers, crawled out, thanked the cow, and went on a stroll. He needed to be away from his brothers and think, think, *think*.

Why did he know Audhumla was a cow, her horns were horns, tail – a tail, but he didn't understand the dispensers and the milk-carrying growth? Would they eventually empty it completely and then milk-less Audhumla would be ready to eat and wear? Also, how were they supposed to eat her if she vehemently disagreed and probably outweighed all three brothers together?

He tasted some of the yellow flowers Audhumla munched on and wished he hadn't – they must have only been good for cows. It was difficult to say who celery was good for. Some sort of sticky liquid emerged from the flowers, staining his hands. It was not blood – it wasn't red. It was not milk either, nor was it water. If things that were alive had liquids inside of them, what did that say about the stream? Were there liquids inside the stupid tree? Were trees alive?

Odin flexed and stretched his excuse for imagination. He still intended to impress his brothers – while Audhumla made a *certain* impression, it was not the sort he had in mind. Trees... liquids... flowers that were edible only to cows... there had to be something that came out of the ground, was neither ash nor elm, and wasn't brutally disgusting. There had to be some sort of combination and he was now far away to try out a few things without witnesses.

"Oh, hello," he said lightly a while later, approaching his brothers, nonchalantly biting chunks off something that was neither a lemon nor a walnut. "I was wondering whether you would like to try something that isn't celery, Vili. Of course you, Vé, have no need for anything else..."

His words died out, a chunk of pear nearly clogging his throat forever. The glare Vé responded with felt like a punch in the stomach and Odin had never even been punched in the stomach so far. It was a joke, he wanted to protest, innocent and funny, ha ha... but that look Vé gave him brought the word "death" back into Odin's mind.

Odin needed to find a way to defend himself before Vé introduced him to death more closely.

Vili, who didn't notice anything, squealed in delight when Odin handed him an apple. He chewed on it a bit, and his eyes widened, mouth opened, a drop or two of juice trickling down his beard. A blink later some of the bushes around the river turned out to be various sorts of berries.

"I didn't do that," Vili said, bewildered, when a few of the bushes turned out to have sharp thorns that scratched his and Odin's hands, drawing blood. Same as Odin's flowers. Whether Vé noticed or came up with those himself was not important.

"Vé," Odin just said.

"I'm helping them defend themselves against attacks," Vé said. "You're welcome to them, I'm going to drink some milk."

"What attacks?" Odin asked, but Vé was already on his way towards Audhumla.

"I don't even know which juice is from the berries and which is from me," Vili complained, washed his hands and hissed. Odin did the same, then examined the stinging scratches, some of which were filling with blood again despite being freshly cleaned. He glanced at Audhumla. There couldn't be a way to remove her skin while she wasn't paying attention. His skin wasn't even removed and it hurt with pain. She would definitely notice. They would need to divert her attention very thoroughly and move very quickly. Fast or not, how did one remove a cow's skin at all? Or... or... a God's?

Odin wanted to cry with frustration. The pieces of knowledge that came to him were nothing but random words, the meanings of which he did not know ("anvil," his mind whispered helpfully). The actual inventions, cow aside, were mostly courtesy of Vili and Vé. Once they came up with something, Odin thought of ways to improve it or put things together, thus eventually creating pears, but not before coconuts (too hard) and kiwis (too hairy). The questions kept torturing him, another one appearing before he had a chance to fail at answering the previous one.

What Odin needed was the ability to understand, judge, gather the knowledge and experience. There must have been a word for that, but he'd probably need to find that ability first, which was infuriating. He bit on a plum, chewing, half-delighted at Vili's new creation, half-envious. Vili didn't need to produce lemons or avocados, both of which resulted in a lot of surprised spitting. Vili just got it right with his first attempt and didn't seem to even think about it.

24

Vé approached, grimacing, and picked one plum. He examined it as if it were the most un-aesthetic thing he had ever seen, then ate it. And another. And another. His stiff expression suggested that they were disgusting, but not enough to stop eating them.

"Ow!" Odin cried and spat something out. An irregular rock hid inside the plum.

"That's not me!"

"Of course not," Vé snorted. "Only you would create defenceless food. No needles, nothing. We could eat through all this and then what? Create more, eat that, create more, and spend our lives doing that?"

"So you're defending the food from us?!"

Vé didn't answer, but his grimace cracked, his expression turning into a smile that was not a smirk, at least not entirely. He was finally pleased by something that didn't draw blood. This should have been worrying. Odin, however, didn't feel like worrying right now. He was relaxed and full – no longer *hangry*, his mind suggested. Odin shrugged to himself, knowing this wasn't even a real word, not knowing how he knew that.

Vili was staring at nothing in particular, massaging his belly, smiling to himself. Whatever he was thinking about was not going to be important. Vé, however... Odin took another plum and, with his fingernails, split it in two. Sure enough, there was a rock inside it. *Defenceless food.* That suggested Vé intended for the food to be attacked and he couldn't have meant by the three Gods or Audhumla.

If music had been invented by now, it would have been ominous. As things were, the stream quietened. Sun seemed to shine less bright. Danger was in the air...

"What *is* that?!" Odin cried, waving his hands around

in terror, trying to drive away the attackers. Vé just screamed wordlessly, slapping and slamming the air, some of which was suddenly visible and silently spun, danced, slashed. Fast, ruthless, colourful chunks of Gods' inevitable doom. *This is called "Ragnarök,"* Odin's last thought said.

"Butterflies," said Vili, grinning.

Sorry, Odin's previous thought added sheepishly. *I really thought I was the last one. Carry on.*

Odin let his hands drop. The ragnaröks, also known as butterflies, did nothing to him. They dispersed in all directions, flapping in such a way that they remained in the air, sometimes shining various colours, sometimes turning invisible. One of them sat on Vili's hand, slow-flapping. A colourful shape, a thin line, colourful shape again. "Isn't it pretty?" Vili asked.

Vé extended his hand to poke the thing. The butterfly flew away before Vé's hand got near, and both Vé and Odin squealed in fear. "What are those for?" Vé demanded. "Will they poke our eyes out? Fly into our mouths?"

"They're just...pretty," Vili said, uncertain. "Completely harmless. Look, one is sitting on a flower. Now they are even prettier together."

"Lies," said Vé. "Air is – air. You can't even see it. There's no need for it to be pretty. Tell us the truth."

Vili blushed. "It just felt unfair that the soil was getting everything..."

"As long as you leave the sky alo – Odin. Just look at that."

"They're clouds," Vili said. He tried to look ashamed, but the glimmer in his eyes betrayed his delight. "Little fluffy clouds. They are made of flying water."

"They're moving," said Odin, staring at the little fluffy clouds.

"Water always moves," said Vé. "How did you make it fly?"

"More importantly, why?"

"Well," said Vili, fiddling with his own fingers, "it just felt unfair to water…"

"Next there will be Audhumlas all over the sky," sighed Vé. "And their milk will be big fluffy clouds."

"Oooh," said Vili.

"Don't you dare," said Vé.

Odin produced a sigh so deep that all of the soil seemed to join in, then frowned. Vé pointed out something important. The streams kept running away, the water always moving from nowhere to somewhere. Now it was even flying in the sky. It was bound to run out eventually, like the defenceless plums – wouldn't it be handy if the rocks inside turned out to produce new ones? – unless one of the brothers devoted his life to producing water. Which would then escape into the sky, where they couldn't reach it. Surely, it would be more practical to create water that didn't keep running away? Especially as he needed a drink after all the sweetness of the fruit.

"Audhumla," he said. "Please stay where you are. Vili, Vé, do please join Audhumla. Do not panic."

Vé crossed his arms on his chest. "What if I say no?"

Odin shrugged and created an irregular lake. One that just happened to exist, among other places, right where Vé was standing.

"Finally," Odin said, ignoring Vé's cries and burbles. "This water won't escape or fly in the sky. No need for it to defend itself either." All this thinking was exhausting and he didn't feel as though he was receiving enough accolades. As in, any at all.

The cow immediately began to drink. So did Odin and Vili, dropping to their knees. Vé emerged on the shore, wet, shivering, muttering something, and suddenly the soil bit into Odin's knees. "Gravel," Vé explained as Odin grunted and grumbled, wishing he'd learn how to curse already. "Very useful. Like rocks, but very small."

"What is it useful for?" Vili asked, lifting himself up and massaging his knees. The gravel left tracks on them, but at least this time there was no blood. "Oh, look! When the sun moves down my little fluffy clouds get even prettier!"

"The sun is going down," gasped Vé. "Why is that? Does it want to drink some water? Send more water in the sky, Vili!"

"It's moving away from his clouds," said Odin weakly. The sun was heading towards the soil, colouring the clouds shades of pink and red that were indeed pretty. A nice last view of their lives. He should have figured out that the sun was alive, too. Hardly a surprise when it kept moving. Now it was heading to drink water, eat soil... and maybe a God or three.

"Moo?" Audhumla asked.

"Stop," said Vili, his voice breaking. "Come back. My clouds need you."

"*We* need it, Vili. I command you, sun. Listen to us Gods," Vé said, his voice dropping to a whisper. "Please."

It was getting darker and colder now. As Vili pleaded for the fate of his fluffy clouds, Vé's and Odin's eyes met. That was it. The Gods had appeared under the Bad Tree That Wouldn't Listen, had strolled around creating mountains, streams, berries, butterflies, and one cow. Now the Bad Sun That Wouldn't Listen would end all that. This was going to be their legacy, left to...nobody.

"Our time is over," Odin said darkly, as seemed fitting. "Once the sun eats us, there will only be cold and darkness, and those will want to eat, too. Everything that moves must eat or get eaten, and we can't eat the sun. Goodbye, brothers. Goodbye, Audhumla. Vili, you made some pretty butterflies and clouds. Vé, you... eh..."

"My time is not over," Vé said. "I'll make something for the darkness and the cold to eat."

"Moo," encouraged Audhumla.

"It has to be hot and bright," Vé continued. "It has to eat something we have a lot of and nobody is eating yet. Something that's big and won't run away..." He snapped his fingers and a bunch of trees appeared. "Look at this!"

At first it didn't look extremely impressive, a lick of light that moved fast, like the butterflies. Only on trees. And it kept expanding, greedy, eating the trees, growing taller, wider, hotter, brighter... The heat and light lived, letting out crackling sounds that must have been laughter, turning the trees into clouds of smoke illuminated by the *fire* itself. And it grew. And grew.

Audhumla trumpeted in terror, a sound not dissimilar to the one Odin and Vili made... and so did Vé, who was supposed to know what he was doing. Vé's cry scared Odin more than the fire that grew.

And grew.

The heat was strange, wrong, dry. Odin's sweat seemed to immediately evaporate. He had to take a step back.

"Shrink!" Vé bellowed. "I command you!"

Fire paid no attention. Audhumla mooed again and

ran away, into the darkness. The light was more terrifying.

The Stupid Useless Tree and the sun didn't listen to the Gods' commands either, but they were already here when the brothers showed up. Gods' inventions, so far, did as instructed. Not this time. The fire just consumed, flames shooting higher and higher. The heat became unbearable, forcing the Gods to move away. It was the same as with Audhumla, Odin realised. He'd wanted food, drink, warmth all at once, and got it. Vé wanted light and heat that would be so dangerous that it could defend itself. It was doing all those things so well, especially the defending, that the brothers couldn't even approach it anymore. It ate, as intended, and provided light and heat, as intended. Much, much more than necessary.

"Make it stop!" Vé yelled. "Someone help me! Go away! I command you!"

The fire was eating the trees, Odin thought, stepping away further, and now something should eat the fire. Darkness and cold should be eating it, but they couldn't, being eaten themselves, the fire's greed seemingly infinite. He coughed, then again – the fire was eating air too. There was hardly anything left that he could think of until his foot landed in the shallow water of the lake he had created earlier...

The fire hissed in protest, a furious sound as Odin caused Vili's fluffy water to fall from the sky down into the air, heading towards the soil, eating the fire. The heat and light were gone now, but he couldn't stop, his angst pushing for more and more and more, until a sober thought reminded him that they would eventually run out of water.

Odin stopped, breathing heavily, coughing, inhaling something that wasn't quite smoke but whatever it was that fire and water produced when they met. Everything was now pitch black, wet, and freezing cold. Vé had caused destruction, then Odin caused the destruction of destruction.

"That wasn't too bad," he coughed. "Let's do a fire again, but not so much of it. A small tree, and just one. Then, when the fire eats it, we'll make another one, and then another, and then..."

"No," Vili interrupted. "We'll...never have time...to make...anything else again." His teeth made a curious sound, a bit like unimpressive clanging. Clattering, Odin decided, subject to change. "Let's make a few... very big trees that d-d-drop bits, and then we put those bits in our small fire. Or we'll have no soil left, only stinking bits of small trees, when the d-d-dark and cold end."

"If they ever do," Vé muttered.

Now that Vili had come up with the idea, it seemed to be the only sensible thing. Odin wasn't surprised to discover that Vili's version of fire was pretty. Even its crackling sounded inviting, rather than horrifying; the flames no longer roared with fury. It was warm, but not burning hot, unless you were bits of trees.

Odin forced himself to thank Vé for inventing fire. Vé, sounding just as excited, thanked Odin for inventing rain. Both turned to thank Vili for making it pretty and found out that at some point he had broken.

"What's wrong?!" cried Odin. "What have you done to him?"

"Why me? Maybe it was you?" Vé's mouth opened and a strange, long *oooooaaaahhh* sound came out. "Do you know," he said, his voice weird, strangled, "I feel very...tired. I need to break."

"No," pleaded Odin, terrified, "don't leave me alone!"

It was too late. Just like Vili, Vé fell to his side. A blink later, a strange sound came out from his mouth. It sounded like...*sawing wood*, Odin's mind suggested, which was stupid, because no such thing as "sawing" existed. At least he knew wood. Wood was the thing he would put in the fire soon... once he got some rest...

The same strange, loud *oooaaahhh* sound nearly tore his face into two, causing his jaw to protest. A yawn meant that Odin's body wanted to fall and saw with his mouth. Recover.

Once the dark and cold went away, Odin promised himself before the recovering swept him away that he would become wise enough to understand all of this. *Sleep.* That was... the thing... he... was...

...SITTING.

Not on the soil or on a rock, but on a...thing. His body was wrapped in another thing, and he held a long stick in his hand. Under his feet was something that was not soil... he gasped. His feet were covered in some of Audhumla. Only she no longer made sounds and there would definitely be no more milk.

This wasn't real. Everything else could have been, but he knew Audhumla too well. She was not the type to generously part with some of her skin so that it could wrap itself around Odin's feet. He was experiencing something that didn't exist. Unless...it was the soil, sky, and fires that didn't exist, and this here was the exis-tence that really existed?

He needed to find out – somehow.

Resting on the stick, Odin took a few careful steps, Audhumla's disapproval radiating from his feet. He approached a hole in the thing that surrounded him, for instead of all the soil there was now a thing around him, one with holes. Out of this hole he could see a lot of everything. And there was so much of it now! Trees, flowers, bushes, alive things that skipped around or jumped around or ran around or ate each other or did something he didn't know how to name, but it seemed quite personal. The things were of different shapes, colours, and sizes. What baffled him more than anything was that some of them looked like Gods. And there were many more than three. It was obvious this existence was the non-existent existence, unlike the other, existing existence, in which he was not wearing Audhumla on his feet.

Odin knew none of this was real, but still felt the bite of anger mixed with apprehension. There was no need for more than three Gods. In fact, now that he was thinking about it... one seemed like a good number; best, in fact. A God that was wise – a thinker. One that understood everything had to eat something. That not everything should draw blood and not everything needed to be pretty. That the defences of berries and even fire had to be broken somehow, or the berries and fire would take over the entire soil. There was only space for *one* thing that couldn't be eaten, unless it wanted to, which it probably wouldn't.

That would be Odin.

Those other Gods he could see through his looking-hole seemed very varied. Smaller, larger, differently coloured, dressed, even shaped... The not-real Odin shook his head. They couldn't all be Gods. Vili alone, if unsupervised, would cover the entire soil in flowers and butterflies. If all those started creating all over the place, nothing sensible would ever get done. They should be... not quite Gods. There should be someone who would have control over them.

That would be Odin.

He withdrew back to the construction he had sat on earlier and only now noticed that his brothers were nowhere to be seen in this...different reality with not-quite-Gods that occurred during recovery from doing things. Those were too many words. Sleep and dream – there we go. Only a thinker like Odin could make things so simple. *Only* Odin.

There was no way around it. Vili kept creating. Vé kept destroying. Neither of those things should stop, yet, at the same time, they had to stop. No – they had to be thought about, thought Odin, thoughtfully leaning forward and supporting himself with his stick, lost in his thoughts, thinking like the thinker that he was.

Once they were fully recovered, they should sit together. Vili and Vé would listen carefully as Odin, the thinker... the Thinker, actually... would tell them what they were and weren't allowed to do. No matter what Vé thought, gravel was *not* useful. Neither were butterflies. No, Odin hadn't invented fire, although he definitely could have if he'd tried. He hadn't invented flying water either. But he guessed one would destroy the other before the fire destroyed everything.

Unfortunately, it was Vili who had both created the clouds and turned the fire into something useful.

Even in his dream-sleep Odin continued to think and worry. His brothers simply threw around streams, mountains, celery, multiplying them randomly. When Odin had come up with apples, Vili and Vé produced hundreds of different fruits. Odin placed more water on the ground, but Vili sent it into the sky. Which wouldn't be so much of a problem, had they not been doing it in rather limited space. While dead things, like mountains and possibly streams – Odin couldn't make up his mind on those – needed the Gods' help, Audhumlas and trees should multiply themselves without the Gods' involvement. Just not too much. Especially not fire.

On the other hand, since there were only three of them, no matter what the dream-sleep showed him, why bother? They could find a nice spot, which would be easy, as all spots were identical until they got to them. Somewhere far away from the Rude Tree That Wouldn't Listen. Vili would make the place aesthetically pleasing, filling it with butterflies and flowers. Surely, Vé could be persuaded that since nothing was attacking anything else, needles and thorns were unnecessary. He could always play with his fire at a safe distance. The rest of the everything could do whatever it wanted. Which was nothing, because soil was even less creative than Odin.

The vision was tempting, but unrealistic. Vili couldn't be stopped and Vé couldn't be reasoned with. Once they decided on that spot, Vili would make it too pretty to fit any food, then Vé would add thorns to Vili's flowers, and surround the streams with gravel. They would need to keep moving and moving around the soil. No wonder he could see so much of everything when looking through the looking-hole. It looked like so much work that just the thought made Odin feel less recovered than he was so far. Maybe they should create some less creative but productive Gods to help with all that...

On his construction, Odin leaned back, holding on to his stick, massaging his temples with his other hand. There had to be multiplying, but not too much. There needed to be limits on all the multiplying. Everything had to eat something else. So much work. So much thinking–

"Odin! Odin! Odin!"

The dream broke.

ODIN'S NOSE WAS ITCHING. Bright light penetrated his eyelids. With a grunt-gasp he sat up to discover that the land had returned the sun. Strangely though, it had sent the sun to the other side of the endless soil. Odin rubbed his eyes, which seemed to be the right thing to do. The fire was gone, replaced with a pile of black pieces and dust that used to be wood and now weren't anymore.

"Odin!" continued Vili. "Odin!"

"I can hear you. What is it?"

"The sun is back! The sun is back!"

Odin sighed, rolling his eyes, although it wasn't that long ago – specifically, a blink before the sleep ended – that he couldn't say for sure either whether the sun would return. "It is called 'a day'," he explained, letting his thoughts spill out of his mouth, listening to himself in surprise. "It's for doing things. When it's dark, that's 'night'. It's for not doing things. Night is for dream-sleep. Even Audhumla knows that. Where is Vé?"

"I don't know. But I was thinking..."

Doubtful, Odin thought, but he kept it to himself. Vili might be useful against Vé. Not that there would be need to do anything against Vé, as long as he'd listen to the voice of reason...

"...that you said Audhumla is to be eaten and then we can also wear her. I tried to bite off just a small bit of her tail and she kicked me in the stomach. She's very nasty, do you know? We need to create small edible Audhumlas and ones to wrap ourselves in, because we can't walk around and carry a fire, and I am still cold."

Rolling his eyes was a strangely fulfilling thing to do and Odin decided to do it more often. "Audhumla is made of food that is wrapped in her skin, and she keeps the milk inside all that. Once you eat her, there will be no milk, and once you take her skin off, she will fall apart."

"That would be awful," Vili breathed. "How do you know that?"

Odin blinked in surprise. "You don't?"

"It's your cow. You made her. Oooh... or do you know everything about everything?"

"Uhh... yes, of course. I was thinking butterflies should be easy to eat. If they just sit on you when you want to..."

"No, they are not for eating. Just to look nice," Vili said.

"And what do *they* eat?"

"Flower powder."

"Flowers have powder?"

"You don't know that?"

"Ah, yes, of course," Odin answered, feeling his face getting warmer. "I forgot for just a blink. Well, no harm done, I suppose. As long as there won't be any more of all those."

"So," Vili said, looking at the remains of the fire,

"speaking of that. While you were asleep, I came up with something."

Odin stopped breathing. In no way could this be good news.

"It's a lot of work, creating everything one by one. And there's all this space."

"Yes, exactly! I was going to say that. Audhumla, for instance—"

"So," said Vili, avoiding Odin's gaze, "I had this idea that maybe they could create themselves."

"Ah, yes," said Odin. "I was thinking the... same..." Vili's expression, together with the careful admiration of his steepled fingers, suggested the worst. "Butterflies?!"

"Well, maybe, who knows with those things, it's all complicated, but as I was saying, small Audhumlas..."

Odin gasped, then looked around. "Where are they?" *Small.* "How small are they? *What* are they?"

"Warm," Vili mumbled, "and with this..." He pointed at his hairy chest. "But much more of it, so they're warm too, until we take their skins off. And hair. Then the food will fall out and there is no milk, so no problem."

Odin failed to imagine small, hairy, milk-less Audhumlas. "Where are they?"

"Well," said Vili, leaning forward to take a very close look at the remains of the fire, "would you believe that? It's still hot!"

"Where are they?"

"There's this problem..."

"Where. Are. They."

"Don't be angry."

Not once in the history of the Universe, although so far that did not mean a lot, had those words actually calmed anybody. If Odin had created Frigg yet, she would have been able to use her future-telling skills to exclusively reveal that this would never change.

Odin closed his eyes, swallowed a few times, considered counting to ten, then remembered he didn't know how to do it. "Tell me."

"It's difficult to say."

"Then show me!"

"If you insist..."

"Just do it alreaaaaahhh!!!"

A furry creature shot away from them faster than Odin could imagine anything moving. It rubbed against his ankle, a strange, soft feeling. No blood. The creature was so thoroughly gone that it could have as well been yet another dream.

What if sleep and dream were not the same thing...?

"They keep doing this," Vili mumbled. "Both the boy bunny..."

Odin squealed as a blur flew past.

"...and the girl rabbit..."

This grey ball of fluff hit Odin in the belly, bounced, then also departed, although somewhat slower. It headed towards the part of the forest the fire had not eaten, then disappeared there. It had big, fluffy ears instead of horns – sensibly – and was, indeed, all covered in fur.

It was also gone, same as all the previous ones. And Audhumla herself.

"I was thinking maybe the boy should be the rabbit," said Vili, "and the girl – bunny... are you feeling well?"

Odin said nothing, massaging his stomach.

"I wanted to talk to them," Vili continued, "and explain that we are friends and have no bad intentions, but they won't wait. It's like they can sense..."

"I found a way to stop them," said Vé, and both brothers winced. "Show me how you make bunny rabbits, Vili, I missed it."

"Don't encourage him," Odin groaned – too late. More furry bunny rabbits shot away, heading towards the trees... but one of them didn't make it.

A cry, a protest, a moan. A growl, a grunt. Cracking, slurping, munching. Shiny eyes as the latest creature glared at them, its elongated mouth dripping with blood. Almost immediately, it lost interest in the brothers, returning to what it was doing. Which was eating the bunny rabbit without even taking the skin off to wear it. Understandably, as the silver-grey creature already had its own hairy skin.

It was also terrifying.

Vé crossed his arms across his chest, looking very pleased with himself. "Vili's idea was very good," he said. "There are now boy wolves and girl wolves, and you need both to produce a new one. When bunny rabbits get to producing new ones, more wolves will produce themselves, so we will never have too many bunny rabbits. And of course if we discover there are too many wol—"

The wolf looked at him and let out a low, menacing snarl. Its teeth, chin, even nose dripped with blood. What little was left of the bunny rabbit did not move or make a sound.

Odin stopped breathing. Vé's voice died out. He took a step back, stumbling, raising his hands as if trying to push the wolf away. "You *like* me," he said, visibly trembling. "I– I created you. Listen to me. You only eat bunny rabbits. Not Gods."

"And not Audhumla," added Vili, his voice coming from behind Odin.

The wolf's guttural growl continued, a low wave of warning. It took a step towards the Gods, then another, still snarling. Vé let out something like a sob.

Odin suddenly remembered his dream. Nothing would ever eat him. Especially not some wolf.

"Get out of here!" he boomed.

The growl stopped, cut short. The wolf blinked before turning away and shooting back into the forest – in exactly the same direction the bunny rabbits had. A long, high tone arrived – a howl, it was called – and another one sounded in response from somewhere else.

"How many have you created?" Odin asked.

"F-four..."

Odin sighed in relief.

"...hundred," Vé finished weakly. "To begin with. But don't worry, they ran away in various directions! So there are only some left here and the rest are just all over the place. If we're lucky, we'll never see one again."

Odin couldn't even count to ten and here was Vé, creating four hundred menacing howler-growlers that turned bunny rabbits, and possibly Gods, into...

His belly ached, stomach simultaneously cramping and suspiciously full, as Odin examined the remains of the bunny rabbit. It did not work as simply as he'd imagined. The hairy, grey skin, mostly discarded, still had the head attached to it. The head said nothing when Odin poked it. The pieces of food Odin expected inside were there indeed, sort of, protected by some sort of construction. One he could only compare to trees, if they were made of rocks, and also were planted inside animals.

Bones. What an ingenious construction. Of course, if it was just made of food and blood and skin, the bunny rabbit would just splosh around instead of running. Adding the bones holding the pieces together was quite a smart way for food to transport itself around. The bones were partially broken now, some bits of the bunny rabbit probably missing, eaten by the wolf. Odin couldn't tell what was still there and what wasn't. None of the remaining bits, however, looked appealing. All of them were sticky with thick, red blood, as was the skin and, now, Odin's hand.

Absentmindedly, he licked his fingers, then scowled. Blood seemed to be the drink equivalent of celery. Odin couldn't even wipe his hand on his clothes, since he hadn't created any yet. His stomach churned again, then even let out a sound. It felt full, but in some sort of wrong way. Odin tried to ignore it, gawking at his bloodstained hand. He did not want to think the thought that was forming.

When they got scratched by Vé's berry spikes there was blood on the skin.

Which meant...

That...

Gods weren't all that different from rabbits. Odin also had bones and bits and *blood* inside him, wrapped in skin. That made him walking food too, as the wolf had already indicated. Someday a very big wolf might appear, out of nowhere, and do exactly this: tear Odin's skin, spit out his head, and let his blood spill around. Vé's insistence that creatures needed to defend themselves made sense now–

Odin's stomach told him in very clear terms that he had to immediately stop thinking, grab his backside, trot into the woods, and remain there for a short while.

WHEN HE EMERGED, feeling both relieved and awkward, his brothers were missing as well, possibly doing what he had just done. Despite the lake's coldness, he went straight into the water to cleanse himself. He was glad to get rid of the feeling of wrong fullness. It ranked high on the list of the most unpleasant things he had so far experienced. Most probably not as unpleasant as death, although Odin couldn't tell for sure due to not having tried being dead yet. Apparently food that he placed in his stomach to stop being full underwent a transformation. Its effects were not something Odin wanted to carry inside. Or smell.

Except now that the wrong fullness disappeared, he was hungry again.

When his brothers joined him in the lake, none of the three acknowledged the others. *We will not talk about it* hung in the air, so clear they could practically hear it, which was very handy, as they couldn't read yet. Odin got out of the water first, leaving Vili and Vé behind. While the wolf had left some pieces of food inside the bunny rabbit, there weren't enough for three.

Soaked and cold, Odin produced a small fire near the remains, then sat down to warm his back and examine the wolf's victim. The bunny rabbit looked nothing like Audhumla, although in its current state it was hard to say it with absolute certainty. How could the disgusting bits inside have been food? Odin picked something and held it with two fingers, grimacing. The thing was somehow simultaneously soft and hard, connected to other bits, and covered in blood. His mind, normally so impatient to throw up words, seemed unsure as to what he was holding. A lung? Heart? Stomach? The only thing those parts shared, apart from blood, was that he *really* didn't want to eat them.

Odin stood up to warm up his front, holding on to rabbit bits, his hands dripping with blood. This was *made* to be food. The wolf had eaten it. If Vili's creations worked like Odin's did, Vili couldn't have mistakenly created food that was good only for wolves, because at that moment they didn't exist yet. Perhaps the lungs, hearts, and all the other stomachs were a bit of an acquired taste? Unless the wolf ate everything there was to eat and those... those... his own stomach refused to contemplate them. He'd accidentally tasted some of the blood already and this was dripping with it.

Some parts of Odin started to feel too warm and he took a step back, still contemplating the "food." His foot landed on something wet, slippery, and disgusting. Odin screamed and jerked forward, only to abruptly stop before accidentally jumping into the fire. Where the bunny rabbit food had already fallen.

"What's going on?" asked Vé, approaching, shaking his head, scattering drops of water.

"It fell in the fire! We need rain!"

"Absolutely not! Just make the fire smaller. What fell in the fire?"

"Shrink, fire! Shrink! Vé, it doesn't listen and it's burning!"

"Take a deep breath," said Vé. "Not in the smoke. Spread the fire with a stick. Why are you covered in blood?"

"Later," said Odin, already following Vé's advice. The

flames had mostly died out, but the embers remained hot. The bunny rabbit parts were smoking, destroyed. There was nothing left to rescue. The sticky blood on Odin's hands attracted dirt and dried soil. He left Vé and his questions behind and returned to the lake to wash his hands.

Vili stood there, still dripping with water, staring at the lake with such intensity that Odin immediately felt a bit sick.

"What?"

"Ah, ahaha," said Vili and quickly retreated towards the fire.

Odin knelt in a spot mostly free from gravel. As he washed blood off his hands he also watched the colourful beings – fish – that moved in the water, looking as confused as he felt. Vili had done it again. More colourful, pretty creatures that apparently didn't even need to walk or breathe, just existed in the water as if that were perfectly normal. Had Vili thought of what they would eat? Gravel? Someone – that might actually be Odin – should eat the fish in return. They were moving and they had skin, so inside would be bones, blood, and those chunks of–

Odin's thoughts dispersed as he sniffed the air. There was more than just woodsmoke. There was, somehow, a hint of deliciousness. He hurried back to the fire, where he found Vé poking at the remains of the bunny rabbit, now completely brown, free from blood, and producing black smoke that smelled...appetising.

"Aha," said Vé, lifting some of the brown, smoking chunks out of the fire with two sticks. "Mine."

"Why yours?" Odin immediately countered,

searching for longer sticks and good arguments. "We're brothers. Shouldn't we share everything?"

"It's risky. You might get your fingers burnt. It might make you sick. I'm very brave to help you like that." Vé swallowed loudly.

"I created this bunny rabbit," protested Vili, "and I want those. As a keepsake."

"It's *very* hot," said Vé, dropping the piece he tried to touch, blowing at his fingers.

"That's how fire works," said Odin.

Vili said nothing. He just grabbed a piece and put it in his mouth. When his eyes popped out, light seemed to beam out of them. "It's howibwe," he said, reaching for more. Vé's stick smacked his hand.

"Stop that," Odin said, carefully dropping more hot, smoking remains on the grass. "There are more bits." He carefully picked one, burning his fingertips, bit half off and passed the rest to Vé. The burnt rabbit-food was black on one side and pink on the other, but it smelled or tasted like nothing they had eaten so far.

So, this was the *meat* Audhumla was practically bursting with. And there was so much of Audhumla. Odin suddenly found himself very concerned about the cow's whereabouts. Hopefully she didn't get lost. He'd miss her very much.

Vili, done with his small piece, hovered around them, radiating rather unattractive greed, as Vé and Odin exchanged bits that turned out to have different tastes. Odin sniffed one and handed it to Vé without a word.

"Here you go," said Vé, passing the darkened chunk to Vili.

In disbelief, Odin watched ecstasy appear on Vili's face as he chewed on liver, a part so foul even the wolf wouldn't touch it. Were they really brothers if one of them liked *liver*?

As always, the moment Odin's belly stopped complaining, his head started demanding answers. Fish swam in the water without breathing. He, a God, couldn't do that. How did the butterflies just – be in the air, when he couldn't? He was supposed to be the God here, yet some dumb butterflies laughed in his face. At least they had the decency to do that silently. And from a great distance. Come to think of it, butterflies generally seemed quiet.

"Vili?"

"Yes?"

"Do fish speak inside the water?"

A moment of silence followed.

"What?" Vé asked.

"Go look in the lake," Odin sighed. "So, Vili, do they?"

His brother shrugged. "We talk enough."

True, Odin thought, lifting himself to join Vé at the lake. If fish started talking, together with the butterflies, they would all have opinions and demands. Vé was staring intently into the water – a bit too intently. Odin was already dreading what he was going to see. It *had* to be a giant fish to end all smaller fish…

"SCREECH!" announced a new creature, flying into the air, its long, flat arms flopping. Half of Odin attempted to fall forward, face down into the lake, the other half more interested in dropping on his backside. As a result he landed sideways on the very useful gravel.

"Which of you made that one?!" he cried.

"Screech," creature answered from above.

"Why are there more air things now?!"

47

"Wait till you see what they do with fish," Vé muttered.

Odin pointed up at a dot in the sky. "Avoid it?"

Vé frowned. "Let me take care of that…"

"No! No making bigger flying air things to chase smaller air things! Wait, wait," Odin said in a very different tone. "Can you make one slowly?"

"How do I make one *slowly*?"

"I want to see how they go into the air. Then we will follow them."

Vé just blinked in confusion.

"I know what he means," said Vili and created a peacock. "Off you go, air thing, but slowly."

The peacock spread its feather tail.

"What?" said Odin flatly.

"They come out of his ass," said Vé, and a brief silence fell upon them. This was not a safe direction to go into after what had happened in the forest earlier in the day and how much washing it had required. "Is that how it goes in the air?"

"No, that's art," said Vili. "Show them, air thing!"

The peacock threw them a bored glance, collected its ass-feathers, then strutted towards the woods. A wolf's growl made the creature stop, then jump and flap its arms, just long and hard enough to land on a branch. The peacock made itself smugly comfortable. Now the wolf could growl as much as it wanted.

Odin and Vé were already running around, flapping their arms as fast and hard as they could.

"Stop!" Vili yelled. "Stop! You don't have the right arms!"

"My arms," said Vé between pants, "are perfect."

"They need to have the ass-feathers, but not on the

ass! You created that..." Vili looked in the sky. "That thing that's gone. It had feathers on its arms."

"Did it?" Vé asked, somewhat sheepishly.

"You don't know?" Odin asked, surprised. "How did you create it?"

Vé shrugged. "How do you create things? I thought it up."

"Yes, but what exactly did you think of?"

"Something that attacks from above... attacks fish, mostly fish."

"My poor fish," cried Vili.

"So it must come down eventually," continued Vé somewhat weakly. "When it gets hungry. It was too fast to take a closer look at its arms."

"Like my bunny rabbits," Vili nodded.

The same happened with Audhumla, Odin remembered. He had a general idea and then there was a cow...

"Where's Audhumla?" asked Vili. "I think I'd like to eat some of her now," he confessed in a whisper, looking around.

Odin's stomach seconded the motion. "Audhumla!" he bellowed. "Come to Daddy!"

A wolf's howl was his only response. The peacock jumped back down and paraded, presenting his ass-feathers proudly. Odin had to admit it was an unforgettable sight, colours and shapes that probably had no names yet, taking place for no reason other than that they could. "Art." Vili was getting better and better – and more self-confident. Still, Odin would bet he'd never thought of what the peacock would eat. "Will there be two of those to produce even more?" he asked, curious how the other one would be decorated.

"Like with everything," said Vili and another creature

appeared. The first one clucked and seemed to expand even wider. The other...didn't, shaking its unimpressive butt to no effect. Its eyes narrowed and it looked accusingly at the three Gods, trying to figure out which one was to blame.

"Now he knows you're the girl," Vili explained.

The girl peacock screeched and Vili hid behind Odin.

"She's missing the..." Vé started and paused. "The... wait for it..."

"Yes?"

"It's called comedic effect and you're ruining it. She's missing the ass-thetic."

Complete silence from Gods and peacocks ensued.

"This is where you laugh," huffed Vé. "It's called 'stand-up' and... never mind. So now there are those two and how does the next one... you know?"

"When they... when they do what they know they have to do... the new one has to appear."

"How?" asked Vé.

"I was thinking it would come out of her ass," Vili mumbled. "So that it could also be useful for something..."

The peacock ground the teeth she didn't have. She screeched, her feather-arms allowing her to lift herself into the air just enough to not quite be on the ground. When she dropped back down, seething with fury at possessing neither ass-thetics nor arms of sufficient flappiness, Odin briskly moved out of her way.

"It will be in a container!" Vili cried. "It will be in a nice round container! You won't even notice and it won't get all...squished!"

"That is the dumbest thing I've ever heard," Odin said to the peacock, withdrawing further as she headed for

Vili, and barely avoided tripping over something small and very loud. "Goodness me, what are those?!"

The new flappy arms tried to flap their arms, looked at each other with slight confusion, then raised an accusing gaze at Vé.

"This is a hen," said Vé. "This is a rooster. They can flap their arms as much as they want and they won't go into the air."

"That's not how flappy arms work…!"

"Quiet, Vili. Those we can catch and put in the fire."

The screeching roar the rooster answered with deafened Odin, and scared the girl peacock, and possibly all other randomly alive things and creatures in the everything so far. The hen just… sort of… clucked. "And," Vé added, unmoved, "the hen will also produce small hens in containers that come out of her ass. And we will eat them."

The hen clucked again, sounding a bit desperate, as the rooster attempted to grin. He too had a nicely decorated, container-free ass.

"That's so cruel!" Vili cried, watching the hen and rooster departing in as great a haste as they were capable of, followed by the girl peacock. The boy peacock spread his ass-thetic one more time, looking both smug and relieved, then turned to follow his container-producing companion. He didn't make it far before a wolf ended his triumphant strut.

The wolf didn't even bother with eating the peacock, just bit off his head. Here, the wolf seemed to say, you did not manage to jump on a tree this time, did you? No, in actual fact you did *not*. The headless peacock left behind, the wolf returned to the woods. His point had been made.

The Gods stood in complete silence, even Vé seeming too shocked to say anything, just watching the flappy-arms-that-couldn't-flap storming away.

The next thing that happened felt too personal to watch. Unfortunately, it was too brief for the Gods to modestly avert their gazes.

The hen stopped to cast one final glare at the brothers and the rooster...seized the opportunity. The hen barely had time to squawk in protest before he left her alone again. She lifted herself and shook some dust off. The rooster seemed as proud of himself now as the (currently dead) ass-strutting boy peacock used to be. The hen could finally cast her glare at the brothers before strolling away in a way that suggested all of that was planned.

"That was horrible," said Vili, his voice strangled.

"If she's going to push things out of her ass, they have to get in there somehow," said Vé. His shrug suggested he was the one who had planned it, but the shakiness in his voice betrayed his shock.

"It's not going to be her ass," said Odin weakly. "We all have asses and this could get confusing. She's going to have an...extra...not-ass to..." He ran out of words. "Well, she will not... anyway, you can stop holding on to yours! You know what comes out of them and it's not containers."

Containers. Only Vili could come up with an idea like that. Also, could Odin decide that the hen would have an extra non-ass for containers, or was it too late, or had the hen decided...? That was not possible. The hen didn't get to decide anything. Yet, somehow, Gods clearly didn't either.

Audhumla would not have containers, Odin knew

somehow, the little Audhumlas would just climb out of her non-ass. If someone had created Odin, he'd be thanking that someone for not having been given visual imagination... there was something wrong with that thought. The brothers were *creating* things – the peacock wasn't there until it got created, and then he was there. Vili had given it certain parameters, mostly related to flying slowly and looking pretty. The rest of the thing... filled itself in. The wolf killed the peacock, but not for eating, and that was even more confusing. However, it seemed to reveal something about Vé.

Odin felt his shoulders relax somewhat when he realised that otherwise they'd have to come up with every single bit separately. Breathing, jumping, liver, smell, number of legs, voices of fish and butterflies... They'd still be fighting about the first Audhumla's number of dispensers if that were the case. They were being helped.

By whom, though?

ODIN SILENTLY WATCHED his brothers placing various things in the embers of the fire to see what happened, starting with apples and celery, then continuing with rocks (Vili) and the dead peacock (Vé). When the colourful feathers caught fire, the stink turned out to be unbearable. Vili and Vé yelled at each other, Odin grabbed the peacock's feet and threw the whole thing in the lake. Whatever feathers were good for, it was neither eating, drinking, nor warmth. Who needed things that had completely no use apart from looking pretty? This nonsense needed to stop before Vili began to insist that his "art" had some sort of value, then demanded to be rewarded for it.

When the wolf bit off the peacock's head, blood poured out of the neck. Could that mean peacocks had skin under those feathers and, once the "art" was removed, the brothers would find meat? "Vili," Odin started, "are the peacocks for—"

Vé interrupted him, handing him a hot apple on a stick. "Did you see what that rooster did to the hen?"

Odin shivered.

"Do you think she liked it?"

"Who could like something like that?!"

"I think that could be done better." Vé's voice took a sort of dreamy tone and Odin felt something called goosebumps. He made a note to create a boy goose and girl goose sometime later, but the important thing was that Vé was clearly approaching *the* discovery.

Bunny rabbits, boys and girls, would produce more and more bunny rabbits. Those would be killed by boy and girl wolves. What about those? The first wolf, the one that gave them a look Odin didn't like in the slightest, made him believe they didn't need many more of those at all. Not even one more, much less four hundred "to begin with." Hopefully the bunny rabbits would produce lots of new bunny rabbits really fast to appease the wolves' appetites. The flappy arms – birds, he decided to call them, a less unwieldy phrase, and shorter – mostly departed into the air, hen and peacocks excepted. More birds of all sorts would come from rounded containers. They would need to eat something and be eaten by something else. Eating birds would clearly require even bigger birds, which would soon lead to a thick layer of giant birds covering the entire sky, then filling the air until the brothers had to push their way through bird-eating birds. The wolves could be killed by bigger wolves, and then what? *Even bigger wolves?* Something was necessary to get rid of those. Wolves would dispose of excess bunny rabbits, yes, but they looked as if they could also dispose of excess Gods. And Odin, for one, saw himself as essential.

Odin didn't want to get killed and eaten. Wolves didn't want to get killed and eaten. Only one side could get what it wanted and that side was currently outnumbered. If boy wolves and girl wolves were to produce more of themselves, the Gods needed to find a way to do it as well. They needed girl Gods, but ones that wouldn't run around creating more Odins, Ves, Vilis. Half-Gods, or maybe even not-really-Gods. The ones he saw in his sleep-dream.

"How do bunny rabbits know which one is a boy and which is a girl?" asked Vé. "Without the decoration?"

"I don't know," said Vili. "They just do." He sighed. "I should have invented art earlier."

When making new Gods, Odin thought, ones that couldn't create wolves and butterflies and gravel, he had to ensure the girl Gods were different from boy Gods... He glanced at his brothers, comparing them with the parts of himself he could see. Shorter beards should do the trick. Although... surely it would be easy to make girl Gods prettier than his brothers?

"Why do you only put art on boy birds, Vili?"

"Birbs?"

"Flappy arms. Don't you think 'birds' is a nicer name? Shorter? More convenient?"

Vili gawked at him.

"This is why we need a leader," said Odin. "Someone who thinks about those things."

"You're right," said Vé. "As the greatest leader this… everything has ever known, I promise to never fail the trust you put in me. Thank you, thank you."

Odin simply snorted. "You? A leader? I'd like to remind you that it was me who came up with our cow, Audhumla, whereas—"

"We were supposed to eat her and wear her! Where even is she?"

"What a good question," said Odin coldly. "Probably killed by the wolves that *someone* thought would be a good idea."

"Vili," said Vé, "tell *your brother* that my wolves are nice creatures that would never do such a thing."

"Vili," said Odin, "tell *your brother* that wolves already kill nice creatures, like peacocks and bunny rabbits."

"Vili, tell *your brother* that his nice Audhumla attacked me when I tried to eat her, and I even said 'please' and 'thank you.'"

"Vili, tell *your brother…*"

"Stop!" Vili cried. "Do you know what you sound like? How old *are* you?"

Vé and Odin looked at each other. "Two days," Vé said.

Vili pursed his lips and looked away. Odin followed his gaze and saw a rainbow unfold in the sky. A few butterflies arrived and–

Swash, snap, swish.

"Take your flappy bird away from my butterflies!" Vili cried.

"Done," said Vé.

"Before, not after!"

Vé shrugged. "It's not my fault that your butterflies don't defend themselves. They should have known."

"When the wolf killed our peacock," huffed Vili, "was it 'defending' itself?"

Odin winced. Of course Vili had to say something. The bigger wolves were coming any moment now.

Unsurprisingly, there was a low growl.

A mass of brown fur, taller than either of the brothers.

A mass of *confused* fur.

"This is a bear," said Vé. "It eats fish," he said, pointing at flickering, colourful creatures in the water. The bear let out a grateful sigh and got to it. "It kills wolves too," Vé added, in a whisper. "Fish eat...flies." A fish shot into the air to grab at something that wasn't there a blink earlier. "Flies eat..."

Odin couldn't afford to wait any longer. Those were his decisions to make before Vé inevitably ended up with something that ate Gods, then continued indefinitely.

He cleared his throat.

The first man and woman looked at each other, wide-eyed, then at the Gods, two of whom were at least just as baffled. The bear seemed unimpressed. The fish did not comment.

"Those are people," said Odin, trying to contain all the feelings that arose inside him. Excitement. Fear. Relief. They were *his* people. "The one that looks like you and me is a man. That's a boy people. The one with the..." He swallowed. Despite lack of feathers, the girl people was surprisingly nice to look at and caused even more feelings to arise. "The one without the beard... is a wo-wo..."

"Why do I have those and you don't?" asked the woman, pointing at the meat sacks hanging off her chest. "They're heavy. And where is my peeing dispenser?"

As she tapped her foot, awaiting the answer, Vé and Vili just silently stared at Odin.

Odin fixed the problem. Everything ate something, but people – and Gods, in fact mostly Gods – ate it all. Who ate bears? People did. Who ate wolves? People did. Who ate celery? Wrong example, but still, people *could* if there was nothing else around.

Now he just had to explain this to bears, wolves, and celery.

"I like this," said the first man, poking the woman's nipple. "What does it do?"

"Keep your hands to yourself!" The woman slapped the man's bearded cheek. He stumbled, letting out a surprised gasp. So did the three Gods.

In Odin's urge to create the solution, he'd elevated problems to a whole new level.

He made the same mistake as with Audhumla, creating something in a hurry, with vague parameters. Boy and girl people, so they could reproduce. No ability to create anything, artfully shaped tools for milk production, beards so short they were practically invisible. Done. The point of them, the only reason for their existence, was to keep the wolves, bunny rabbits, and other butterflies in check. Of course that meant they had to be unruly, nobody could eat a wolf nicely, and, as Vé would say, they needed to be able to defend themselves–

"Oooh," said the first man, pointing at the other woman. "I like this one better than you."

"She's mine," barked the second man.

"What are you talking about?" asked the third woman. "Who are you all?"

"Hey, hey," said the third man, pushing the first man away. "Don't touch the lady until I give you her permission."

"Stop!" Odin cried. "Who's making those? I didn't permit—"

"Your hair is ugly," said one woman to another.

"How dare you! My hair is the ultimate in the history of hair! It's the longest, the shiniest..."

"Not anymore," sniggered Vé, his new creation proving that black could outshine gold.

"My dispenser is bigger than yours!"

Vili looked down at his own, then shrugged. Vé did the same and frowned.

"Why are they different colours?" groaned Odin, quickly adding more men, trying to keep count. "It's you, Vili, isn't it?"

"Don't you think they look nice without hair?" Vili asked instead of apologising. "Or maybe this sort of hair?" More people kept popping around, each of them different. "Art is all about making mistakes on your way to perfection..."

"Hair keeps them warm," said Odin, adding some fur on selected men's chests, arms, backs even. He found that women's chests had a certain *je ne sais quoi* that, in his opinion, shouldn't be covered. Since art turned out to have some value after all, he created a few more mood pieces. Vili had an excellent point when it came to colours, shapes, sizes, hair...

"Why don't I have hair on the meat sacks? I'm cold and it's unfair," scoffed one of the women.

"I will keep you warm," panted one of the men. His peeing dispenser didn't look good, all swollen and sore. Odin's brothers seemed to be experiencing the same affliction. So did Odin.

"She's mine," growled another man. The woman's expression suggested she'd rather bite her head off and eat it than touch either of the men with a long stick.

"I like you," one man said to another. The other one smiled uncertainly. At least they didn't yell at each other or push each other, but any illusion of control Odin still retained was gone now. Also, he liked both of them too… In confusion, he let his gaze wander. There were people everywhere, some fighting, some pressing their mouths to those of others, some doing things he didn't understand, but suddenly wanted to. How did *they* know?! The noise was becoming unbearable as more and more people kept appearing, distracting Odin further and further…

The bear rolled its eyes and left, uneaten. The people didn't even notice, busy with everything at once, Vili and Vé in some sort of artistic race. None of this was going well.

"Stop!" Odin screamed at his brothers, his voice barely drowning out the bickering. "There are too many! They will all want to eat!"

"I want to eat," one immediately declared.

"Me too."

"And me!"

"See what you've done?" Odin hissed at his brothers, neither of whom paid him any attention.

He'd intended to create *two* people. They would then use their own, very limited production abilities to make *some* more. As Vé kept creating bigger and bigger things that would eat each other, those *very few* people would always remain on top. If that bear started getting ideas, it would find itself dead and eaten, and it'd be really surprised. All those people would require feeding multiple times a day, though – every day. Odin was already hungry and none of those had had a meal in their entire lives. The Gods would now have to run around the entire soil, producing endless quantities of Audhumlas and bunny rabbits and fires, chased by constantly multiplying people and their demands. Unless he found a way to stop his brothers, he *would* have to figure out how to keep the number of people in check as well, and since nothing was supposed to kill people...

"Vé, what are you doing?" Vili asked.

"That's not me," Vé said. "They're doing it on their own."

The people that looked more similar to each other seemed to form groups. Those groups yelled at each other. One of the women pushed another. A man kicked another one in the ankle and cried out in pain, holding on to his toes, as the kicked man laughed. Ankles were tougher than toes, Odin noted. But why would anybody–

Vé laughed as well and the question was answered before it formed. Odin's idea was ruined. Vili made it pretty... which was distracting... but Odin had no complaints... *anyway*, Vé had made them snarl at each other where they were meant to *cooperate*. Defend themselves, yes. Together. Against the wolves and the bears and everything else. Instead, they seemed determined to battle each other. They were grinding their teeth, their hands folded into fists, glaring at others. More and more others.

They reminded Odin of the wolf that bit off the peacock's head for no reason.

"Vili... could you stop..."

"This is the best time of my life," panted Vili, ignoring the people's pushing and growling, producing all sorts of men and women of all shapes, sizes, colours, hair, eyes, differently sized peeing and milk dispensers. Women had to pee somehow, a thought reminded Odin too late. Some were drinking water without needing to be instructed. One grabbed an apple, and it was the Gods' apple, and maybe they didn't want to share it. The people didn't ask permission, though, figuring things out by themselves. The ones who were already busy working on producing new ones were the most distracting.

"Vili, Vé, please," Odin groaned. *Queen Victoria, Queen Victoria, Queen Victoria*, he thought, trying not to look at the producing. Some men and women tried to pull others away and stop the production process, others yelled, there was more pushing. Vé kept sniggering and Vili sniffled.

A small group made it near the brothers – too near.

"Keep your hands off me!"

"She's mine!"

"Actually, I'm hers," said one of the women. "If she wants me."

"She doesn't! You, leave my woman alone!"

"You don't belong to anybody!" Odin yelled. "You are free to choose! But not now! Now we must—"

"What are you doing to her?" demanded another man, pushing the first one away. "I told you she's mine!"

"The boy is mine!"

"No, he's mine!"

"Get away from me!" growled someone and Odin broke down.

"You've made too many!" he yelled in Vili's face. "You've made them – like that! Now they'll have to be eaten too! Can't you see they're already making more and more of – OW!"

The air pinched him.

Then again.

Vé screamed, performing something of a dance, waving his hands around. So did the people, no longer fighting or producing, except the most dedicated ones. Only Vili stood still – until Odin's hand grabbed his throat.

"What is this?!"

"Let go of me," Vili croaked. "I just did what you asked for. Now people will be eaten, too—"

"Aw! By air? Why is air biting *me*?!"

"It's not air. They're called mosquitoes. You'll see. They'll eat the excess people soon."

"They're eating *me*! Why are they not biting *you*?"

"Because I am a God," said Vili. His voice had never sounded like that before, calm, strong, decisive. "And my creations love me... no, no, not my mosquitoes! Nooo! Stop them!" Dark birds that disappeared in the sky earlier, returned in style, their movements fast and assertive. Loud, sharp, nasty sounds – crowing – left no doubts as to who created them. Some flew around, eating the biting air. A few, however, aimed for people's eyes. Fish remained unperturbed.

"*You* are a God?" snapped Vé. "What about us? Who

are we, in your humble opinion?" He pushed Vili in a manner identical to how some people pushed others.

"Obviously, you are my brothers," Vili said, his voice strong enough to overpower the people's shrieking. "We need a leader. Someone with imagination, someone of greater importance..."

Odin's face reddened. One side more than the other, as he slapped his own cheek when another mosquito bit him. Now he slapped Vili's and that felt much more satisfying. "You? *You* are the leader?"

"Help!" cried the people. "Help!"

"I see something!" one shouted and suddenly most of the people were running away, heading towards the big tree. Yelps and cries followed, as they slipped, fell into streams, or found Vé's useful gravel with their feet. The shouter ran first, leading them without the Gods' permission...

"You're not the leader!" Vé yelled, pushing Vili again. "I am! I understand the value of defence! How do we defend ourselves against your air that eats *Gods*?"

"Only the unimportant ones," said Vili in this new voice of his, then smiled sweetly.

The sky darkened and cracked with jagged light. A loud rumble followed, one that sounded as if the soil itself stood up to defend Vili. No bear or wolf could produce a sound so petrifying. Water – *so* much water – began to fall from the sky. It hit the Gods harder than the air could bite, slamming, punching, all the new words, all the new pain. "No more destruction!" Vili yelled, his arms raised to the sky as another thunderclap shook the ground, the bright light cutting through the black sky. "No more ugliness! No more—"

It could as well have been an accident, Odin and Vé

would mutter to each other in the future if they were to find themselves in a particularly forgiving mood, which would happen never. For some unknown reason, all of a sudden Vili was on the ground, motionless and quiet. Water stopped falling from the sky that had turned blue again, an enormous rainbow connecting one side of everything with the other. The angry birds were gone and air was no longer eating the Gods. Vé and Odin froze in place. So did Vili, but differently.

The rock that had made a large hole in the back of Vili's head was sharp and tall. It wasn't just a bit of blood that came out of his head, like when Vé's defensive plants scratched their forearms. Vili did not lack any body parts, his skin was mostly intact, but the back of his head... it was just... meat, bones, blood, a soft mess that *poured* out of Vili.

Vé quickly removed the rock and Odin placed Vili's head on the ground. Vili's eyes were open, unblinking, his mouth half-open, no sound coming out. Nevertheless, Vili was a God. He'd fallen like this once before, although a bit less, and recovered. Most of his head was still there, very much unlike the peacock's. In fact, at certain angles Vili looked really quite unbroken.

"He's been working very hard," Odin said, the words brittle. "Maybe he just needs rest."

"Then he'd have his eyes closed..." Vé lowered his voice to a whisper. "Maybe he's pretending. To make us feel guilty."

It was working.

Odin cleared his throat. "I apologise," he said. His mind, normally so good with words he never asked for, was taking a sudden vacation.

"We both do," said Vé, his voice breaking. "You can be

65

the leader…every now and then. When the sun eats the ground again."

Vili did not answer.

"Even before it eats the ground," Odin tried. "Like, now. You can be important from now until the next sun is up."

"And you can make everything as pretty as you like." Vé sounded as if his words were boulders he was pushing uphill.

There was nothing. If *that* wasn't enough, nothing would.

The brothers' eyes met, Odin's blinking, uncertain, Vé's narrowed and sharp.

"You made my brother dead," Vé said in a slow growl, a bit like the bear's.

"*My* brother fell on *your* rock," Odin answered, his voice high and shaky. He hated himself for that. "And, and *you* pushed him."

"Liar…!" Vé's fist stopped right before hitting Odin's jaw.

Neither of the brothers breathed for a bit, Vé's hand dropping slowly, the fist opening, as if he were hoping that it could retreat unnoticed.

"I– I, of c-course, would never d-d-do it, because I am, ah, a…" Vé inhaled sharply and his eyes narrowed again. "I'm not like *you*. I would never touch my brother."

"You pushed him," Odin hissed. "You 'touched' him so hard he fell."

"If you don't stop with those accusations…"

"Then what? Hmmm? You'll do it to me too?"

"What have you done?" a woman's voice asked. Odin nearly jumped out of his skin. Vé choked on a gasp.

Not all of the people had escaped. Odin and Vé – and Vili – were surrounded by a small group of men and women, all of them clearly unimpressed. Vé's and Odin's eyes met for a blink.

"He is resting," Vé said, standing up.

"Yes, yes," Odin agreed, also lifting himself, so that he could look at the people from above, not below. Unfortunately some of them were so big that he was still looking at them from below. A few crossed their arms on their chests and Odin discovered fear. "Th-that's exactly what he is doing. Resting."

"He got tired of creating too many of you," said Vé. "He needs lots of rest. Go away and let him rest in peace."

Another unspeakable thing happened. A man – tall, big, beardless, the top of Odin's head barely reaching his chin... slapped Vé, nearly sending him to the ground. It must have been one of Vé's own, Odin realised in shock. That would be exactly the sort of Vé's creations' behaviour. Vé's creations would make wolves look sweet and friendly.

"We don't like this," the man grumbled. "We don't like you. You go away."

Folded fists, growls, snarls, hissing, whispering.

There were many people around. And only two Gods. Those people did not like the Gods. Something needed to rescue Odin and Vé, something that would attack people, but not the Gods. Odin's decisions ruled out everything. Almost.

He sighed.

"He's touching your woman," he said to the tall man.

"He isn't!" the woman protested. "Whoever he is!"

"I'm going to touch you if I want," another large man

announced, extending his hand to grab the woman's arm. His peeing dispenser pointed upwards, which would make peeing very awkward. Yet somehow it looked just right, albeit in the wrong way. "He won't stop me and you won't either."

"Leave me alone!"

So predictable, Odin thought, *so sad*. It had worked as expected. He wished it hadn't. He and his brothers had created non-Gods that seemed to only want to eat, produce more non-Gods...and fight. So, exactly how Odin had envisioned them.

The tall man turned away from Vé, approached the other one, raised his fist above his head, and lowered it. The big-dispensered man simply folded, falling on his knees, then down, on his face.

This was a good time for a sharp intake of breath, but Odin simply stopped breathing.

"Who's next?" the tall man asked quietly.

"Here," Vé whispered, picking the rock still wet with Vili's blood and handing it to another large man. "You'll need it. They hate you."

"Who's they?" the man asked, bewildered.

Vé pointed. "He does, and she does, and this small one the most. They all envy you. They want to hit you."

"I don't envy him at all!" The small one's voice sounded a bit choked, possibly because he had to look up. "He's, he's ugly and smells bad, and..."

"How do you know what he smells like?" another one asked. "Did you go and check?"

"I'm not ugly!" The knuckles of the hand wrapped around the bloodied rock whitened.

"Who's next, I asked?"

Vé and Odin communicated with a quick nod. Grass,

yellow and dry, grew under the bickering people's feet. Before anyone had a chance to comment, flames shot up. People of all colours, shapes, sizes screamed, jumping, crying. The only space free from the fire was the circle surrounding the brothers – and a straight path that hadn't existed until just before right now.

"Run!" Vé screamed. "Save yourselves! Do you see this big tree? It's the only safe place!"

People of all colours, sizes, shapes turned as one and ran, heading towards the Potentially Useful After All Tree. They were followed by wolves, bunny rabbits, a panting bear, even some of the birds.

"Why there?" Odin asked, waving away the smoke. The grass burned high and fast, the flames already replaced with lazy smouldering, the brief heat gone.

"Because we're not going there. Now we are safe." Vé paused. "Completely safe."

The lie rang so clearly even Vé blushed. Each of them was in mortal danger until the other one was gone. They were too smart and too afraid for their own good. Without Vili, the two lacked balance.

"Maybe he had enough rest now," Odin mumbled, pointing at Vili. "Let's wake him up."

Vé put his finger in Vili's nose. Odin poked his ribs. Vé pulled at his hair and Odin at his beard. Vili remained as he was; unmoved and unmoving, his body turning cooler, arms and legs stiffening. His eyes were still open, looking at nothing. Not even at his sky that he had wanted to make prettier with clouds and rainbows and flappy birds and butterflies, but through it. Odin's guilt had left by now, replaced by something else, something that brought the goosebumps back.

"Why did you tell them to go towards that tree?" His

hand inconspicuously wrapped around a rock. The rock was too small and now he had to inconspicuously unwrap it, then search for a bigger one.

"There were many directions it led to," Vé said, sitting cross-legged and, terrifyingly, doing nothing inconspicuous that Odin would detect. "Haven't Vili and I said it? You picked this place. Everything that happened here is your fault. I'd have gone elsewhere."

"And you would have done what in that elsewhere, brother?"

Vé nodded towards Vili's unmoving body. "Not this, for sure."

"We both know who did this."

"Yes," Vé coldly answered. "You did."

This rock was sharper, larger, wet with blood and whatever else used to be inside Vili's head. Excessive self-confidence, probably.

Vé, empty-handed, smirked, that grimace Odin hated so much. "Is that all you've got?" he asked. "A rock? I created those."

"Yes," Odin said. "This is indeed what you have created. Rocks. You wanted to see more blood. You wanted this to happen. Now that our brother's blood is all over your rocks, I imagine you're delighted. His blood is on this rock. Here, take it and cherish it forever."

"If you don't stop..."

"Then what? More rocks? More blood? Go under your tree, find your people, make them fight, kill each other. Like you've always planned. I made things useful, Vili made them look pretty, and you made them sharp, pointy, biting. Find a place of your own, take your people there and make them all like this." He pointed at

Vili. "Once you run out of people, make more and more, enjoy yourself. Far away from me."

"I see it differently," said Vé quietly. "I will find all *my* people, yes. And then they will find *your* people. Once your people are gone..."

The rock in Odin's hand was already heading towards Vé's temple, but his brother was faster. His fist smashed into Odin's jaw. Odin fell, dropping the rock, his hand desperately searching for *something*, throwing a fistful of gravel into Vé's face.

"Here!" Odin screamed, lifting himself to his knees, throwing one handful of gravel after another at Vé, forcing him to back off. "Here's your useful gravel!" A tree appeared out of nowhere, and as one of its branches fell off, Odin picked it up, then smacked Vé's arm with it. "Here's your biting tree!"

Out of nowhere, rocks appeared in the air, falling upon Odin like sky-water had before. Sharp rocks. One hit Odin's leg, drawing a scream and blood, always the blood. The branch he held exploded in flames. Vé gasped, leaning back, as Odin lunged forward, heading for Vé's beard.

A short, jagged sound made Odin turn just in time.

The wolf, already mid-leap, found itself heading towards the burning branch, rather than Odin's back. The creature screamed, a shriek and growl and roar and fear, flapping its legs, trying to change the direction of its jump. Odin dropped his branch, squatting, and the wolf flew above his head. Vé's laughter was cut short by the creature snarling at him.

A huge bird descended from the sky, aiming for Odin's face. Fire. Fire scared them. A tall, leafless bush shot out of the ground, already burning. The bird flew into the flames. Shriek, crowing, panic, pain. The wolf rolling on the ground, its fur aflame. Noise, so much noise, too much noise and too many flames, Odin himself screaming, slapping his face with his hands, his beard hairs curling from the heat, the stink, the smoke. Water falling from the sky, extinguishing the flames, drops sharpening into small white rocks. Sky gravel. Rough wind blowing everything Vé's way, rocks, branches, blood dripping off Vé's forehead, more birds, Odin falling to his knees, more birds, more sky gravel, white, painful, more fire. Blood on Odin's knee. Smoke that suffocated and blinded. Cries, howls, sharp, brutal, black, white, red. So much noise, noise, creatures and Gods that would destroy everything in their attempts to over-create the other–

When Odin tripped over Vili's body and fell, the darkness and silence brought no dreams.

ODIN OPENED his eyes and screamed. A man and a woman bending over him, staring curiously from way too close, both winced. He would have too, had he not been lying down.

"Aha," the woman said. "I told you he wasn't going to rest as long as the other one. The other one will not stop resting."

"He will," said the man. "This one did, that one will too."

"It's not true. You know nothing, man."

"And what can you know?"

"Excuse me," said Odin, "I'd like to sit up, so move away. Who are you?"

"You tell us," said the woman.

"The other one will stop resting," the man insisted. "I just have this feeling that he will. And I know better, because I am a man, same as he is here."

"I am not a man, I am a God, and my name is Odin."

"What does it mean that you are a God?" asked the woman, frowning.

"It means you must listen to me, because I created you."

"You don't create anything, only destroy. We watched you. You call this 'creation'?" The man pointed at the smoking remains of the bush. "And this?" A dead bird. "And this?" Vili. "Is he created or destroyed?"

"Or *resting*?" the woman added with enough sarcasm for Odin to hear the italics.

"It was all…necessary. For, ah, your protection. Where is my brother? That other one? It was all his fault, by the way."

"He ran away."

Odin chewed on this for a moment. "Just like that?"

"Well, she yelled at him," the man said. "And she's so ugly that he ran away."

"I'll give you ugly! I yelled 'what have you done now, young man?!' and he was so ashamed…"

"Yes, and the dogs and crows were also ashamed…"

"Where did they all run?" Odin interrupted.

The woman pointed towards the tree.

Odin bit his lip. He was almost sure which ones were dogs and which were crows. His mind would need to see them again in less emotional circumstances.

"How did you create us?"

"I felt that you would be useful."

"Useful for what?"

"I don't know. For asking questions, I guess. Bring me some water."

"Create some," said the woman, "if you are a God."

Odin ground his teeth, caused some sky water to fall, opened his mouth, caught much less of it than he would like, then stopped the sky water. That was bound to impress even the sarcastic woman.

"Now we are wet and cold," she said. "If that's what a God does, do it somewhere else. See, man? Even that didn't un-rest the other one. He's... God, what's the right word? What is he?"

"We should try fire," insisted the man. "You, God, put fire on his toes. *That* will wake him up."

"Only a man would come up with that! You're really as stupid as those Gods. Haven't we had enough fire?"

"Something has to be done with him," the man said, ignoring her. "There's enough mess as it is. We can't have him lying around here forever. Are you going to do something, God? Huh?"

"No!" cried Odin. "I mean, yes! I don't know! This never happened before!"

"Will it happen again?"

"How did you do it?"

"Why did you do it?"

"What is it that Gods actually do?"

"Why are we not Gods?"

"Because you're useless," snapped Odin. "Leave me alone. Go hide under the big bad tree."

"We're not stupid," said the man. "If it's a bad tree, we're not hiding under it. We've been hiding among those trees there, but it's too cold. Make us warm, God. And feed us. Unless you can't?"

"We should have followed his brother," the woman said.

Many conflicting feelings fought inside Odin. Part of him wanted to impress the irritating creations. Part wanted to scream very loud, while hurling rocks at them. Unfortunately, man and woman had a point. There were enough dead creatures and Gods around. For there was no way to pretend that Vili could possibly have any life left in him if Vé's and Odin's battle hadn't woken him up.

Shame felt even less pleasant than fear, even though all of this was almost definitely Vé's fault. "Fine," he sighed. "Bring me dry wood and I'll make you warm."

"Why do we have to do things? Create, God, create!"

"Or is it *another* thing you can't do?" the woman asked, italics dripping from her voice.

Odin's anger returned much faster than it had disappeared. "You owe me respect! And if you continue asking me stupid questions, you too will rest for a very long time!"

"There's no need to yell," the woman said. "We hear you perfectly well, so-called God. Dry wood after you made all this wet water fall? Why don't you just ask for gold and jewels?"

"Come, woman," said the man, assessing Odin's expression. "We'll find something."

As man and woman bickered on their way into the still smoking woods, Odin closed his eyes and finally invented counting to ten while breathing deeply. He recognised those two. They were the first man and first woman he, Odin, had created. Along with them he created irony, as they forced him to acknowledge how much destruction he had caused. Around him were answers to questions he hadn't intended to ask. The smoking bushes, puddles of water, a dead bird... a dead brother. Odin's legacy so far.

No wonder Vé had run away. Odin wished he could run away too, leave all this behind, pretend it didn't happen. Wake up under that tree again and let someone else make decisions. Someone...wiser.

"Wisdom" – knowledge and understanding, both of which Odin lacked – needed to be built bit by bit, with time. He had no time. Nothing and nobody had time if he was going to keep destroying things in his attempts to create them. If he kept developing wisdom this way, even the bad tree would eventually keel over and die.

Assuming it was alive.

He didn't even know *that*.

Odin sniffled once or twice before the powerless frustration of *just not knowing* was replaced by a new feeling. One that followed sending people for firewood, then seeing them return, each carrying...

One stick.

"There you go," said the woman. "Make us warm, God."

Red flashed in front of Odin's eyes. "My name is Odin. And if you don't give me the respect I deserve, I won't make you warm, I'll make you dead."

"What's that?"

Odin pointed at Vili. "He is dead. Deceased. Expired. Kaput. He'll stay like that forever and soon you might join him. Wolves will appreciate more food."

"I'm glad to hear there's something for wolves to eat," said the woman. "No food for us, I notice. And I'm still cold. Why aren't you doing your job, God Odin?"

"If you are a God and we aren't, what are we?"

"What has this poor other God done to you? And now you threaten us as well? What next? Have you no shame?"

"Why do you have a name and I don't, God Odin? Give me a name. What's my name?"

Something broke inside Odin.

"Ask!" he yelled. "Because all you do is ask! Do this, do that, what is this, what is that! *I* am the God here! You will do things for me!"

"Has no manners whatsoever," the woman judged. "What is my name, then?"

Odin was about to scream in her face that her name was also Ask, and briefly considered Shut Up, when he realised something. Nothing was keeping him here. Answering their questions wasn't his job and neither was keeping them fed and warm. They could fend for themselves, and if they were to fail, he wouldn't shed a tear. If they were not happy with his creations, including each other, they were free to do a better job.

Vé sent all those other people, some of whom were bound to be less irritating, under the tree. From there they could go in all the directions. So could Odin. There was a direction somewhere that had Vé in it, but there must have been many more that didn't. He'd carry a long stick, conveniently suggested by his dream, in case Vé suddenly appeared. Odin, too, could create something to defend himself with from any unpleasant people or Gods he might walk into. Eventually he was bound to find a nice, secluded place free from wolves and sarcasm. He'd make it beautiful, in Vili's memory; useful, because he was responsible; and as difficult to enter as possible, in case Vé found it.

"Well? Did a wolf eat your tongue? What is my name, God? Where is my food? Why are we still cold?"

"Your name is Embla," said Odin calmly.

"That's not even a name. That means 'elm'. I want a real name."

"Too bad. It wasn't nice knowing you, Ask and Embla. Search for the cow Audhumla, find out how to get milk out of her. Don't let wolves or whatever else kill you, or they'll get in the habit. Enjoy your day and good luck with the fire when it gets dark."

"But, Odin...!" cried Embla as Odin examined various sticks, then picked one he could comfortably lean on. "We don't know how to make fire! What is a cow? What is milk? What habit?"

Odin's mood brightened with each step that brought him closer to the tree he no longer considered useless or irritating, not in comparison to what he was leaving behind. There might have been very few questions he knew how to answer, but he knew how to make fire whenever he felt like it. If he wanted another cow, he could create her. What would boy cows look like? He couldn't wait to find out. He had learnt a lot already and would learn even more. There must be so much more to do and discover! As a God, he had an especial duty to advance his knowledge of all sorts of art, as Vili described men and women...

"Hey, you there, God Odin! We're sorry, okay?"

Ask's screechy voice again pierced the bubble of serenity, just as Odin was about to progress from positive thinking to affirmations. His grip on his stick tightened. Those two were just failed sketches, an early phase in his artistic career. Very early. Very failed. Sketches that criticised the artist.

Was this red fury what Vé felt all the time? Had he just been forcing himself to stay more or less polite? If the screechy sketches didn't actually have a point – there were enough dead bodies around – Odin would destroy them. Together with all the wolves, the biting air, the birds, everything. He'd burn the woods, create more woods, then burn them too. But Odin was nothing like his brother. Odin was a thinker, a visionary, a creator, the only one left around, unless Ask and Embla accidentally did something useful. He was also thirsty.

An unexpected warm feeling spread inside him. The cow produced a drink called milk. Water produced a drink called water. While Odin couldn't tell the future, somehow he just knew that he would become peace and love itself once he'd invented a drink that was neither water nor milk. Inventing – that was what Gods did. This... the deaths, the fire, the fights, Ask, Embla... all of it was but a slight mishap on his way to becoming really good at the God thing. A good lesson, if painful. For others.

Perhaps creation and destruction weren't mutually exclusive; perhaps they needed each other; perhaps they were one and the same. Odin didn't know that yet, but he would find out soon. Over a drink.

The up-and-coming All-Father smiled, leaving behind the place that would one day be called Midgard and would be populated entirely by descendants of Ask and Embla, ones so stupid they'd kill each other and pray to die with his name on their lips.

79

LOKI RUNES EVERYTHING

"FBI," mumbled Odin. He didn't know what exactly that meant, but it felt like almost the right thing to say at this difficult time. Just like the diagram covering half of his new world, Ásgard. It felt like it was almost right. Except for the parts that weren't, which were all of them.

First of all, he still had to distribute the countless creations all over multiple worlds, not just Midgard. He'd left all the mosquitoes in there, because Ask and Embla deserved that. This meant that the creatures eating mosquitoes had to find something else to feed on. As the diagram continued to expand, the second problem struck him. Odin had turned out to be really bad at drawing. After a while he couldn't remember which circular shape with two/four/six/eight legs/arms and one/two/three heads was which. When he tried to put checkmarks next to them, he ended up with a ram and a stag. Admittedly, horns were a very interesting invention, even somewhat aesthetic, but that simply wasn't the point.

Odin was lost.

Note to self, he thought, come up with a way to make notes to self about thoughts, before the thoughts inevitably became memories which – just as inevitably – escaped his memory.

The elegance and roundness of the thought delighted him enough for him to forget what the latest circle with sticks was supposed to symbolise.

Ásgard might have been on the bijou side, but that allowed Odin to turn it into a half-opulent-residence-worthy-of-the-greatest-of-both-Gods and half-soft-clay-to-draw-on. There were some mountains; a bit of snow; flowers; fruit and vegetables (no celery); plus animals that didn't eat each other or Odin himself. No rats or porcupines were produced in his lovely, lovely, rodent-free world. The only things allowed in Ásgard were ones Odin wanted in there. It was the one topic on which his diagram was very clear.

Even this posed a problem.

Odin spent an awful lot of time walking under the roots of the Tree, and there were *so* many worlds he felt responsible for. He distributed his creatures and creations as he saw fit, but that didn't stop them from travelling the same way he did, redistributing themselves. In particular, bunny rabbits were everywhere by now, even in Ásgard. Still worse was a cute squirrel he'd named Ratatosk and had petted for about as long as a blink takes before it ran away and shot up the Tree. If Odin couldn't shoot up trees of any calibre, there was no way some squirrel should be able to. Ratatosk didn't seem to know that, though.

The worst of the worst were, of course, people. They walked underneath the roots, commenting on the views and complaining about lack of entertainment, then invariably got into fights. Which provided some entertainment to those not involved, but it was only a matter of time before they found out how to reach his not-yet-gated community of one.

Odin had to come up with something again, but he was so *tired*. He was aware that burnout would need to be invented some day in the future. Nevertheless, it was a creation he preferred to leave to someone else. Ideally, his brother Vé.

It was Vé's creation that forced Odin to take action.

Vé's world, Vanaheim, was green and rich (Odin might or might not have carefully stolen some ideas and seeds from it). People of various sorts inhabited four more. Ásgard was Odin's own and precious. There was also Niflheim, the land of ice and fog, which was as exciting as it sounded, and Múspelheim. Odin hadn't intended to discover Múspelheim, exhausted by the number of worlds he'd already felt guiltily responsible for, but after he had created bees (which produced honey, which was eaten by people and bears, while bees were mostly eaten by dogs, which were like wolves, but stupider and less murderous)... in any case, what had chased him all the way to Múspelheim was almost, but not entirely, a bee.

Odin had made two discoveries that day. 1) Apparently a land of ice and fog needed a complementary one consisting of fire and smoke. 2) The thing that managed to sting him on his arm so painfully it made mosquito

bites seem like a gentle caress, was almost like a bee...
but vile. Vé was corrupting Odin's creations. As should
have been expected.

If Vé were to keep his little monsters to himself, he
could do whatever he wanted. Ásgard, though, Odin's
domain, could not contain wasps. (Or Ask and Embla,
who kept appearing in his nightmares.) The Tree wasn't
some sort of touristic attraction. The stinging reminder
that vile things were vile was a sign. All this mingling
had to end.

It hadn't even been difficult. Odin had already found
out that the same Tree grew in all of the to-be-
confirmed-but-hopefully-not-many-more-number of
worlds. The protective barrier he had built around the
Tree was made of terrifying and sickening dark magic,
the secret essence of celery and wasps. Once he had
protected Ásgard, the barrier repelled all creatures big
and small that were located in the to-be-confirmed-but-
hopefully-not-many-more-number of worlds. Now
every living being, including Ask, Embla, and the
mosquitoes, would avoid the Tree. The only ones who
could cross the barrier were those who also possessed
magic, i.e. other Gods, i.e. his brother. He wouldn't,
though, not now that he couldn't bring a single wasp
along. Ásgard was protected.

Odin took a day's rest after this, then returned to
work. He felt safer now, knowing people wouldn't
follow him back to Ásgard. His bijou world, as elegant as
it was with special bushes designed solely to relieve
himself, felt a bit lonely. The story of his life kept
growing longer and he hadn't had a single line of
dialogue yet, except "FBI." Which *wasn't* it.

"PSB," he said, then sighed. This wasn't it either.

If he wanted to have dialogue in Ásgard, he needed to stop keeping it to himself.

A plan began to sprout in his mind, leading him to also create Brussels sprouts. They were very quiet, though.

IN LOVING MEMORY OF AUDHUMLA, Odin created extra cows wherever he went. He made both girl cows that carried milk and boy cows that didn't. As he travelled, Odin thoroughly investigated people of all shapes and sizes, casually letting it slip that he was the All-Father. Those who gasped in awe were allowed to investigate Odin in return. Those who asked questions received gifts of tiny, personal clouds hanging above their heads, which produced heavy rain until they got the hint.

When Odin revealed to his latest human lover that cows provided more than just milk and meat, he was stunned by the result. Whatever Odin had imagined as clothing was *not* an entire cow skin, still warm and wet with blood, with a hole for the wearer's head cut in the middle. It was a bit like a cloak, his confused mind whispered, except a bit too *organic*.

"It's very simple, All-Father," explained the overjoyed and bloodied lover. "You simply take the cow and a very sharp rock, then…"

"Yes, thank you, that's enough," croaked green-faced Odin. He was slightly dying inside at the thought that he was *really* wearing Audhumla now. The skin stank, and attracted flies, and the blood dried on Odin's own skin. He thanked the lover profusely, if briefly, grabbed his stick, and departed in a hurry. He couldn't wait to take the possible Audhumla off and wash her blood off his body. Human inventions seemed to mostly revolve around very sharp rocks and lots of blood.

He would never kill a living being, Odin decided, immediately stepping on a snail – he'd forgotten what snails were for, but they were evidently not for being stood on. He'd killed again! Was there no way not to?! The melancholic "moo" of Audhumla sounded in his mind, her big eyes appearing in his imagination as if The First Cow were truly staring at him. Odin felt sick. Yes, he'd created cows with the express purpose of being drunk from, eaten, and worn, but – but nicely...! *This cow died for you*, his mind kept telling him, *so you might as well have eaten it.*

"Shut up," Odin said aloud.

Mmm. Steak. We'd love steak.

"I said shut up," Odin huffed, marching back towards Ásgard. Flies, too afraid of the Tree, remained behind. The smell, stickiness, and guilt didn't.

DURING HIS INVESTIGATIONS, Odin realised something disturbing. He might have been the only one who created things, inconvenient brothers aside, but people were the ones who invented uses for them. (And made them sharper.) All he'd told his lover was that cows could be used as attire. He'd barely had time to blink before he was presented with a ready-made... cloak.

Odin didn't want to know how they'd convinced the cow to part with her skin, using a very sharp rock. On his own, he hadn't come up with anything but "pretty please?" which suggested that people could be smarter than their creators... no, *creator*, Odin decided. There was only one All-Father and one At-Best-Uncle. And one Madame A, who possessed knee-length boots, while Odin stepped on snails barefoot.

He visited Madame A with certain regularity, since she had turned out to be the most investigable specimen so far. The reasons were purely scientific – as the All-Father it was his duty to become acquainted with her many interesting talents and inventions. As she kept him busy, or the other way round, it had never occurred to him to ask where the boots came from and whether he could he have some.

Back in Ásgard, Odin rested his weary, snail-stained feet, trying not to smear his diagram with his cloak. He had to admit that the magically-cleansed dead Audh – *clothing* wasn't entirely unpleasant to wear. It really made him warmer and the heaviness of it was strangely comforting. It fit him like second skin, one could say. No matter how well his mind advertised the steak, though, all he could think of was the melancholic "moo" and big, disapproving eyes. His therapy bills would be enormous one day, his mind pointed out with unneces-sary snark, making Odin so upset that he refused to talk or listen to it until it understood what it had done and apologised.

With his mind offended, Odin proceeded to doing things mindlessly. He picked up his stick and began adding more and more legs to the elongated shape he was sketching, which was originally meant to be a worm (which ate the soil, and which was eaten by birds, and which did not need all those legs, but Odin's mindless creativity didn't really extend past adding appendages). As he continued turning the worm into a not-worm, the word "legs" led to "feet," which led to "snail," "eww," and eventually "transportation." With way too many worlds to take care of, plus one where Vé was doing Vé-knows-what, Odin couldn't afford to waste time dragging his bare feet around and mumbling "DDT." (Which also didn't feel like the right thing to mumble, but he needed to mumble *something*.)

So far, all that he had to help him move from one place to another was his stick. He was aware that he could invent Nordic walking by simply grabbing one more stick, but this one was a branch that had fallen from *the* Tree. It was, possibly, the first branch to ever fall from any tree at all. It made his feet, as old as the Universe, slightly less weary, but it didn't make him any faster. It didn't help when he stepped on useful gravel or a snail either. Even if he were to get some boots from Madame A, at this pace he would never finish creating everything that appeared on his ever-growing diagram.

Odin needed not just to create a means of transportation, but invent it first...

"Perhaps," he said aloud, "I should create a – a Lamborghini."

"Absolutely not," Odin answered himself. "That would require gas stations, gas station attendants, gas itself, and it would eventually cause everything to turn into Müspelheim. It's enough that one world is constantly burning."

"Well," Odin said, spreading his arms, "then I don't know. Do you have any ideas?"

Odin responded by clearing his throat in a way that signified he was done with this conversation. Now he wasn't speaking with his mind *and* with himself.

"We'll see," Odin sighed, then finally looked at his new drawing. It looked quite a lot like a peeing dispenser, but it was covered with legs, which briefly made him grateful for his lack of visual imagination. The arrows pointed towards it eating leaves of plants, while being eaten by birds, wasps, and... whatever the leggy dispensers were, something needed to eat them, and fast, he decided. "Or," he said to himself, shakily adding another arrow, "they could turn into something else. Like... like... butterflies!"

This idea brought double relief. Finally. A way for butterflies to multiply. This also meant the leggy dispensers – that name was even more disturbing than the sight and he quickly changed it to "caterpillars" – wouldn't last long. And wouldn't be larger than baby butterflies. As to the exact process of transformation, Odin left that up to the caterpillars themselves.

"See," he said triumphantly to Odin. "I *am* creative."

"See, see," Odin mocked in response. "Where exactly will I see them?"

Odin shuddered. "Not here, for sure!" This was followed by a sigh, for it meant another trip. The butterflies were created in Midgard, the world of Ask and Embla, who deserved to be covered in a thick layer of caterpillars. Madame A, though, also resided in Midgard, and the last thing Odin wanted was to be surprised by a sudden caterpillar or two while they were... researching.

Perhaps the caterpillars should live on trees, or something, especially as they were apparently eating leaves...

"You see," he said to himself, then fell deep into thought. "See..."

"Well," huffed Odin, "the problem is that I don't."

He rubbed his eyes, tired, and realised it was true. His diagram covered so much space by now that he would need to hover above the middle part just to figure out what he had created, which wouldn't help, because the drawing would inevitably look like a squished circle with sticks symbolising legs, arms, and everything else. "BMX," Odin muttered, then closed his eyes in an attempt to kick-start his imagination. Which, unfortunately, he still did not possess.

"I see..." he said, his eyes closed, his hands moving in mysterious gestures through the air, "I see... I see..."

"Well?" Odin urged.

"I see...*horse*." Odin said the first word that popped into his head and sounded vaguely transportational, just so that he would stop bullying himself.

When he opened his eyes, he saw a small, wriggly creature. It was yellow. It was also very unhappy, judging by how it threw itself around, erasing part of his diagram that might or might have not been a unicorn, until its spiral tail – the horse's, not the unicorn's – stopped moving, together with all the rest.

"KGB," he sighed, dropped on the ground, and hid his face in his hands. *This isn't quite what horse should be*, his thoughts insisted. It was a see-horse, although what those two words had to do with each other was beyond him... "My unicorn!" he cried, jumping up, grabbing the see-horse and throwing it away in a random direction, destroying what might or might have not been a centaur.

The unicorn and the centaur shared something. They both had four legs sticking out from an elongated circle... and... and there was something else...

Had Odin even created the centaur and the unicorn yet, or only drawn them?

. . .

89

WITH A SIGH so deep it nearly swept half of his diagram clean, Odin decided his work was done for the day. He built himself a nice fire, over which he absentmindedly cooked simple split-pea soup with spinach and barley. Next, predictably, Odin burned his fingers while removing the pot off the thing-to-hang-pots-on-that-he-forgot-to-name-because-he-didn't-make-a-note-to-self-to-do-it. He then looked at his simple soup, nearly sobbing with frustration. A stick was perfectly adequate to stir it. But not to eat it.

Odin needed help. In order to get that help, he had to – a shiver went through his body and Odin moved closer to the fire, careful not to set his cloak alight – create *someone* who would help with the creating. Someone who could tell what would be necessary to do things like eating soups and satisfying stockholders of fossil fuels companies. Someone who knew the – the – the future...

It was getting dark, though, and the All-Father was tired. He needed some sleep in order not to end up with a future-seeing okapi. Once he got some rest he'd see everything, including his diagram, much more clearly. The simple split-pea soup with spinach and barley wasn't *that* bad when it was cold – he could slurp it out of the pot. Also, maybe the dream would turn out to be... some sort of... helpful... prophecy...

"My love," a seductive voice whispered in his ear. "I will always be here for you."

"Mmmm," he sighed, rather pleased with the dream so far.

"Hold me close, my great, big All-Father, I must be in your strong arms right now! Let's make sweet, sweet love!"

Grinning, Odin turned to see a giant, green cater-pillar extending all of his appendages towards him.

With a shriek, Odin jumped up and decided to never sleep again. There was something he liked about this dream, though. He would like someone who would call him "great, big All-Father" and demand to be in his strong arms. Just not too often. A Goddess that could tell the future as they made sweet, sweet love.

He rekindled the fire and wrapped the cow-skin around himself tighter, scowling. The magic he'd used had stopped working when he had fallen asleep. The "cloak" stank even worse than the day before, which he felt was a suitable punishment for telling people to murder Audhumla and her friends and family. A blink later Odin decided he was sufficiently punished and, again, removed all the stink and stickiness of the blood from his cow-skin. One day in the future, he mused, once the Goddess told him what to do... He could make a list... no, he couldn't, because he couldn't write. She could tell him how to make a list. Yes, such a Goddess would be very useful.

Having finalised his decisions about her internal characteristics, Odin moved on to the important part. She should be a... his hands moved, as if probingly... well-endowed Goddess. But maybe not too well. Just right-endowed. She should look like... definitely nothing like Madame A, because the last thing he needed was to call one of them the name of the other. Madame A would never forgive that.

The new Goddess's name would be... actually, Odin pondered, since she could see the future, maybe she had already figured it out? No, she couldn't tell him what he would have decided... had decided... Frigg, Odin decided, just to avoid further grammatical complications. Short, sweet, and absolutely nothing like "Madame A." She should be incredibly attractive... but not too incredibly, perhaps... in case someone else tried to lay their filthy hands on Odin's Frigg.

Maybe she should be completely *not* attractive, so that Odin wouldn't end up laying his hands on the Goddess that would be able to tell in advance whether he was going to do it? *But then...*

"KLF!"

There he was, trying to predict the future, when the whole point of Frigg was to do it for him. When Odin had decided to create food, drink, and attire in one piece, the... Universe... or something... delivered a complete Audhumla. Frigg would be Frigg, Odin decided, sweeping aside a worried thought that suggested she might turn out to be a cow.

"Let there be Frigg," he said. He intended to continue along the lines of "...and there was Frigg, and I saw Frigg, and she was haaaaawt" but before he got there, the freshly made Goddess slapped him in the face.

"That's for cheating!" she screamed. "I'll give those floozies a hard time, those hussies, those..."

"What is cheating?" mumbled Odin, holding on to his cheek and taking a step back from the angry Frigg. "What are floozies?"

Her breath slowed down. "Not yet," she said, a half-statement, half-question. "Still, you will, you womaniser. And maniser. And you'll brag about it, you little..."

"Hey, hey," Odin protested. "I am the All-Father!"

"Yes," said Frigg, rather coldly. "Many of those trollops will agree about the 'father' part. Why do I have to know that? Oh well, we might as well get married already, so you can start cheating on me, the faster the better, I suppose. I take you as my husband forever and for always." A deep sigh. "You take me as your wife, not that it will make much difference. Done."

Odin didn't even have time to protest before a horrifying thought appeared in his mind. So far, Frigg was less of a "take me in your strong arms, O All-Father" and more of an Embla.

"Have you built us a hall yet?" Frigg asked, looking confused, then she looked around, taking in his complicated drawing, the fire, and spilled simple split-pea soup with spinach and barley. "This is very confusing. We are in Ásgard, aren't we?"

Odin carefully confirmed.

"I won't hit you again," she said. "No, that's a lie. I won't hit you very soon. I think." Her forehead wrinkled and she stuck her tongue out, scratching her cheek in thought. Frigg looked rather attractive when she was thoughtful, Odin decided, which was followed with something like an internal blush. So far she did not seem to find *him* attractive at all. Certain women and men definitely did, as his research had proven, but his own wife should, too. Shouldn't she? She had a duty to like him, Odin was almost certain…

"What is a wife?" he asked quietly.

Frigg blinked a few times. "Oh, that's a thing people invented. Or maybe will invent. It's hard to say. It means that you have to be faithful to me, not that you'll care, and that we have to live together, not that I will want to, and – maybe I shouldn't have hurried so much. Oh well. What's done is done."

Odin also blinked a few times. He understood her

words, but not the sentences they apparently formed. Why did he create her in the first place...?

"Oh, I know. I need transportation—"

Frigg shut him up with a glance. "I will have a hall, please. Doesn't have to be very big to begin with, it will be a while until I gather maids and servants. And some sort of wardrobe, I'm not going to walk around naked, am I?"

"I – I don't mind."

"I will need bras without wires sticking out of them, Manolos, linen," Frigg said. "Needles, a dishwasher, concealer. Silk will take a while, I feel... or is this cotton? What are you wearing? Is this a dead animal? Why can't you dress in black leather like normal..." She sort of wavered. "I think I need to lie down. It's a bit overwhelming."

"All the cotton and stuff?" Something told Odin not to touch upon the topic of floozies again.

"Everything. I can foresee everything and everyone."

"Oh, good."

"At once."

"*Oh.*"

Frigg looked around. "Where are the beds? Mattresses, pillows, duvets? How do I charge my phone? Where is my organic wood-burning pizza oven?!"

"Please slow down...! I will never remember all of this, any of this! I created you so that you can tell me all those things, but... but in order!"

Frigg sat down, fanning herself with her hand. "This is the worst thing that's ever happened to me," she sighed. "No handbags either? Does anything at all exist? Really, no pillows? No books?" Her gaze landed on his bare feet. "No boots?!"

"Ah, ah!" Odin cheered up. Finally a word he knew. "I can arrange boots!"

"Size 7, or 38, depending on which world you're buying them in," Frigg said. "Flats. Are there stockings yet?" She sighed. "Wish Loki were here, he'd know exactly what I need. No stockings, no pillows, and whatever it is that you are wearing, I don't want any of it. What else is there? Oh, goodness me, if I am foreseeing it, that means it's in the future, doesn't it?!"

"I suppose," braved Odin.

"I need Eir to come up with relaxing herbs," Frigg sighed. "So, we'll need Eir. Wish Idunn was around already. Bring me some boots and something to wear... what *is* it that you have on?! And why?"

"It's a cow-skin," said Odin. "When I raise my hands you can see the little Odin!"

Frigg didn't seem amused by the presentation. If anything, her frown deepened. "Two eyes. I should have noticed. Go, hang off the Tree already," she sighed. "With the spear and all that. Men never remember what to buy without a shopping list. Will you remember this one? Just two things: boots and something to wear? Can you do that with two eyes?"

"Do I have to walk again...?" squealed Odin.

"Odin," Frigg said in a way that suggested her husband was, so far, ranking way below her expectations. "I'm here to tell you what to do. You're here to do it. Once I have my boots, you'll get your 'transportation'. Now, off you go. I'm going to lie down...somewhere."

"If you could just try not to ruin my diagram..."

Frigg rolled her eyes and gave the slightest of nods. "It wouldn't make a good pillow, trust me. Not that anything here would..."

95

Odin retreated before hearing the words "so-called God" he remembered all too well. As always, his mind confirmed the existence of pillows and dishwashers, but wouldn't show him what they were until he saw them. His steps quickened as he realised that in order to investigate boots he had to visit Madame A. His own wife had told him to do that, although she'd phrased it differently. He had no choice.

He also wondered what Frigg meant by "two eyes."

And whether Madame A was a floozy.

MIDGARDIANS, or humans, were neither the brightest (those would be the dark elves), nor the best looking (jötnar, no contest), but they were the strangest, which made them the most interesting. And if strangeness and/or interestingness were a competition, Madame A would win it without breaking sweat. Her own, at least.

As he neared Madame A's office, he heard a crack, then a man's cry, and realised she was working. His appointment was still days away. Nevertheless, he was the All-Father, and that man was... not the All-Father. Once his session was over, Odin would enquire about boot production, perhaps also about...

"You naughty cow-skin-remover!"

Madame A held a whip.

Crack – the man's cry – Odin's sympathy cry – Madame A's surprised glance – "harder, Madame, please!"

"Why does he like that?" Odin asked, bewildered.

The man gasped and tried to jump up, but she simply pushed him back on the ground with her tall, fur-lined boot. *Note to self*, Odin thought hopelessly, *I'm here for boots...* "Oh hello, All-Father. I wasn't expecting you today..."

Odin frowned and cleared his throat.

"I mean, I wasn't expecting you at all..."

Odin cleared his throat more meaningfully.

"It's...some other All-Father," Madame A said to her client, sounding resigned. "Not Odin. A whole different one... *ouch!*"

The man freed himself, causing her to fall, and he tried to run, screaming, holding on to his precious bits, only to fall flat on his face a moment later when a rock struck his skull. Madame A, scowling, dusted off her hands and shook her head.

"I can't believe that bastard pushed me. Don't worry, All-Father, he's been using the special mushrooms. When he wakes up, I'll tell him it was a vision."

"I thought you were opposed to violence," Odin said.

"I am. Everything I do, I do lovingly."

"This?" He pointed at the whip.

Madame A smiled warmly. "There's nothing that could make him happier."

"But... but why would anybody want this?! It hurts!"

"Pain is the same thing as pleasure, only more," Madame A said. "Not all pain, of course, you need experience and wisdom to achieve my expertise. The new clients ask for a little spanky, but this one's quite experienced. See the scars on his back?"

Odin swallowed the rock that had suddenly appeared inside his throat.

"He begged. I did it for his pleasure. I would never hurt a living soul... That rock I hit him with might turn out to be the most exciting experience in his life. I believe that what they'd really like is to get as close to death as possible," she continued. "Then, right before it's too late, spill their seed and survive. Like the rituals in your honour, only, you know …unfinished."

"Like the – ah, those rituals with the hooks and all?" Odin snorted. "How is that going to bring them closer to me?"

Madame A smiled. "How do you know about the hooks?"

"How do you think? I had to go and watch. It's – amusing to think that those people think I like watching it… well, I do, in a way, but only because it's so stupid… why are you grinning like this?"

"They want to be close to you," she said. "And, when you're there to watch, they *are*. My client here got very close to you."

"I hope he forgets about it," Odin muttered just as the client groaned a bit louder. "Look, I've got to go. So, you're doing it for their pleasure and they pay you?"

Madame A stretched, purring seductively. "Next time you come over I could show you…?"

"No, no, thank you, I'm good with the egg whisk," Odin quickly said. "Perfectly fine."

She made a face. "Not the feather duster?"

"Take good care," Odin said, his voice somewhat strangulated, "of him and yourself, and, and yes, the feather duster, please thank you very much. Oh, oh, I had a question!"

"Please hurry, All-Father," said Madame A, kneeling next to her client. "Naughty cow-skin-remover? Can you hear me?"

"Harder," the client grunted. Madame A looked at Odin and rolled her eyes. "So," she hissed, "the question?"

Odin was so shocked by the final "harder" that it took him a while to remember. "What is a spear?"

"This," she said, pointing at a stick with a sharp rock somehow attached to one end. "It's his. You can take it. My clients always pay..." She paused, looking at him in a strange way, then let out a tiniest sigh. "He'll pay with this spear in addition to the gold."

"I also need some rope."

Madame A slowly shook her head, then passed him the red rope, his favourite. "*Please* go, All-Father."

"All-Father...?" groaned the client.

"I said 'I'll do it harder'," Madame A said, then sighed. "I hope he won't end up with a headache. Can you please return my rope tomorrow, not-All-Father?"

"I, ah, I have an appointment," Odin said and retreated, wondering why anybody would willingly get close to death when the egg whisk and the feather duster existed. Not that he could remember how *exactly* they came to exist. Or why.

Odin needed to find someone who knew what they were doing, because he sure didn't.

WHEN HE WATCHED HUMANS' rituals, he was both disgusted and fascinated by the many things people did to themselves, ostensibly in his name. Most of those things were painful and bloody. Nine men, nine horses, nine goats, nine cows were put to death, their blood collected, and so on. Odin would mutter something along the lines of "KKMF," and busy himself with creating nine new horses, goats, and cows. There was no need to create new people – there were probably ninety-nine more born before the ceremony ended.

Madame A had a point. They got close to him, although technically he got close to them, and it was hard to tell what benefits exactly they got out of that proximity. Possibly because they were either barely conscious from the special mushrooms, or dead.

Odin stopped in his tracks.

There was madness to this method, which meant it probably made as much sense as anything else that had happened since he and his brothers had come to exist. If someone smarter – *not you then*, his mind whispered in a voice weirdly similar to Frigg's – were to work on this method a bit harder... not Madame A harder... or... perhaps?

Her client found himself right next to Odin and the only reason he might not be able to tell the tale were the special mushrooms – and a rock that almost, but not quite cracked his skull. Nearly. Very nearly. Was there a point where one could be simultaneously dead *and* alive? To get so close to death as to smell it, but not inhale?

Odin inhaled so sharply his lungs protested in surprise. He'd sure get very close to death once Frigg found out he'd gone straight to Madame A – with the best intentions, of course, and for no other reason than to ask about boots and the other thing that he had forgotten – and he'd proceeded to talk about everything but the boots. Odin was also nearly certain that Madame A was someone Frigg would describe as a "floozy."

What was it that Frigg had said about the spear and the Tree helping him make shopping lists? "Hang off the Tree with the spear and all," she'd said – strange that he'd remember this, but not what the other thing was on the list that was not boots. Odin had seen hangings from trees. None of them involved a spear. Also, all of them ended, indubitably, with death as those nearby confusingly chanted Odin's name. What was he supposed to do in order to speak with the management that took his confused requests and turned them into Audhumlas and Friggs? Sacrifice himself to himself? Did the management have a name he should chant while not dying?

Odin held his stick in one hand and the spear in the other. They were not all that different, except the spear had a sharp rock at one end. It wasn't difficult to figure out how it worked. He touched the tip and hissed. The sharp rock was *sharp*.

"No mushrooms," he muttered to himself, his surroundings disappearing as his imagination and creativity struggled to come up with something. "No food and no water at all." Hanging off the Tree... Madame A had shown him the ropes, but when she did it, it wasn't quite deadly at all. It was rather lively, in fact, greatly enhancing the effects of the egg whisk and the feather duster.

Odin looked at the spear again and gulped. It was so entirely unlike a feather duster that he'd have a hard time trying to come up with something even more unlike a feather duster. Yet it had to be used. Worse – it had to be used in a *nearly* deadly way... this required some thought...

You will notice the title mentions Loki, literature said.

"What is a title?" asked Odin, confused.

The sound of literature's sneakers as she sprinted away was his only answer, but he didn't have to wait long.

"Hello," said a familiar voice. "I am a stranger in this world. Could you point me towards…something?"

Odin froze into a statue, inventing statues as he did so. This voice was so familiar it could almost belong to a member of his family.

"Of course," the voice continued, on the verge of tears, "I wouldn't want to interrupt if you are doing something important, it's just that I am rather lost…"

"How…?" Odin cried, turning very slowly, not wanting to see the source of the sounds. "Why…? What…?"

Vili stared at him, looking more confused than Odin himself. "This might be hard to explain," he said, "but apparently I have died."

"Yes," said Odin weakly. "V-very difficult. Do you mind if I sit down?"

"Not at all. May I join?"

"P-please and also go on." *How does one kill a dead God? Just in case?*

"I found out that the dead go into a land that's made entirely of ice, snow, and fog," Vili said, frowning. "I did not like it much. Then I found this big tree, like the one here, only it was there… I don't know how to explain it… and I told them all to join me, because at least it didn't snow underneath. They didn't want to. They seemed very confused in general, but they especially didn't want to come close to the tree."

The magic was working even on dead people, Odin's mind sighed, relieved, then shook its head. It was, but not well enough. *Shut up*, Odin told his mind, *we're busy panicking.* Oh, the mind said sheepishly, *that's only too right. I forgot. Please carry on.*

"I couldn't convince them," Vili continued, "so I just

walked around a bit... and... now I am here. Where is here?"

"It's Ásgard," Odin groaned. "No, hang on. This is Midgard. I'm a bit shocked."

"Oh no, can I help?"

Yes, Odin's mind said, rather crankily, *by remaining dead*. "I'm – not used to – uh. So... what do you remember from before being dead?"

"You don't remember anything from before being dead," Vili explained. "That's how being dead works. That's the only thing we, the dead, know. That we are dead. Actually, if I am talking to you, does that mean you're dead as well?"

"Not yet," Odin said weakly. "So... since you... I wonder if... what would you say is...your name?"

Vili looked thoughtful, then shrugged. "I don't remember. Yours?"

Odin's mind threw itself into a sprint. Should he answer? If yes, then why and what? If no, then why and... he had to say something. What if Vili remembered...? "The All-Father," he finally said.

"Oh, that's very impressive," Vili said. "All? The dead people too?"

"It's a metaphor..."

"I just thought that sounds like a lot of fathering. What is a metaphor?"

"Uh, it's like a simile, but different... actually, well, my name is Odin." *Now or never.*

"Odin," said Vili, nodding slowly. "Odin... Sounds familiar..."

Odin stopped breathing.

"No, sorry, doesn't ring a bell. So, as the All-Father, you must be very important?"

"Yeah," Odin muttered, "I'm kind of a big deal." He gulped, wishing he had something – a kale smoothie, ideally – to drink. "I could, in fact, tell you a lot about...yourself."

"You could?! Are you also Me-Father? I feel like we're very close, if you don't mind me saying it."

"Doubtful," Odin croaked, then cleared his throat. It didn't help. "I am, for instance, not dead. I can, however, exclusively reveal that your name is L-Loki." Frigg mentioned a Loki. "You live in..." *Not Vanaheim*, his mind hissed. "Ásgard! Yes, that's where you live, together with me and my wife." How was it possible for his knees to turn into jelly when he was sitting? "You will have to get used to new things, other than ice and fog..."

"I don't mind," said Vili-Loki, shuddering. "I really don't."

"It's nicely decorated," Odin continued weakly. "Half of it, at least."

"What happened with the other half?"

"I – I will need you to help me with it. You're good with aesthetics... is... is my feeling. Ahahaha. Can I touch you?"

Vili-Loki blinked convulsively. "Is this an indecent offer?"

"N-no, I just wanted to see what being dead... how... it... feels."

Loki extended his hand and their fingertips met.

No ominous music sounded. There was neither thunder nor lightning. Not even the slightest buzz. It felt like touching someone's finger, which was both reassuring and disappointing.

"How peculiar," Odin muttered. "How about the back of your head?"

Loki instinctively reached to pat it. "It's also dead, I think," he said.

"May I see?"

There was nothing unusual about it. Loki looked very much alive, except for being Vili and also dead. *Note to self*, thought Odin hopelessly, create some sort of place where the dead go *and stay* before they work out how to get around his barrier and use the Tree to come over into Ásgard.

"When you and I reach Ásgard, I will show you the beauty of, uh, half of it. You will also get to meet Frigg," Odin said. He lifted himself to his feet rather clumsily. "That's my wife."

"I don't know her," Loki said, then frowned. "Oh, wait, you said I live there. Do I know her?"

"No. Neither do I. She's brand new. Truly one of a kind." Odin wiped sweat off his forehead with his forearm, nearly poking his eye out with the spear. Frigg seemed to be an assertive dame and, so far, he had done nothing to soothe her nerves.

THERE WAS ONLY one thing even more important than Frigg's disposition – keeping Vili… Loki away from Vé, the only other one who could recognise him. Frigg knew the future, but not the past, which meant that Odin could write literally any convenient backstory for Loki. Unless Vili was simply Vili, alive and lying, in which case what Odin said didn't matter at all.

What the backstory needed was an explanation for Frigg as to why Odin had left to bring her boots and the other thing and had returned with a dead brother. All of which Frigg had most probably predicted by now.

"Can you tell me something more about me?" Loki asked as Odin led him back towards the Tree.

"Glad you asked!" Odin enthused weakly. "You, Loki, are a son of... a... giant and a Goddess... who both... died. In an accident. They were very important themselves, although not as much as me, I'm afraid. But! You are, in fact, a God yourself."

"That's so nice!"

"With asterisks and small print," Odin muttered.

"Excuse me?"

"Nothing, nothing. You have returned from the dead, so I hope you can see how important you are..." *Is this the right thing to say?* his mind suddenly worried. Odin had not been prepared for his brother's resurrection. No, not a brother. For completely unrelated Loki's resurrection. Loki needed to remain on Odin's side, where Odin could keep an eye on him. Flattered enough not to throw himself into Vé's arms, but not enough to think that maybe he was, after all, as important as Odin. "You are welcome to live in Ásgard... ah, yes, you already live there, or rather used to, before you died. Together with your parents. Before the accident."

"What happened?" asked Loki, his voice slightly choked. "Did we suffer?"

"Absolutely not! Not even for a blink. It's better if I don't tell you, because you would be very upset. Do you need a hug?"

Loki eyed the spear. "I'm fine. Please carry on. Oh no! I need to go back to the dead world, find my parents and bring them back!"

"No, no, you absolutely can't! It is a... universal law. Only you are so important. They, I'm afraid, as nice and, and very good-looking as they were..." Odin quickly invented a handkerchief and dried his forehead. "If everyone could come back from the dead, we would have to accommodate them all. Overcrowding is a real problem that our societies will have to face sooner rather than later."

"What?"

"It's not realistic," said Odin. "It's just not realistic. Certain things, I mean people, are simply too... too dead. You are" – a gasp of awe – "exceptional."

"True, true," Loki agreed. "I feel quite exceptional. I can't wait to see Ásgard! Maybe my memories will come back once I enter our family hall?"

"It...is also gone," Odin croaked. "It was a very thorough accident. Nothing left, not a stitch. Gaaah!"

"What happened?!"

"I thought I saw a caterpillar," Odin said weakly. *That was the other thing Frigg had requested. Something to wear.* If Odin were to bring a very sharp spear instead of so much as a stitch, whatever that was, he'd probably have to return from the dead himself. He needed an excuse much better than that his only association with boots was Madame A, who'd made him forget about a lot of things, not just shopping for clothes.

The spear, the Tree, and the hanging suddenly felt safe. Relaxing, actually. Calming. Maybe he could learn how to meditate while he was at it? Once Frigg found out that he'd nearly died in the name of her shopping lists, she couldn't possibly be angry.

"I'm afraid I forgot about something very important," he said, stopping. "We must first go to Álfheim."

"What's Álfheim?"

"It's a very special place, free from the ice, the fog, fire and smoke, and..." *Anybody I know. Especially Frigg.*

"It won't take long." *I hope. Some of those rituals went on for nine days.* "You see, I must perform a certain ritual for the good of Ásgard. Actually, the good of the entire Universe..."

"For the dead, too? They're so unhappy." Loki sniffled.

"Possibly, possibly," said Odin nervously, hoping the answer was negative. "I will need your help."

"Why mine?"

"Because you came back from the dead and I will need to nearly get there."

Loki seemed to chew on that. "Why?"

"For... reasons. God reasons. Look, it just has to happen. And if I, myself, happen to die, then you can remind me who I was. Am." Odin crossed his fingers behind his back, wishing he could simply leave some notes for himself. This whole spear-hanging for the... God of Gods? The Divine? All-Grandfather...? – whatever the management called itself – better be useful.

"I hardly know you, though," Loki said.

He was right. Unfortunately, the only other person who actually knew Odin was Vé. Frigg was simply too fresh. Madame A knew *certain* things about the All-Father. In his quest to populate the worlds with caterpillars and birds that ate them, and to spend every night in somebody else's bed, Odin hadn't made any actual friends. The worshippers he had met would simply inform him that he loved nothing more than watching animals and men die slow, bloody deaths.

Gee, his mind said, *I wonder who could have spread the rumour that you are someone that craves pain and death so much that he killed his own bro–*

"I didn't do it!"

"Excuse me?"

"Ah, uh, I was just talking to – well. So. I must suffer," Odin explained. The handkerchief would have been more handy if he had more hands. "Badly. This is called a sacrifice."

Loki winced.

"It makes you even more important," Odin explained.

"Why?"

"Suffering brings you closer to G – to the Div – to senior management. Of the Universe. That's how you get promoted... look, it doesn't matter. It just has to happen. And unless I quickly create a God of Piercing Me with This Spear in a Not Quite Deadly Way, you're my best choice. You have suffered enough to be very, very important."

"Piercing? You? With this *spear?*" Each word seemed to be more italicised, with "spear" practically fainting on the page. "Only you, though, right? Not me? Because I feel important enough already."

"Oh, look," said Odin weakly. "This is Álfheim. Lovely, innit?"

"It's very pretty," Loki agreed. "Can we eat something here? I'm starving. I don't think I have eaten anything since I died. Was that long ago?"

"Maybe I could offer you a simple spinach and goat cheese lasagne?"

Loki looked positively shocked. "Goat cheese? No, thank you, I'd rather eat grass. How about beef?"

"Beef...? You mean meat?!"

"Of course, is there any other beef?"

"I did not create tofu and soy so that I'd eat beef," Odin huffed. "The nutritional values of soy beans..."

"You wouldn't be eating it, though," Loki said. "You can have your goat cheese."

"I won't be having anything," said Odin. "It's a part of the ritual. A quick kale and white cheddar soufflé? Grilled vegetables with red pepper hummus?"

Loki's eyes, already big, opened even wider. "Kale? Hummus?! If you have to suffer, you should prepare me a steak. I like it medium-rare, please."

"I'd need to create a cow—" Odin's throat closed for business.

How did Loki know that he liked steak, or what it even was, if he'd just returned from the dead without any memories and hadn't eaten anything there...?

He's lampshading, literature said.

"What is literature?" asked Odin, confused.

Only the sound of literature's sneakers as she sprinted away and Loki's puzzled look were his answer.

"Let's just do your ritual," Loki said, "then we can both go home and eat. I'll meet your wife, Frigg, whom I still don't know." His shoulders sloped slightly. "I don't know anyone, even my parents. I wish I could meet them."

"When I'm doing this ritual, I have to be on the verge of death and life. If I see them, I will give them your regards."

"Oh! That's so nice of you! Thanks so much! Then let's pierce you."

"Not so fast," Odin said, unsettled by both Loki's eagerness and his fondness for steak that wasn't even well done. "The hanging goes first. Madame A always starts with the bondage." He tried to scratch his chin thoughtfully and smacked himself in the forehead with the spear. Frigg's explanation lacked some detail. *Hang off the Tree with your spear and all.* He didn't have the *all.*

"Who is Madame A?"

"My advisor," Odin said shortly. "Let's just do it. I'll explain as we go." He tried to swallow, but his mouth was dry. The hanging wasn't the problem. The nearly-but-not-entirely mortal wound was. He needed an internal organ to volunteer.

None of them seemed enthusiastic. In fact, the internal organs seemed to be pushing each other to the front, which made Odin really nauseous. Most agreed it was the liver that should get speared. *Absolutely* not the kidneys, said the kidneys, they were in fact the worst idea possible. Very mortal. As mortal as mortality got. Liver it is, nodded the heart, which knew it was safe. *Absolutely* not, the liver protested, I am so disgusting because of my great importance. I'm saying the bladder must go. I must go, the bladder agreed sarcastically, which is why I am staying.

Lung, the other organs agreed when Odin had stopped breathing from just imagining the pain he was going to be in very soon, thus taking away the lungs' ability to protest. Lung is good, the bladder agreed. Due to Odin's throat currently not operating at full throttle, the lungs failed to file an appeal quickly enough. Lung, the heart agreed. The right one, it added. Keep that spear away from me, or I'll stop beating and we'll both regret that.

"I already regret that," said the right lung, and therefore Odin himself. None of the other organs could express itself as loudly as the lungs, but they didn't care, busy celebrating their safety.

Odin cleared his throat, instructed his lung to keep its opinions to itself, then turned to face Loki again.

"First of all," Loki said, unprompted, "I would like to thank you for the trust you have placed in me. I am truly proud and humbled. I would like to thank my parents, whom I don't remember, your wife Frigg, although I still don't know her, and your advisor Madame A, but mostly you, of course, for giving me this opportunity. I shall not fail you. Thank you, thank you," he bowed. "I promise to be here as long as it takes. Unless it takes too long, then not."

Odin gulped.

"What do I do with this rope, then?"

"My advisor would know," Odin muttered. If only Madame A could somehow appear here, perform the bondage part without asking any questions, then magically return to her office... Perhaps, he cheered himself up, he would possess this sort of magic after the hanging and spear and all were completed. "Let me explain to you what a legs up-balltie is."

"Maybe you could draw that," Loki suggested. "I'm a visual sort of person."

A few bent sausage-y shapes with sticks and circles representing the rope later, Loki was solemnly grinning. "This is the most exciting thing in my death," he announced.

"Gmpf," answered Odin, who just hit the ground for the fourth time. Perhaps what Frigg meant was that Vili-Loki should hang from the Tree. If Odin didn't feel guilty enough about having killed his brother once already, although in truth it was Vé's fault and not Odin's at all... "Can you please do it a bit tighter?"

"Are you sure it's 'balltie' and not 'ball'" – an excoriating pause – "'tie'?"

"Very," said Odin shortly. There were sorts of suffering he was not willing to experience for Frigg's shopping lists. Also, Madame A knew her job much better than he knew his.

And then...

...it worked.

Frigg's wrath couldn't have been half as painful as this.

The ropes were almost-but-not-quite pulling his limbs out of their sockets, almost-but-not-quite cutting through the skin to make him bleed. The legs-up balltie was not created with hanging from trees in mind.

"So, what do I do with the spear?"

"OMD," muttered Odin. He'd forgotten about the spear and now, due to being tied and well hung, he couldn't point where his terrified lung was. "Just – just stick it in my side."

"Like this?"

"Ouch!"

"I'm so sorry... I'm worried about you. Are you *sure* this is the right thing to do?"

"No," admitted Odin. "But poking me definitely isn't. Push it in, because when you do this, you are tickling me, and not in the right way."

"There is a right way?"

Every question intensified Odin's suffering. "Just do it! Harder! Deeper! AAAAHHH!!!"

"Oh no, oh no," cried Loki, running around Odin. "I hurt you!"

"Deeper," groan-whispered Odin. The spear went

just deep enough to reach an internal organ of its choice before Loki took it out. "And leave it there!"

"All-Father, I don't want to kink-shame you, but..."

"DO IT!"

And Loki did it.

ODIN CAME to when Loki threw a bucket of cold water at him. Now, in addition to everything else, Odin was wet, cold, and plagued by the question as to where Loki had found a bucket.

"This looks so bad," Loki cried. "So bad. You are bleeding."

As he struggled to answer, the wounded lung crossed its arms on its chest. *Maybe you should have picked a kidney after all, huh, quiet man?* "Hhhhh," Odin finally said.

"I am very worried about your health. Do you drink enough? Because dehydration might really kill you. Should I bring you some water?"

"Zmf," Odin managed, the pain intensifying to the *near* unbearable level.

"I knew it. You can't talk, because your lips are too dry," said Loki. "I will bring a wet cloth. Do you have health insurance?"

"Gmm!"

"There is also the question of nutrition. I don't think you have thought this through, oh dear, oh dear. How about we try again? I'll take you off this tree, I'll cook some rabbit stew... ah, you've mentioned, you don't like meat." Loki swallowed. "I do. And I haven't eaten since I died. Will you be okay on your own for a while? I mean, considering? I'm just going to pop out hunting for a sec and catch some rabbit."

Odin's eyes narrowed to slits that he imagined as being red when he saw Loki turn into a wolf. He would have gasped, if not for the circumstances. There was Vili-Loki, and then there wasn't, but there was a wolf. A very realistic one. Very...real.

The pain, confusion, pain, the sensation of hanging upside down from a branch of the Tree, being tied up by someone who was not very good at it, and also pain were now compounded by sheer terror. What had his brother become? How did he make it out of the world of the dead, through Odin's barriers...?

Mercifully, he passed out for a while, only to be woken by Loki, slapping his cheeks gently. Ish.

"Are you feeling well, All-Father?"

"Gwwm."

"I would feel much better if you did this under medical supervision."

"Gwwm!"

"Should I try and find your wife Frigg, although I still don't know her? She might be worried, waiting with dinner since yesterday... possibly going out of her mind with worry..." Loki sighed. "She should know. I will go and—"

That did it. Even Odin's lung had enough of the Helpful Questions. "Go away!" Odin cried. "I am trying to almost die here!"

Loki, his eyes wide, withdrew a bit. "Of course, of course. I wouldn't want to interrupt that. If you are absolutely certain, then I am just going to build myself a little fire here and bake my rabbit. You won't even smell it. Unless the wind changes."

Odin slipped into the merciful unconsciousness again. He couldn't tell whether he remained in the non-state for a blink or three days before he was woken up by something very heavy and pointy.

Loki's stare.

"I'm just sitting here on those rocks," Loki said. He wasn't even blinking, his fascinated gaze fixed on the spear. He took a bite of some random rabbit bit and Odin would have winced if he remembered how. "Keeping an eye on you. For your own good, of course. Because I am very caring. Also because you know more about me than you said so far. Much more, don't you, All-Father?"

Odin's innards stiffened, and not just because of the smell of baked meat.

"I felt so lonely there with the dead. They're not very talkative. As in, not at all. They don't seem to have any memories or know anything." Loki paused. "I hope you don't die, All-Father. Because if you did... I don't think you, your wife, or I would like that. Imagine being at the mercy of someone who has information about you, but you can't get it out of that person." Another bite, a sound that had no right to be so loud, and a flash of Loki's white teeth. "Also, I like being the only one to ever make it back from the dead. Wouldn't be good if others started doing it, would it? It would make me look less important."

Odin was aware that he should be feeling threatened. Maybe he even did. He couldn't tell anymore, couldn't differentiate between feelings, physical or emotional. His mind was in such a haze he could have as well been imagining Loki now. Was it a good idea to ask him, out of all the few people and deities that Odin knew, to pierce him with a spear and hang off the Tree? Was any of this a good idea? Even if it was solely to make the Universe a better place and avoid Frigg's wrath? He hadn't known her long enough to tell whether she was the easily wrathed type. Wrothed. Wrothy. He couldn't even into wrathing anymore. His mind was becoming blank, which was actually not entirely unpleasant, until Loki spoke again and brought Odin back to a reality in which he was in *lots* of pain.

"This is very amusing, if you don't mind me saying."

Odin minded it very much but was currently unable to express himself.

"That you would put a spear through – well, obviously I helped, but that the importance would require the hanging, not eating, not drinking, the spear... It's been days. Why would anybody want to be so important? Yet," Loki continued, "I...like watching it. Watching your quest for promotion to higher management. I hope they are impressed by your devotion to your job. The All-Fathering." He paused. "I wonder what your new title will be..."

The rest – Loki clearly liked the sound of his voice very much, even if the audience remained mostly passive – blurred into one sound, the non-state Odin had experienced before. The realisation that Loki found Odin's predicament amusing, exactly how Odin perceived humans' sacrifices, lasted forever and for a blink, just long enough for one extra thought. Surely... he hadn't sacrificed himself to Loki?

The thought made Odin feel nothing, because he was nothing now, nothing and nobody and nowhere and never and not.

Except.

Somehow, in his All-Father career, there was *always* an except, a but, asterisks, and small print.

I have a charm for you, his mind said. *Hello? Anybody there? Can you please let me continue nearly dying?* Odin thought desperately.

In the dark void of nothingness, tiny lights – so tiny they didn't exist, until an infinity of them joined to become a near-invisible-and-yet spark that joined more and more others, formed an orb of pale green light.

The first is called Help, because it can comfort grief, lessen pain, and cure sickness.

Well, Odin thought, *that would be useful. Right now.* If someone could utter it for him.

The second orb of light looked like pale gold.

The second is something that every healer needs to know.

Maybe you should give it to someone who—

The third: while in fight, I can blunt the opponent's blade, so he can't wound me.

A bit too late for this one, Odin thought, nevertheless admiring the red light. It didn't seem to have a source. It just was. He wasn't seeing it as much as experiencing.

His mind was sometimes so irritating, though, that he really hoped it wasn't the Divine.

The fourth: if someone should bind us hand and foot, the charm will release us, so we can walk free.

Now you're just taking a piss, Odin thought. *Leave me alone.*

I am literally your mind. I can't leave you alone even if I wanted to. The fifth charm, by the way – if you see an arrow in flight...

Please stop, Odin thought, *you are worse than Loki.*

...you can catch it.

What is an arrow?

Ask Frigg. The sixth: if anyone wants to kill us using a stick engraved with runes...

Hey, hey, wait, Odin thought.

...that one will only destroy themselves. The sev—

No, go back, runes, Odin thought. *I'm here for those, aren't I?*

Oops, his mind said, rather sheepishly. *I think I got the order of the charms wrong. Interestingly, though, if a roof bursts into flames...*

Runes.

Can I interest you in witches flying on rafters?

Runes, I said.

But do you KNOW what? This one is good. If we see a hanged man swinging from a tree, his heels above his head... The mind paused for effect. *Or maybe I should leave me alone.*

No, no, go on, Odin thought, *what do we do with that hanged man? Is there a spear in his lung?*

We can cut and colour the runes so that he will come down and talk to us.

What? Cut? Colour? Runes? This is brand new information!

I'll be back some other time.

Why? Give me my runes!

I am you, the mind sighed. *I can't give you what you don't know.*

But you gave me the lights!

Charms, if you please, and that is because the Norns have provided us with those.

Norns? Are Norns like runes?

The mind sighed. *And you called Ask "Ask" because he*

kept asking and asking. We have to be in pain for a while now, Loki wants something.

Odin's consciousness did the worst. Namely, it returned.

"...rope. I could just fix it a bit so it wouldn't make your feet, you know, they're a bit blue. Would you like that? Or do you like them blue? This is *so* interesting. Maybe I should only do one foot, and then you can tell me which one feels..."

The mind, charms, runes, or Norns took pity on Odin and he floated away again, into something that was neither time nor place. This time, finally, there was no "except" waiting for him.

IN THE BEGINNING, there was confusion, but not for long. The fog that had no colour began to split into green, yellow, blue, grey, white. Non-fogs. Objects. Sun. Sky. A path appeared under Odin's bare feet, with eternally slow immediacy; a path surrounded by grass and flowers more beautiful than anything he had ever created.

Dressed in something that his mind informed him was a *tunic* held around his waist by a *belt*, Odin stood in that one spot, looking around, utterly confused. Had he died, he should be surrounded by ice and snow, according to Vili-Loki. Therefore, he hadn't died. And...? *And breeches*, his mind said belatedly.

He had found the Divine, Odin suddenly realised, and nearly whooped. He would feel more whoopily, had the Divine not so far consisted of a path and greenery... and a bird. A bird suspended in the air.

Odin approached the creature and looked at it closely, yet carefully. The bird could have been some sort of a trap or a test. Something that would explode in his face or drop a container from its non-ass on his booted – oh, how nice – feet. It was a colourful bird, neither a peacock nor a crow, rather small, carefree and unmoving. He bit his lip, unsure what he was seeing and why. Very carefully, Odin extended his finger and touched the bird.

It was real.

Or was it?

What even *was* "real"? Was Odin real?

The bird was tangible, Odin corrected himself. To the possibly-real-unless-not form Odin was currently in, whatever that was, the bird was something that the form could touch. Perhaps the bird was a form of something else, too. Or just a bird, only... impossible.

Was Odin possible right now?

If he'd had a chance to watch cartoons from the 1970s, Odin's eyes would currently look like question marks. Alas, neither cartoons, nor question marks had been invented yet, although the latter were going to become necessary as soon as the next sentence.

"What are you doing here???"

With a gasp, Odin turned to see a woman. She looked angry. She was also dressed in something that was not a tunic and not breeches. Something that caused his mind to let out a little squeal and hide instead of searching for words that could describe the...attire. There was something extremely unsettling about the woman. She shared something with Odin. Neither of them *were*.

"A manifestation," Odin said, snapping his fingers.

That was it. He was currently a manifestation and so was the woman. "Good... eh... day to you."

"Get out," said the woman. "You can't just be here with us. It's not possible."

His eyes widened. "Then how am I here?"

"I don't care as long as you leave."

"But I don't know how," Odin said. "Really. I was there, hanging from the Tree with a spear in my side as you do, when suddenly..."

The woman rolled her eyes. "My sisters know what to do with you. There," she pointed, "walk down this path."

"And – and you?"

She showed him an object she was holding. It was green, bulbous, with an elongated beak, and a flower on its side. Some water spilled out of the beak. "And I water the flowers, because what else can Verðandi be good for? Of *course* good middle-aged Verðandi waters the flowers. When I am back, I am making tea. You..." A smirk replaced the irritation on her face. "Are their problem. You are there. And don't touch this bird, because that potentially creates inconsistencies."

"How?" Odin asked.

"I give them an inconsistency one day," she hissed, already marching away with her... *Watering can,* his mind whispered helpfully, *and for your information, I was not hiding, I was, ah, regrouping.*

The Divine was turning out to be very different from what he couldn't even imagine.

HE FOLLOWED the path until both the path and Odin turned and stopped abruptly at what appeared. His feet grew roots, although not literally, not yet – who knew what manifestations feet were capable of in *Odin's mind gestured at everything*? The vision was confusing. It was also gasping.

Behind a big chunk of wood placed on smaller chunks of wood – *table*, Odin's mind whispered, *note to self, this looks very useful* – two women sat on a mid-sized chunk of wood placed on even smaller chunks of wood – *bench*, Odin's mind whispered, *note to self*.

"You know the note business never works," Odin barked at his mind. Unfortunately, he did it aloud and the manifestations noticed that.

"You will get out of here," said the one on the right. She looked young. Apart from that, she also looked like every woman at almost once, giving Odin's manifestation an immediate headache. He loved women, but at slower pace, even if there happened to be more than one around.

"He does not leave until Verðandi has returned," said an old woman to her left. There was nothing unusual about her, apart from the fact that she didn't exist. "Good day to you, Odin."

"G-g-good day to you, er…"

"My name was Urðr," said the old woman, "and I was a representation of the Past."

"Not manifestation?"

She frowned. "You had better watch your words when there were ladies around. And Skuld."

"Urðr!"

Odin accidentally glanced at Skuld, and his manifested – or represented – stomach protested.

"Who are you?" he asked.

123

"I will be the Future. A better question will be: who will you have been?"

"I am Odin," Odin reminded. "The old w – Urðr knows me."

"I knew you ever since this Universe had manifested," said Urðr. "That was how you should have correctly used that word."

"So, I will not know him," said Skuld, bewildered.

"You have known him since Verðandi returned and this moment had passed."

Odin blinked. Urðr sounded the way Skuld looked.

"Oh, you should have sat down," sighed Urðr. "But not have touched the tapestry."

The entire table was covered with something that made Skuld look grey and ordinary. Colours and shapes meandered, disappearing where Urðr sat, appearing – blurry and unclear – on Skuld's side. Right in the middle was the only spot, or line, or thread, that looked sharp.

"You had ceased to exist," explained Urðr. "Once this moment has passed, you should have begun to exist again, unless you have died."

"Have I?!"

"Skuld will know."

"I will not tell even him if I will know," Skuld said. "As far as he will be concerned, he will exist and he will not exist until he finds out. Schrödinger's God. Fingers!"

Odin, who was about to place his hands on the table, withdrew swiftly.

"Where did Verðandi go?" muttered Urðr. "This required tea."

"She has – had went to water the flowers," Odin helped. He had not yet been introduced to grammar or copy editing, but whatever those women were have will been doing intimidated both of those things. "What's tea?"

"I am back," Verðandi interrupted. "I suppose I am supposed to make tea now?"

"You will please ensure that he will not mess with the tapestry," said Skuld. "I will make the tea."

"What's tea?" asked Odin.

Verðandi clucked her tongue.

"It was invented soon anyway," said Urðr. "Every Universe invented three things, greed, intoxication, and tea."

"What's intoxication?"

"You noticed that he didn't ask what greed was," Urðr said to the air. "Verðandi? Was I right?"

"There is no thread for him. Are you introducing me already?"

"Ah... I had been thinking maybe it would be best if you did it."

Verðandi sighed. She looked neither pleased nor pleasant. "I am the Current. I am the Moment. I am the Now. The old woman is the Past, she is all the moments that have come to pass. The child making tea..."

"Verðandi!"

"...is the Future, she is all the moments that will come to pass later."

Odin took a confused look at the three, or rather two and a half to avoid the Skuld-related headache. They looked similar. Like sisters, in fact. He used to have two brothers. They could not be present here due to... circumstances. He was outnumbered.

"We are Time," sighed Verðandi. "Do you understand what Time is?"

Odin instinctively looked at the sun. "Early afternoon?"

Verðandi hid her face in her hands.

"All of Time," said Urðr. "I was, Verðandi is, and Skuld will be. Together, we have been Time, capitalised, since the beginning of time, no capitals. The difference is very important. Someone like you should have understood that."

"Like me?"

"You are Odin," said Verðandi. "You are the All-Father, although people call you many names such as the Wanderer, the..."

"Not yet!" cried Skuld. "They will not call him that to his face yet! You will not listen to her, Odin. What sort of tea will you have?"

"They haven't discovered it yet," said Urðr. "He looked like the lapsang souchong type to me, though. Don't have dared to put sugar in it."

Odin was handed a small cup, so tiny it felt like he'd crush it from just looking at it too hard.

"Be careful," Verðandi said. "This is our good china with hand-painted periwinkles."

"He will still have to invent periwinkles," said Skuld. "And china. You will be more careful with your words, please."

"Biscuit?" Verðandi said, and Skuld and Urðr ground their teeth in unison. "What? If he is not aware of tea yet, he is not aware of biscuits either. What's the difference?"

"Maybe you will also give him AK-47s and pocket calculators while you're at it," muttered Skuld.

"So, I am sitting here with time?" Odin asked, paying

less attention to Skuld's words than he will think he should. Had. Would have will.

"*Time*, if you please. With a capital T." Verðandi handed him another tiny piece of good china with hand-painted periwinkles. It was small and round, with something even smaller, brown and oval-shaped, placed in the middle. Odin gawked at the construction. "It's a biscuit," she said, irritated. "You eat it. The brown part, not the plate."

Odin didn't dare not to and the biscuit melted on his tongue into a combination (*note to self: invent "symphony"*) of tastes, all of which were wonderful. The tea smelled and tasted like a bonfire, which was the most unusual smell for a liquid. It was hot, as the bonfires' reputation would dictate, and his manifestation or representation burnt its tongue.

"BMW!"

"What?" asked Verðandi, but Skuld silenced her with a gesture.

"He came for runes," said Urðr.

"And we give them to him? Just like that?"

"We have given them to him," the Past sighed. "Hadn't you heard what he was doing?"

"I never know anything," Verðandi said. "Please enlighten me."

"It was a bit of an experiment," Odin quickly said. "With a spear and the Tree. I sacrificed myself to the manag – the Divine. Which of you is the Divine? Or are you all the Divine?"

Verðandi blinked. "We are the Norns. We are Time. You are the Divine."

"No, you don't understand. The other Divine. The

one who created me and my – companions. I have a few questions."

"Too bad," said Verðandi. "You are It."

"I sacrificed myself to myself?!" Skuld snorted. "You will not be the brightest lightbulb in the...lightbulb store."

"But how could I have created myself? That's impossible."

"You and your brothers had not created yourselves," Urðr said. "You had begun to exist together with this Universe. Each Universe had a beginning and an end. The unusual thing was that all the previous Universes developed worshippers who then had made up their Gods, not the other way round."

"I am not made up," Odin answered, crossing his arms on his chest. The old woman was overstepping. "Are you telling me the spear and the rest were unnecessary?!"

Urðr just shrugged. "Without them you would have never made it here. The only way to have found yourself in the moment, but not earlier or later, was from becoming alive and dead at once."

"Right at this moment the ropes are tied around nothing," said Verðandi, grimacing. "You don't exist in space now."

"Long enough for you to have fallen..." Urðr interrupted.

"On his face, I hope..."

"Silence, Verðandi. You should have gone searching for the user manual." Urðr turned towards Odin again. "Loki had questions to which you did not have answers. If you told him about us when you returned, he would have found us too...and we have had to have given him something."

Verðandi cast a doubtful look at Skuld. "Is he getting the runes then?"

"You will know very well that I won't be able to tell you..."

"Did he look like someone who would have left without runes?" Urðr asked. "We couldn't have worked with him here. He would have had to have died. Here. Did you think we wanted a dead Divine here? Just have given it to him already."

Odin tried to think multiple thoughts at once to save time. He wasn't *entirely* sure what runes were, but if they were going to help him write down what was eating what, or what Frigg wanted him to bring from Midgard, or simply come off the bloodied Tree, remove the spear from his lung – logistics of that to be confirmed – and eat a simple spinach and feta quiche, he was not leaving without them. Ever. Whatever "ever" meant when he was sitting with Time.

"I also want the bee squids," he said, "and the tea."

"It doesn't matter what you want," said Verðandi. "You are given what you are given. Take it or leave it. Are you forgetting the cockatoo already? The bird you were trying to touch?"

Odin blinked.

"I am the Current, I am the Moment. I am right now, nothing before, nothing after. Once I get bored of right now, or I feel sufficiently motivated" – for some reason, Verðandi glared at the other two with impressive exotropia – "I move the tapestry of Time to the next moment. Skuld, here, is the one who settles it. And Urðr is the one who checks the previous moment for inconsistencies. You," Verðandi said, pointing at him with a tiny silver spoon, "are an inconsistency. As of right this moment, you do not exist anywhere in space. You are dead and alive at once. And you are the Divine," she added, grimacing as if her biscuit had been replaced with a cunning slice of celery. "The One That Is."

Odin didn't bother trying to understand most of what was being said. He knew he wasn't smart enough for it anyway. What mattered was that he was the Divine, which meant that his brothers weren't. Vili-before-he-was-Loki and Vé hadn't been here. Or... had they? He had to come up with really good excuses why they shouldn't be.

"Do I get some sort of badge?" he asked. "One that says 'The Divine'? Or a diploma? Certificate?"

Verðandi just rolled her eyes. "There it is," she said, producing a thick, rectangular-shaped, white item and showing Odin its front side. "Fingers! Don't touch the tapestry!"

He gawked at the black shapes that seemed to be drawings so small and crooked even his peeing dispenser with hundreds of legs made more sense.

"Don't have been like that," sighed Urðr. "Just have told him already."

"User manual for combo-microwave oven," said Verðandi. "Available in the following languages..."

"Verðandi! That was not funny!"

Odin gulped. "Combo-microwave oven" sounded like a charm potent enough to make him sweat. Frigg would definitely demand one of those within a few... moments... after his... return.

"Okay, fine," Verðandi groaned. "Now, Divine All-Father Odin. Listen carefully, for I am saying this only once..."

. . .

WITH A THUD, Odin fell on the ground, landing on his butt rather than face, presumably disappointing Verðandi. It must have been Skuld's fault. From what he had understood, she will have has... no... he'd forgotten how to speak normal Goddish, but will soon have remembered... for now, he had the runes and the seventeen charms. Which was really quite exciting, but not as exciting as the forest fire raging way closer to the Tree than it should.

"Loki!" Odin cried out. If his brother were to repeatedly die and return, Odin's nerves simply wouldn't be able to take it. Was one out of the seventeen charms useful for burning forests? No, for un-burning them? Odin produced a quick downpour, then tried to sigh in relief.

Oh.

The spear was still there. His lung had only shouted for Loki because it had been too distracted by the blaze.

"My fire!" Loki cried, appearing next to Odin. "It was so pretty!"

"Mmpf?"

"I was sitting by a fire, when you were—" Loki gestured "—and it is so beautiful to watch. I love beauty. What's more beautiful than beauty? More beauty!" He smiled. "One day I'll create the biggest fire ever... oh, my apologies, how selfish of me. Here I am, talking about my hopes and dreams for the future, while you still have that spear in you."

Odin nodded weakly.

"I stand here, doing nothing but talking about my taste in decoration," Loki sighed. "Maybe I could create an eternal fire. One that no rain could extinguish, swallowing the entire Universe..."

Loki is foreshadowing, said literature.

What is literature? asked Odin's mind, since his actual voice was currently unavailable.

There was no answer, apart from the sound of literature's sneakers as she sprinted away.

"Sorry! Sorry! The spear. Can you tell me what to do with it? No, you can't. Hmmm. I think your wife will be very nervous by now. You look really bad, too. Maybe you should bathe a bit. You're a bit...covered in blood. Do you think you could bathe with that spear?"

Odin coughed and a wave of pain went through his entire body.

"It's just that I don't have experience with removing spears from All-Fathers," Loki said. "Through your back, no? Because otherwise the... spear-head goes through you again and that's going to hurt worse. Oh, hang on. Hahaha, I made a joke! 'Hang on', so good. I'll keep it in mind. Anyway. Do you still need to suffer?"

Even if Odin could utter one of his brand new seventeen charms, none of them would shut Loki up. He could only glare and wait.

"I'm going to pull it through your back. Ready? Three... two..."

"Aaaaaahhhhh!!!"

"This is sharp!" Loki cried. "I didn't even get to say 'one' and I cut my finger! Now I have a boo-boo. Look!" He nearly poked Odin's eye out as he demonstrated the scratched digit. "See? And I can't even ask my Mummy to kiss it, because she's dead!"

"Kiss what?"

"My boo-boo... I feel very strange," Loki groaned, slowly dropping to his knees. "Very strange."

Odin, who had just finished hanging from a rope with a spear through his deeply upset lung for nine days, had very little sympathy for Loki.

"Your blood flows in my veins now," Loki intoned. His voice turned lower; somewhere between confused and menacing. Like an angry bear handed a bee squid.

"It's barely a drop," Odin said. He was somewhat shaky, both from the pain – the lung was not impressed by any of what had happened to it recently – and Loki's transformation. "In fact, it's not even a—"

"We're brothers," Loki whispered.

"No! We are absolutely unrelated! Not even in the sl—"

"We are *blood* brothers," continued Loki in this new, unnerving voice of his. "A part of you is a part of me now. But the pact is not finished yet." He cut his finger with the spear in one decisive move. Without mentions of boo-boos, he stuck the bleeding finger straight into the hole in Odin's side.

Only the combination of charms #1 and #2 saved Odin from passing out. But not even all seventeen of them could take away the *change*. Loki was neither lying, nor making it up. A small drop of his blood mixed with Odin's was more than enough.

"Blood brothers," Odin whispered.

Through a haze, a blur, he watched Loki, cross-eyed, trying to simultaneously suck at his cut digit and complain about his suffering. Odin couldn't hear. He was busy experiencing the eighteenth charm.

He could have guessed that seventeen was not a number holy enough. It didn't divide by three.

The eighteenth charm appeared in his mind. The charm that could never be shared with anyone – the charm that only he and Loki would ever know. It sounded deceptively simple for something more important than the Universe, something not even the Norns could understand or control. It explained the very existence of Odin and his brothers; it explained the Tree; it nearly explained what a combo-microwave oven was.

"FML," Odin muttered. That was it, finally. Fehu. Mannaz. Laguz. Runes that nobody but Odin could utter or write, at least at the...moment.

Loki's complaining stopped, as it cut with the spearhead, only longer and with a more convenient, short handle. "What did you say?"

"Frigg, My Love," Odin said. "A charm that celebrates my wife and will continue to do so forever. From now on, every time someone says 'FML!' they will be offering their endless love and devotion to my wife."

Surely that's worth more than some lousy boots, Odin said to his mind, as they dragged their feet towards Ásgard, Loki carrying the spear, Odin heavily resting on his stick.

Not sure if Frigg will see it this way, his mind answered.

"FML," Odin muttered.

FASHIONTELLER

Frigg sat up in the grass and rubbed her eyes. Little had changed. The visions she called "future burps" plagued her no matter whether she was asleep or awake, reliable in their randomness, expected in their unexpectedness. They gave her headaches and rare glimpses of pleasure, but mostly lots of envy and confusion. The worst thing about them was that if she saw something that wasn't real, it probably just didn't exist yet, which meant she couldn't have it. The burps seemed quite fixated on the first season of *Blabbing with Bjarnisdóttirs*, which was set in a future so distant that if Emma, Lilith, or Tinna's sponsors sent them something new, Frigg could cross it off her mental to-hopefully-acquire list. The list kept expanding anyway in a slightly deluded way, not unlike what would be called TBR piles in the future. Unfortunately, similar to all owners of TBR piles, Frigg didn't know which of her expectations were unrealistic.

The best, as in the saddest, way to figure out what

was or wasn't possible was to ask Odin and assess the degree of confusion on his face. When she asked about treadmills, Odin just gawked at her. The same thing happened when she requested a bong, a yoga mat, and a steam train – Frigg had no real use for a steam train, but it looked like something worthy of a Goddess...for about a blink, after which it was replaced with a vision of a fountain pen.

"A fountain pen?" Frigg tried.

"Yes," Odin said.

She carefully perked up.

"It is a thing," Odin continued, "which is going to start existing one day and then I will let you know." He paused. "Do you like this answer better, Frigg, my love? I have noticed your sadness. I truly want to help—"

"Coffee," Frigg sighed. "*Please* invent coffee already."

Her husband hadn't been entirely useless. He had produced a cave which, as he explained, was practically a hall; large flat rocks, which were practically tables, and small rocks, which were practically chairs. Frigg, who knew exactly what tables and chairs looked like in the future world of *Bjarnisdóttirs*, let out half-hearted oohs and aahs. Hopefully with some more encouragement he'd produce a decent armchair.

Indeed, Odin hadn't stopped there. Small stone bowls with handles placed on slightly larger flat rocks were "the good china, but without the hand-painted periwinkles." Luckily or not, to the best of her knowledge Frigg hadn't seen a periwinkle yet. Perhaps that was what would make Odin's heated water with dry leaves more palatable. Frigg wanted frappuccinos and Odin's "drink" only served as a reminder of how very much she couldn't have them. It also gave her the runs.

"Espresso?"

Odin's infamous blank stare was her only answer.

Frigg massaged her temples. All of that future was giving her a headache.

"Why can't I make a bee squid?" Odin muttered, raking his fingers through his hair. "I have bees. I have squids... Frigg?"

"Please keep the squids away from me!" She couldn't even rake her fingers through her hair anymore, which used to be curly. Now it was something that made her avoid reflective surfaces. "Hairspray? Hairbrush? Rollers? Sham..."

Odin's trademark blank stare was her only answer.

Pooh, Frigg thought.

"I've had an idea," she said, watching him draw arrows between, most probably, bees and squids. "Maybe it will help you find something. I've been watching Loki. He's been shifting into birds, wolves, all sorts of things. You don't need a bus or a Prius, you need an animal. Earlier today, I saw a horse..." Technically – whatever "technically" would come to mean one day – she had seen it much further in the future, in a vision of *Lilith's Little Sweet Sixteen*. Nevertheless, due to the previous sentence taking full advantage of the past perfect tense, "earlier today" it was.

"Not again," Odin groaned.

Frigg's eyebrows wandered up. "You've created one already?"

"N-not completely. Tell me more about the see-horse."

"What? It's just 'horse'. I guess I must draw it for you..." They sighed in unison. In any drawing competition they'd battle for the last spot.

After a few apparently inevitable see-horses, followed by horses d'oeuvres, and a spider that made Frigg decide four legs were a perfect enough number, Odin came up with *something*. The scientific name for the creature was "a limping donkey," but someone, who had spent their entire life unaware of the worlds' fauna, could be convinced that this was exactly what a horse looked like. The key to getting the donkey to do what you wanted him to do was to first lower your expectations, then tell yourself that if he was doing it he was supposed to do it, and if he wasn't, then he wasn't. Still, now Odin had something to sit on and yell at when it didn't listen, and could look proudly down from his perch at small children, animals, and adults sitting on the ground.

As he sort-of began his departure towards Álfheim, looking as dignified as an All-Father on top of a donkey could, he nearly trudged over a beaming Loki.

"I have news!" Loki reported breathlessly. "What is Odin doing?"

"Reversing, I think..."

"FML!"

"I have visited the worlds of the elves, dark elves, humans, ice giants, and—" Loki lowered his voice "—the one where Odin told me not to go."

"Which one is that?"

"The one where I would never go, since the All-Father told me not to," said Loki louder, as Odin limped towards them, massaging the buttock the donkey had kicked. "I can exclusively reveal that people wear sheepskins, rabbit skins, cow skins..." He looked towards the sky, scratched his chin, and stuck out the tip of his tongue. As Loki began to count his fingers, some of them more than once, in clear awe of the number's stupendousness, Frigg held her breath. "One more thing!" he exclaimed and Frigg's lungs nearly burst. "I met two humans who only had two large leaves on their you-know-whats." He pointed towards Odin's you-know-what. "I had to run away, though, because there was a snake."

"That looks more like a worm than a snake," muttered Frigg, looking at the specimen.

"It's cold!" Odin protested.

"No, not the you-know-what! There really was a snake. Snake-sized. They were all talking about apples."

Loki had feasted on those special mushrooms again, Frigg realised. The only consolation was that her gift, once again, had proven to be accurate. She'd expected disappointment and her prediction had come true.

"I could arrange those immediately," Odin said. "The leaves. Not the snake."

Frigg ignored him. "What do they do with those sheepskins?"

"There's this lady called Madame A," Loki said, clapping his hands in excitement. "Odin is besties with her. We should all go together and talk to her about the boots and stuff."

"Who is Madame A?" asked Frigg.

"Sheepskins," said Odin. "I'm sure they're made of sheepskins."

"Who is Madame A?"

"I think I've seen someone wearing a dead wolf around her neck," said Loki, lowering his voice. "I didn't dare approach, though. Could have been alive. The wolf, I mean. You never know with wolves."

"They're getting too creative with the weapons and the killing," Odin mumbled. "A wolf!"

Frigg rolled her eyes. He was the one who created people. It was his own fault that they invested their creativity into weapons rather than couture. "Is that all there is? Dead animals?"

Loki spread his hands.

"A sports bra?" she tried. "Galoshes?"

Loki's hands remained spread. All Odin had to offer was his reliable blank stare. The visions of the future, normally silent, seemed to cackle.

Equestrian apparel, future Lilith suggested and Frigg almost snapped at her. "Go, tell Madame A I said hello, and don't come back without sheepskins and boots."

"I'll just quickly write it down," Odin said, already busy scratching a larger stone with a smaller one. "With my runes. Have you seen my runes?"

"Yes, Odin, frequently."

"You're not curious?"

"I'm curious about Madame A."

"She's quite unique," Loki said. "Aw! Why did you elbow me?"

"This rune requires rapid movement," Odin said, "and you were in the way. Go wait for me by the Tree."

Frigg turned on her heel, then hissed. It was the second time this day alone she'd forgotten that she wasn't wearing heels. Or, at least, flats. *Slippers.* Anything that would stop thorns from finding her heels again and again. If the future had randomly shown her the tool required to remove thorns, she had missed it amongst steam trains and shoulder pads. She waited for Odin, Loki, and the donkey to depart, then sighed, which is a word this book would end up requiring way too often.

Pulling and bending, trying to reach her foot with her teeth, Frigg couldn't even muster the energy to sigh anymore, much to the relief of this book's editor. Thorns in feet must have been why one day someone would invent yoga mats and insist that the position she was about to twist herself into was not only dignified, but also able to cure many ailments. Especially when done at sunrise. But that one day was not today. All that Frigg knew was that thorns and feet were *definitely* invented by now and did not go together.

She now understood what Odin was trying to achieve with his diagram. She knew exactly what boots looked like. *All* the boots. At once. She had the "what," but lacked the "when." Where Odin was trying to make sense of "nature," Frigg had to make sense of "future." Writing things down could be helpful – with her artistic talents there was no point in trying to draw a graph of chronologically ordered footwear.

In the future, Frigg decided, she would show more interest in the runes – and thorn removal tools. No longer biting her fingernails, making them useless, could be a good first step... or twenty-eighth. So far, her future-telling ability had mostly been frustrating and nauseating. It had to change before she started talking to *Blabbing with Bjarnisdóttirs* celebutantés out loud.

"OML" didn't have the same ring to it as "Frigg, My Love," which might have been because, just like Tinna Bjarnisdóttir, Frigg didn't feel like a very loving person before coffee.

· · ·

INSIDE THE "HALL," Frigg piled up dry grass, which Odin insisted on calling "making the bed." She placed herself on top of it and closed her eyes, sliding somewhere between waking and sleeping. The overjoyed future immediately took her into its way-too-many arms and Frigg regretted not having paid more attention to wrestling.

First, she had to stop the random spill of everything. She would never be able to really see the future until she found a way to switch off all channels but one. She needed to close that particular tap – even though as far as she could tell, taps hadn't been invented yet. Perhaps in Vanaheim...? Odin strongly insisted that neither Frigg nor Loki visit Vanaheim ever, due to it being entirely populated with mosquitoes. While telling Loki not to do something was the best way to ensure that he would, even he hadn't gone too far inland. Or so he'd said. What if Vanaheim was The Land of Nice Clothes in Frigg's Size and Also Taps that Odin was withholding for...reasons?

"Focus," she muttered to herself as half of the entire wardrobe department of *The Brash and the Purdyful* fell into her mind. The men's half.

The vision began to declutter a bit as, one by one, Frigg cleansed it of objects that did not spark joy. She was down to just the footwear when all of a sudden countless sorts of sneakers appeared, dancing around her, mocking her with their ridiculous colours and shapes. Even if everyone in all the worlds spent their entire life doing nothing but making all of these, who would wear them? Ridiculous, Frigg decided, and absentmindedly waved away *all* of the sneakers before seeing herself gasp and sit up, shocked by the ease with which it came to her, immediately replaced by...

FRIGG GASPED AND SAT UP, shocked by the ease with which it came to her, immediately replaced by goosebumps of excitement.

She had just seen the future.

True, what she had seen wasn't very far in the future. It wasn't useful, or interesting either. Nevertheless, it was better than the nothing she had managed earlier. She could see the world around her better now that the endless number of futures surrounding her suddenly slowed down to a trickle of men's footwear that wasn't sneakers.

The problem was that if she needed to lie down with her eyes shut to see the near future, all of *her* future was bound to consist of herself lying down. At some point, Frigg would foresee herself standing up to empty her bladder, which would be followed by Frigg standing up to empty her bladder. One blink later wasn't enough. She needed two, three, a thousand. As many as it took to witness herself dressed in... in... whatever was not a single leaf or a sheepskin.

Frigg stretched semi-comfortably and shut her eyes again.

THIS UP-AND-COMING-AT-SOME-POINT Future Frigg seemed asleep on a pile of something that Current Frigg identified as probably sheepskins. She – the Future one – was clad in rabbit skins that were somehow connected to one another. It was easy to recognise the rabbit skins, as Frigg and Loki indulged in various rabbit-based dishes when Odin was not around to lecture them about the vegetarian lifestyle. The skins would be easy to obtain, but how did they remain next to each other, though, instead of slipping off? Were they glued with blood?

Without warning, she slipped on the surface of time and landed somewhere – no, some*time* further.

Current Frigg found herself right next to Future Future Frigg's bare feet. What lay next to her feet must have been foot wrappers, an easily remembered name for something one wrapped around one's feet. If she had to bet, she'd hazard a guess that the name was picked out by Odin. Now that Current Frigg could see what they were, she made another definite discovery...

Current Frigg sat up without a gasp or a jerk, buzzing with excitement. She was definitely heading somewhere useful with her erratic journeys. While she couldn't tell how long it would take for the foot wrappers to turn into polyester socks sold at supermarkets, she had managed to figure out the *order*. Of *two* things and events, out of *all* the things and events that would ever happen. It was still two more than before.

Even though Current Frigg was slowly starting to have problems differentiating between herself, herself, and herself, not even a steam train could stop her from continuing. What was the worst that could happen? Getting stuck in a future that included socks? She'd take the risk.

The Even-Further-in-the-Future Frigg was napping in an armchair. Ignoring the furniture, Current Frigg assessed Napping Herself with a certain disappointment. Apparently, one day she would be wearing sweatpants, a worn-out Deep Purple t-shirt, and…fluffy pink slippers. The Current Frigg could only try to guess what would possess her to combine those items. On the plus side, her grey – Current Frigg shuddered – hair would be clean and combed. Not even the matriarch in *Blabbing with Bjarnisdóttirs* would be caught dead with grey hair and clad in sweatpants…

"They're comfy and they have pockets," the Far-in-the-Future Frigg muttered, not bothering to open her eyes, "and wait until you try your apple and walnut pie."

This time, the Current Frigg did not gasp as she sat up. She screamed. How could the Future Frigg possibly predict—

Oh.

Slightly dizzy at the idea of her future self predicting the visit of her past self, Frigg massaged her temples, thinking as hard as a person deprived of coffee could. There must have been quite a journey between the rabbit skins covering the Nearer Future Frigg and the sweatpants of Far Future Frigg. While witnessing herself at random points in time was somewhat interesting, the real questions remained unanswered. Where would she get the sweatpants from? What was so important about pockets? What even *were* pockets? Where did that armchair come from, what was it made of, *when*? Apple and walnut pie? What was a Deep Purple?

Frigg needed help and didn't know where to search for it. Were there any more accomplished future-seeing Goddesses, besides future herself…? The idea of moving further into the future to ask her future selves how to move further into the future caused her prediction of a future headache to finally come true.

· · ·

WHAT HAPPENED two days later was exactly what Frigg had envisioned and prepared for, without needing to use her dubious gift.

"I brought you boots," Odin announced, clearly delighted with himself.

"They don't fit me," Frigg said.

"How do you know? You must try them on!"

"I have eyes. Haven't you noticed that feet come in different sizes?"

Surprisingly, if uselessly, Odin had more of an answer than his standard blank stare. "I forgot," he mumbled. "What if we cut the toes? From the boots, I mean, from the boots!"

"What this man needs," Frigg muttered under her breath, "is memory. And a thought every now and then. Sit and eat," she said, louder. "You must be famished. I made just the dinner you deserve."

"Lentil paste and kale smoothies?!"

"Cold roast," said Frigg slowly, placing it in front of him, "and celery salad."

Odin's brand new facial expression was worth the suffering she'd gone through trying to prepare a celery salad without looking at it, touching it, or smelling it.

"This is an outrage!" he finally cried. "Repellent magic and a murdered animal! A life destroyed! Is this how you want Gods to behave? Look at our beloved Mr Donnie! Why don't you just kill him too while you're at it?"

"Our who...?"

Odin, his face redder than usual, nodded towards the donkey.

"Ah," said Frigg. "*This* our beloved Mr Donnie." She pulled the meat plate towards herself and slowly, deliberately tore off a chunk. She shut her eyes as she chewed and let out a little "mmm" sound. "How long have I existed now? Have you been paying any attention to me at all?"

Odin's gaze slipped somewhere below her chin before abruptly returning to meet her narrowed eyes. He cleared his throat. "Lots," he said. "Lots and lots."

"Prove it."

"For instance, when I say 'FML!' that means 'Frigg, My Love!' which makes you very important, and then there's the, eh, the…"

"Do you think me too demanding, O mighty All-Father?"

Odin spent a blink too long looking as though he believed that was an actual question with more than one possible answer. "Not really," he decided and Frigg's fingers slowly drummed on the stone table with enough emphasis to break off a small piece. "Not even close," Odin briskly specified. "You are a very giving person, very, um, generous…"

"Loki told me what you did with your spear and the Tree."

"You told me to do it!"

If Frigg's eyes narrowed any further, they would have closed.

"Maybe you didn't say that exactly," Odin said sweatily, "I mean, I – I improvised some parts, but it was all for the good, good of the, the Universe and everything, so now I know the runes and the charms… what exactly did Loki tell you? You can't believe everything he says, you know. Ah, Loki, that trickster, always full of jokes! Ahem. Have I told you there was a charm called Help? What it does…"

"I want a charm called 'sweatpants'," Frigg said. "But I'm not going to hang from a tree with a spear through my lung to get it. My husband, I hear, can create anything. I'll have sweatpants, please. *Now*. And then you can have your kale smoothie and a spinach quiche."

"You've made one?!"

She allowed a trace amount of a smile before picking up another chunk of meat. Odin turned simultaneously red and pale green as she put it in her mouth. "Maybe I have, maybe I haven't. It depends on sweatpants."

"You'll have to draw them for me," Odin muttered, pushing away the celery salad. The rock he called a table wasn't entirely flat and the bowl wobbled back and forth, as if undecided, before falling to the ground. Pieces of celery flew in various directions, causing both the All-Father and Frigg to squeal in terror. Mr Donnie, on the other hand, hee-hawed in excitement.

"Stop!" Odin cried. "You'll hurt yourself! You can't – this is not for eating – why doesn't he ever listen to me?!"

"He's a donkey," Frigg snapped. "How come you're afraid of celery when you're the one who created kale?" She paused. "And...celery itself?"

"It's evil. It is an evil creation! Mr Donnie, I beg you!" Mr Donnie was paying as much attention to the All-Father's commands as was usual. "Leave this poison alone!"

"I asked you a question," Frigg said.

Odin let go of Mr Donnie. Her tone was the vocal equivalent of her fingers tapping on the table so hard the stone broke. Why indeed, he briefly wondered before remembering the truth.

"You're the All-Father," Frigg said. "But not the Celery-Father? Didn't you create the Universe yourself?"

"Eh... I... I made a mistake. Same as with mosquitoes. That's what Vanaheim is for. For my mistakes. I forbade, uh, I requested, I mean, I politely asked you not to visit it for your own good..."

"Odin," Frigg said. She sounded like sentient honey. "I can't see the past, but I can see the future. I will eventually know that is a lie."

"How about we forget about the celery," he pleaded, "and focus on the sweatpants?"

I should have expected this, Frigg thought, as she examined her new attire with the opposite of admiration. She was now clad in what the first Future Frigg wore, rabbit skins held together by magic. The highlight of the Frigg x Odin collaboration *had* to be exactly this. She'd looked into the future, seen it, and now she was wearing it. She'd also be eating nothing but rabbit dishes in the coming days.

Odin finally succeeded in his pleas for a dinner that both looked like and tasted like grass. Chewing on some more cold roast, which by now tasted like wood, Frigg kept searching for a way out of the rut she was stuck in. She couldn't entirely blame Odin for the lack of foot wrappers, because she didn't understand them either. All she'd managed to come up with was that they were not made of rabbit skins, but she couldn't figure out what they *were* made of. Even if she managed to become the best of the early 0th century painters, which depressingly she probably already was, she wouldn't be able to paint material she hadn't even had a chance to touch.

She cut off the tips of the boots. There would be no more thorns in her feet, at least in the near future. That, unfortunately, concluded the list of the footwear's advantages. It also made her realise that there was at least one woman in the worlds that was dressed better than Frigg. A petite-footed one that didn't need to cut tips off the boots in order to make them fit her.

"Would you please tell me about Madame A? I'd love to meet her. What else does she wear?" asked Frigg, absentmindedly picking at one of the rabbit skins that covered her. The rabbit skin, held fast by magic, didn't budge. Frigg's forehead wrinkled. She could tell the perfect, unremovable fit was going to be a problem, but not *why* – not yet. She needed to lie down and take a peek... "Odin? I asked you a question..."

She blinked a few times, then rubbed her eyes. Her husband had disappeared. Bewildered, Frigg looked under the table, glanced into the cave, and carefully examined the men's powder room (some nearby bushes). He hadn't even finished his quiche.

"What just happened?" she asked. Mr Donnie didn't answer, casting pointed glances at the quiche. Frigg sighed and put it on the ground. Odin must have had one of his nervous fits, which struck surprisingly often when Frigg mentioned Madame A. All Frigg wanted to know was where she'd gotten the boots from, as certainly the answer was not "Odin"... ah! Her gentle suggestions had worked. Terrified by the vision of celery salads and murdered Mr Donnie being served for dinner, Odin had understood what she'd really meant. Madame A would be brought to Ásgard as fast as possible, together with her wardrobe. Frigg smiled sweetly and decided that celery had its uses.

The furry not-quite-sweatpants earned their name. Frigg was definitely sweating under the weight of both

the skins and the magic. Why the Future-Future Frigg –
would that be Frigg #3, assuming she was Frigg #1, or
was she already Frigg #2, since she was clad in rabbit
skin sweatpants? *Anyway*, why Post-Rabbit Frigg would
still want to sweat in sweatpants was beyond Current
Frigg. Pockets or not.

She wasn't sure how Madame A's upcoming visit
made her feel. Frigg could do with some company. At
the same time, she didn't want to be seen by anyone
until she was suitably clad. Or at least unsuitably. Odin
and Loki, undeterred by their nudity, kept traveling
around the various worlds. Frigg didn't desire adven-
tures, not until she could rake her fingers through her
hair and/or drink some coffee. Nevertheless... it *would*
be so much nicer if she could meet some other woman.
They could brainstorm about couture in ways that men
simply couldn't understand.

"MADAME A IS VERY TALENTED," said Loki. "One of a
kind."

Frigg scowled. "Does she live far away? I thought
Odin was bringing her over."

Loki half-choked on a snort. "I don't think so. Her
talents are in high demand."

"Oh? What talents are those?"

"She seems to have this... you know? This special
understanding. When I am with her, I feel like... what was
it that made you decide to marry Odin?"

"Stupidity and impatience," Frigg said.

Loki looked thoughtful, then shook his head. "No. I
don't think that's it. She gives me a...feeling. It's a very

nice feeling." He paused. "Very, very nice..." His eyes became a bit glazed. Frigg's darkened.

"She's unique," Loki continued to muse, to himself now more than to anyone else. "Are there more words for unique? She is all of them. I wish I didn't have to share her with anyone. I wonder if the Goddess of lo—"

"A good morning to you both," said a young woman.

Frigg couldn't even gasp, simultaneously shocked, confused, mesmerised, and all that before she realised she wasn't looking at Mr Donnie on stilts. It was a horse. A real, proper horse, just like the one Frigg had seen in her visions and Odin had failed to create. How did one describe the difference between a horse and a donkey to someone who hadn't seen either?

"Loki...?" she groaned. "Is this Madame A?"

The woman snorted. "He's gone already. Shifted and disappeared. As dependable as a fruit fly. Tell me where is Odin, for I much—"

"You know Loki?"

"Everyone knows Loki. Tell me where is Odin, for I much desire to speak to him, crone."

"He's my husband," Frigg answered, blushing furiously. Even when she stood up she had to look up to meet the young woman's disdainful gaze. "Odin, I mean."

"Freyr," barked the woman. "Help me."

Frigg hadn't even noticed there was another horse and rider. He jumped off his horse and helped the woman dismount. That sentence did not describe the apparent difficulty or timespan of the task accurately, but Frigg had no space inside her head for more complex thoughts. Mr Donnie had never been a beautiful creature, but the horses made him look like a turd sculpture. Maybe, Frigg thought feverishly, she could borrow one of them, show it to Odin, and then...

How *did* those horses exist when Odin created everything?

A thud brought Frigg back to reality. The woman raised herself from the ground, snarling at the man – Freyr, her hands patting down whatever-it-was that she wore until it nearly reached her knees again. It was neither her clothes, nor the horses that aroused Frigg's interest the most. When Freyr's eyes met hers, Frigg suddenly felt like the only woman in the world. Technically, this statement had been correct until Freya's invasion. Now, however, things were different. His eyes were so blue that they put the sky to shame. He also had a big, massive, thick, hard...

Yes. That. An entendre so decidedly single that it couldn't be misinterpreted by anyone who had ever been remotely near an entendre.

With certain difficulties, Frigg tore her eyes away from the entendre, meeting the woman's cold gaze. Her new guest's arms and cleavage were bared, same as Frigg's were. The similarities ended there, though. Somehow, the covering over most of the young woman's bosoms made them seem more noticeable than Frigg's completely naked ones. Her knees were dirty from the fall, but her hair... her hair was what Frigg imagined hair looked like when it was not like her own.

Suddenly Frigg no longer wished that Odin were here to reproduce what she was looking at.

The man let out a little cough and Frigg's mesmerised eyes moved back to his entendre. Of course, she told herself sternly, she was simply admiring the...

cut of the mysterious fabric covering it. It was a bit like sweatpants, only absolutely unlike sweatpants.

"Oh, Freyr," said the woman. "Even that's enough for you? Go hump a tree, or something. My apologies, old woman. My brother has no standards. My name is Freya and I am the Goddess of..." Brief hesitation. "Of Vanaheim."

"Ah," Frigg answered.

"And you are?"

"Ah, I... ah, I am Frigg. Yes. That is my name. I am the Goddess of telling the future. Of Ásgard. I mean, the future of everywhere else, too."

Freya let out a little snort. If Frigg had any experience with teenagers, she would have known Freya was the-most-irritating winters old. "I understand you've been expecting us, then."

"Ah," Frigg said. "Yes. I was. Of course. Of course. Completely. Welcome to my, I mean – our, ah, humble abode."

"Humbled," Freya muttered, looking around. "Is this really Ásgard, or did we get lost along the way? I had been led to believe that it was a world where Gods dwelled."

"We're redecorating," Frigg muttered, still processing having been called "old woman." Frigg *was* nearly as old as the Universe, which meant that technically Freya was speaking the truth. There was something about *how* that truth sounded, though...

"We are emissaries from the great Vanaheim," said Freya, "ruled by the even greater Vé, his greatness the greatest of the great... don't you have some sort of a cleaner?" She looked around, pouting. "All I see is dirt. Where does Odin live with his wife? In the bushes?"

Offensive, Frigg decided. Even though Freya still continued to speak nothing but the truth, she was rude and offensive. Frigg un-composed herself, so that anger could overwhelm her before spitting out the answer. "The All-Father is away on an important mission!" "The All-Father," Freya repeated. "Is that what he calls himself? That's just too sweet. I adore children. Did he take his along?"

"Not his, ours! I am his wife, for my sake!" Frigg kept swallowing the words "how dare you," which were completely useless when someone kept daring without any effort. "I mean, there are no actual... it's a metaphor! Not that a floozy like you would know what that means!"

"Floozy?" repeated Freya, looking slightly confused.

"The entire world is our child!" Frigg gestured around.

"Oh," said Freya. She stared at Odin's circles with lines sticking out of them, covering the soil. "I suppose there are exceptions to 'all children are beautiful'. How sad to think this is the best he can do, even given his limitations."

"Limitations?! I will have you know my husband created the Universe! Not just this world, but all the others and everything in them!" Except the horses, apparently, a confused thought insisted. And Freya's clothes.

Freya snorted. "Oh no, darling. He didn't. He might have created this—" she smeared some of Odin's diagram with her foot, ensuring mermaids would never populate any of the worlds "—and whatever it is that you're wearing. Vé, the true All-Father, created *me*."

A snort came from a certain distance, where Freyr

was examining various trees, and Frigg shivered. Was he really going to use his entendre to…

"Fine, Freyr, he created our father and mother, but truth is irrelevant! Oh, darling, I feel so sad looking at—" a once-over showed Frigg that she, not Freyr, was the darling "—this. Perhaps I could send you some of my old clothes? Where I come from, not even the poorest of the poor would consider…" She shuddered. "I don't suppose you've heard about fashion, here, in your… spot?"

Frigg would rather bite her head off and eat it than admit she hadn't. She pursed her lips, failed to look either powerful or intimidating, and settled on disinterested.

"If you want to impress your subjects, not that I see any, fashion is very important. Basically, what you need is what they can't have." Freya looked Frigg up and down again. "Do you know what, darling, I think you've found just the right thing. I can't imagine anybody wanting it."

"Enough! My name isn't 'darling,' it's Frigg. All-Mother if you're nasty! Which you are, and you're also uninvited, so see yourself out and tell your brother to leave Mr Donnie alone."

"Mr Do – Freyr! Freyr! This is a *business* trip! You must forgive him," Freya said, the unspoken "or else" made more unnerving by not knowing *or else what*. "We are emissaries. You can't invite emissaries before any arrive. That is not how emissarying works. We are here on behalf of the *real* All-Father."

"How dare you! My husband is *the* the Real All-Father, the one with capitals! And if you are a Goddess of anything, it's rudeness!"

"You are so right," Freya said. "I am *so* rude. I haven't

even been offered anything to drink, not to mention a place to sit. I apologise for my lack of – Freyr, I told you to leave that creature alone!"

"He kicked me!"

"Good," Frigg muttered.

"I will consider sending you some of my old things," said Freya. "Eventually. Once my maids no longer want them. Darling? Have you considered washing your hair? It's all the rage in Vanaheim. And everywhere else." She laughed. "To think the *real* All-Father worried you might be some sort of danger! Gotta run before I catch something. Toodles!"

Frigg stared, powerless and defeated, at the Goddess – for that was how it felt right now. Frigg was an old, broken, dirty woman covered in the remains of dead animals. Freya was... heading nowhere at all, glancing nervously at her horse.

"Freyr," she hissed, an enviable achievement, since the word had no sibilants. "Freyr!"

"I think you should gallop away now," said Frigg, "for maximum effect. No?"

Freya glared at her, then at her brother, who remained very attached to Mr Donnie. "Freyr! Help me get on the horse!"

"Coming!" A grunt. "Almost there!"

"What's wrong?" Frigg asked.

"Have you never seen a miniskirt? I guess not. You try and get on a horse wearing one... there you are." Freya's voice softened. "Still nothing?"

Freyr shook his head and sighed.

She took his face in his hands and kissed his lips. "We'll figure it out one day, my love. Somewhere else. Let's go."

Frigg watched, with a gentle shiver of happiness, as Freya, huffing and puffing, climbed on top of the horse. Once she finally made it, her face red and sweaty, the miniskirt became more of a belt. Freyr winked at Frigg, his entendre exactly as it was before, before climbing atop his own horse.

"I'll be back," Freya panted. It came out less as a threat and more like a question.

"Do you know," Frigg said, "how sometimes you only find the right comeback when it's too late? I don't even need to wait. Have a good ride home. Is that your only glare? I've seen it already."

Freya departed with her head held high, back straight, posture proud. Freyr waved to Frigg before following his sister.

"...ointment," Frigg heard before the guests disappeared. "Everything below my waist is chafed..."

Frigg sat on a chair – a rock – and hid her face in her hands. No wonder Odin insisted so strongly that she and Loki stay away from Vanaheim. This wasn't just a minor offence. It was a declaration of war and Freya had won this battle without even trying, chafed or not...

"They have pockets!" Frigg yelled, both a lie and too late.

There was a new glint in Mr Donnie's eye as he danced, rather than trudged, into the middle of Odin's diagram. Frigg half-heartedly told him to stop, which the donkey ignored, then she hid her face in her hands. She had a vicious circle to attend to.

While she didn't need a miniskirt, something in her *wanted* one. Odin could only name and recreate things that already existed. Frigg could envision them, but not explain. She hadn't just envisioned the miniskirt, she had witnessed it. Nevertheless, the best she could come up with was "like a skirt, only mini," knowing that Odin would ask what a skirt was. Frigg needed to find out not just how miniskirts were made, but how their successors would be made in the future, whatever they'd turn out to be. The next time they met, it would be Frigg who'd look like a visitor from the future...

"Phew!" said Loki, shifting from a sparrow into his usual form right before he hit the ground. "What a shame I had to go away for a bit for important reasons just before Freya and Freyr, whom I don't know..."

"How do you know them?! Why did you tell me there are no types of clothes other than the skins and... other skins? What does she do with her hair to make it look like that? Why don't I have a miniskirt?" Frigg's voice rose to a shriek towards the end.

"Oh no," said Loki, taking a step back. "I forgot some more important things I must do. See you soon!"

"Don't you dare go anywhere, young...bird!" Frigg waved her fist in the air. Trying to stop Loki was as easy as getting truth out of him or making him follow any sort of rules. He was probably flying back and forth between...

A horrifying thought pierced her not unlike a spear through a lung.

In her confusion caused by *all* the futures...

Supposing there really were two of them...

...had she married the wrong All-Father?

MISERABLE, confused, Frigg selected another chunk of the greasy, wooden roast that made quinoa paste seem appetising. What was it that the other Future Frigg had said? Apple pie? Well, Freya couldn't have it. Unfortunately, neither could Current Frigg, and for some reason that was the last straw.

Screaming her lungs out, Frigg threw the chunk of meat as far as she could, following it more satisfyingly with the rest of the roast. The good-china-without-periwinkles was next. She didn't get any further before Mr Donnie trumpeted in fear and galloped away, his limp suddenly gone. Frigg's anger disappeared as if the donkey had taken it with him.

She expected to feel relief. There was only exhaustion and discouragement. Now her dinner would still be cold roast, but with the addition of dirt.

Forcing herself to breathe slower and deeper, she wiped her hands on her "sweatpants," stopping mid-movement. Freya's miniskirt didn't look like something to wipe greasy hands on. What would hands be wiped on in the future? Was it possible that Freya actually came from the future, one that had fashion and hairbrushes and things to wipe hands on?

Even hot, fresh, dirt-free roast couldn't be *fashion* food. Loki had brought the recipe from Midgard, which meant non-Gods were eating it. Freya had made herself clear: if non-Gods could have something, it was not worthy of Gods' time.

Time.

"Alright," said Frigg aloud. "Beware, future, I am coming."

And she did.

THIS PARTICULAR FUTURE FRIGG, two shiny sticks in her hand, was turning a ball of string into – something. The string was pink. Current Frigg, incorporeal, watched without understanding. What were all those things? Had she been able to bring along Odin with his ability to recognise things that existed, she'd be out-fashioning Freya in no time, as difficult as it was to imagine doing so in pink. Who could predict the twists and turns of fashion, though?

Frigg. That's who.

As Future Frigg continued to turn string into not-string – something like a skin, only free from blood and conveniently shaped for those in possession of one head and two arms, Current Frigg tried to absorb as much as she could. This was not a cave, but a – a space enclosed by flat, vertical…borders made of stone and something that wasn't stone. More non-skins, colourful and pretty, hung from the vertical borders. For unknown reasons, the borders had holes in them and Frigg carefully approached one. They were not really holes; the inside and the outside were divided with something transparent, like ice.

"Those are walls," said Future Frigg, not raising her head, continuing whatever it was that she was doing. "The transparent things are called windows. We are in a hall. Underneath your feet is a shag rug. The wooden part here—" she nodded towards something Current Frigg hadn't noticed yet "—is a door. Stand where you are and don't be startled."

Even with the warning, Current Frigg had barely hung on to the future when the door slammed into the wall and Odin stormed inside. It wasn't just the sudden noise that startled her. Future Frigg looked older, but Odin looked *ancient*. His silver hair was now all the colours of ash, hanging in streaks around his face. She couldn't decide whether the ridiculous, pointy brown hat on top made it better or worse. The beard, also ashen, was unkempt, sticking out in all directions at once. He rested heavily on that stick he always carried around – the only recognisable thing about him.

That still wasn't all.

Sunlight illuminated most of Odin's face – except one of his eyes, which was covered by a shadow that had no right to be there. Or, perhaps, the sunlight stopped short of it. It made the eye invisible. As if it weren't there.

Current Frigg might have been incorporeal, but she still hid behind Future Frigg, afraid of who or what her husband would become.

"Frigg," Odin said. "We must talk."

Future Frigg put down the wool and leaned towards him, resting on her elbows, clearly unafraid. "I know you're going to have a son. What do you expect me to say? Congratulations?"

"How do – it's not my fault that you have never given me children. You never will either, you said so yourself. How can you know?"

"It's my job to know," said Future Frigg.

"I don't understand," Odin groaned. "I drank from the well of Mímir. I paid for that wisdom dearly. Yet women remain a mystery that can never be solved. Do women even understand themselves?"

She didn't even bother to shrug. "I'm never going to tell you."

His wrinkled face crumpled into a one-sided, tearful grimace. "Please?"

"Odin," Future Frigg snapped. "It will never happen. I have foreseen myself never telling you, no matter what.

My hall is nearly finished and once it is ready, you will not be allowed to enter it..."

"I am your husband and the All-Father!"

"Soon to be All-Plus-One-Father," Future Frigg yawned.

"I will destroy that hall and everything you hold dear, like – like this sweater, if you don't tell me!"

"Odin, I *know* what you will do. You can't surprise me. Ever. I know what's going to happen to my hall, when, and who will do it."

"Destroy it?"

"I'm not going to tell you," Future Frigg said.

His eye narrowed. "You can't know it all. Maybe I'll send someone else to talk to someone else, who will..."

"Oh, for my sake! Here it comes, your prophecy. You will choke on a crisp tomorrow at sunset."

"What is a... You know I don't eat food!"

Future Frigg deigned to give him a proper shrug. "You will never hear anything but lies from me."

"What if I promised to never cheat on you again?"

"Odin, I *know* you will cheat on me again. There will be more women, more men. You'll have too many children for me to bother counting. I could help you pick their names, because I already know them, except *I am not going to tell you*. Can I finish my sweater in peace?"

"Frigg... give me a hint. For old times' sake. Please. Is my army big enough? Just say yes or no."

Future Frigg hid her face in her hands, then slowly shook her head. "One day, someone will tell you everything. In great detail. That someone will be a woman. It will not be me..."

"When? Who?"

"You've got a long life ahead of you. Go and live it.

Enjoy each day and every night, because once she tells you, you will never sleep again. You think wisdom made you unhappy? Once you know the prophecy, you will discover what suffering really feels like. Go," she repeated. "Wander the fields, find new flowers to deflower. You've got children to produce. Some of them will be more useful than others when the time comes."

"Why can't you at least yell at me like some normal woman?"

"Because I don't *care*, old fool. I'm very happy for you and your son. Wheee. Hurray. Please go."

"I will be back," Odin threatened.

"I don't mind. I won't be here." Future Frigg picked up her shiny sticks. "Even if I am, I will tell you just what I told you now, same as last time and as the time before. Can I go back to my knitting, *please?*"

Muttering something that was decidedly not "Frigg, My Love" Odin, leaning heavily on his staff, dragged himself towards the door. He didn't just look like an old man, Current Frigg thought, horrified. He moved like one.

"Leave the door open," Future Frigg said.

Odin slammed the door as he walked out.

"And that is how we get a man to close the door," Future Frigg said, then smiled. "Hello. I have promised myself to never knit anything pink beforehand or after-wards, so I know I am here."

Current Frigg couldn't even nod. Being incorporeal had its disadvantages.

"Let me see," Future Frigg said. "I made notes. First, I teach you how to spin wool. Then, how to knit. How to cut fabric. How to sew. We must hurry, though, and I can't give you anything to take back to the past... oh, I forgot I cared about that. That hussy Freya will get punished for her arrogance, more than once. But none will be more unhappy than Odin and I. You. We." She shook her head. "I know you won't listen, because I know I didn't listen. You're shallow and reckless. I didn't stop myself back then, so I can't stop you now." Future Frigg smiled sadly. "You will understand, eventually, when it's too late. Now you're here to learn things you have no right to know. Very well. We begin with spinning wool..."

SOMETHING OR SOMEONE tugged Current Frigg out of the future, where she was about to find out what tunics were.

"How dare..." Frigg began, then rubbed her eyes. Blinked. Rubbed her eyes again.

Next to her sat a young woman... or women... one and all at the same time. Frigg's eyes hurt as she tried to focus her gaze. The young woman? women? kept changing – their skin, hair, clothes, lips, eyes, their *everything*, as if she/they couldn't decide who to be.

"I will be your dream," all the young women in one said. Frigg winced in surprise at how normal their voice sounded. "My name will be Skuld."

"When?"

"Now. We, dreams, will talk differently."

"And look," muttered Frigg. "Do you mind if I..."

"Wh – ah, I will forget, I will never remember the past. I won't really visit mortals. I will mean, immortals. I will mean, I won't visit anybody at all, because I will be a dream. A prophetic sort of dream."

"Unbelievable," said Frigg with a degree of delight. "Are you someone like the supervisor of the future?"

"I, a *dream*, will tell you to stop doing this."

"Which this?"

"You'll be looking into my work."

"What work?"

"Eh... remember I will be but a dream... what will I be about to say... if you will imagine that Future will be a person... that's capital 'F' Future, we will call her Skuld... so, Skuld will weave the actual future, the one with a non-capital F. The one you will look into."

"That's incredible," breathed Frigg. "I am dreaming about the Future! With a capital 'F'! I would *love* to talk to her, if only she were not but a dream. What's weaving?"

The dream ground her teeth. "We will imagine for a blink that you will talk to her. She will want you to stop looking into the non-capital future."

"Why?"

"Because you'll make the Norns' job impossible. There will be an infinite number of futures. Even the smallest choice, whether it will be that of a God, a person, an animal, even the tiniest of butterflies, will limit this number until there will only be one future, which will then happen."

"Why butterflies?" asked Frigg after she'd chewed on all the future tenses for a while.

"It won't matter. Ants, anteaters, no matter what. A mosquito bite on someone's butt will be able to put him in a very bad mood..."

"Oh, yes, I've seen that."

"...and will cause him to start a war he will not have started if he will have been in a better mood. What you will do will limit the futures *in advance*. When you will look at your future self making a dressing gown, you..."

"Is that what it's called?!"

Skuld palmed her face and muttered something Frigg didn't quite catch. "It will not matter. You will be able to call it Susan if you will like. The important thing will be that once you will see yourself making Susan, Susan will have to be made. The infinite number of futures will suddenly be greatly limited, because it will involve you *surviving*, finding out which garments will be made of wool, learning how to use..." She abruptly stopped. Frigg was blushing with excitement, her eyes gleaming, mouth half-open. "All those things will of course not happen," Skuld said somewhat hopelessly, "due to me being nothing but a humble dream that will know nothing. Now, you will stop doing it."

"Or what?"

Skuld's eyes, all of them, no matter the colour or shape, narrowed. "Or there will be consequences."

"Do you mind if I wake up now?" Frigg asked innocently. "I need to pee. And find some sheep to shear."

"It will be too early," Skuld groaned. "And it will also be too late. You will stop doing this. Please?"

"Absolutely," Frigg promised. "Oh, goodness me," she said to the air where the dream had existed a blink earlier. "I have to go back, I will have completely forgotten to tell myself about the socks."

"Socks?"

Frigg shrieked slightly before turning to see something that made her shriek with more effort. A monster crawled into the cave. "Go away!"

"Frigg, my love! It's me, Odin!"

"No, you aren't, foul monster," she said weakly.

"You're something that looks like a cow-skin with some-one's head in the middle... ah. Right. That's my husband, alright."

"Exactly!" Odin stood up and carefully twirled to present his new attire in the limited space. "It's not Audhumla, of course, it's some other cow. Have you ever met...? No, of course you haven't met. Do you want to see something funny?"

"Let me tell you whom *I* met..."

"When I raise my hands you can see the little Odin!"

Frigg, who had already seen it one time too many, i.e. once, did not explode in twinkly laughter.

"I brought another cow-skin for you," tried Odin.

Frigg simultaneously pursed her lips and smirked. "Over my dead body. And my body will not be dead for a long, long time. Grab your notepad – I mean rock – you'll be etching this all down. And listen carefully, because I shall say this only once..."

WHEN ODIN, his eyes two question marks, departed – mumbling something about how he might need a few days to recruit men who knew how to shear sheep, also known as sheep-shearers, and maids who knew how to make tunics out of it, the word for which he hadn't invented yet – Frigg sat down to think. About the wool.

She didn't actually *feel* like spinning wool. It struck her as an un-Goddess-y thing to do. She couldn't afford not to, though. It looked as if Future Frigg was quite good at it, for what Past Frigg's assessment was worth. Which meant that In-Between Frigg would have to do it enough times to learn how to do it well. Only then could she pass this knowledge along to Past Frigg, who –

Skuld, the humble dream, had a point and it was a sharp one.

Future Frigg taught Past Frigg how to spin wool. Now, Current Frigg knew how to do it. This meant that at no point in time had anybody actually invented it.

What *was* time? Was it something else to Frigg than to all others?

There had been a time when she had not existed. Then Odin had created her – allegedly, she hadn't been there to witness it – three, two, one...*boink.* Frigg's existence had begun. Since she had met the Future Frigg, that meant she would continue to exist... for...a while. How far into the future had Past Frigg reached? A hundred days? A thousand? How much more future was there, how much more time? With a shudder, she realised that she had just used some of it – a modest amount, *hopefully* – to think about it. Bringing her death nearer.

And now thinking about bringing her death nearer had –

"I'm going to die," Frigg sobbed, allowing herself a few blinks, where a blink meant a *very* small amount of time and not actual blinking, to experience the terror. When she was done, she straightened her back and cleared her throat. "No! I am not! Ha haa! Haa! Haa! I am the Goddess of the future! I am the future-teller! *Good* future, fortunate future! Oooh, I know, I am the *fortune-*teller! See, dream? I came up with that all by myself!"

Her shoulders were already dropping, voice breaking, back rounding again, hands steepled in her lap. Somehow, all this assertiveness made her feel smaller and more afraid than The Sobs of Terror.

Frigg couldn't explain where the uneasy feeling that

Skuld was not *actually* a dream was coming from. Almost as if the Goddess of future could really speak with the Future herself, and the capital 'F' Future was not pleased with the Goddess. Goddessing, though, had to give Frigg rights, not just responsibilities. What was the point of being able to see the future if she was not allowed to use it?

So, Skuld's job would be harder now. Too bad. Frigg's life would be easier, in fact the entire Universe's (except Vanaheim's) lives would. She'd already seen many things and had no intention of forgetting them.

"Wool," she said to herself, counting on fingers. "Knitting. Looming. Linen. Scissors. Axes..." There was something more she had learned. Something about children.

It's not my fault that you have never given me children. You never will either, you said so yourself. How can you know?

"Itf maf fof," Frigg muttered. She removed her fingers from her mouth. The fingernail-biting, a habit so deeply ingrained she didn't know she had it, had to stop. She didn't need to see Freya's fingernails. She had seen Freyr's. "It's my job," she repeated. Wasn't her job supposed to be being the All-Mother? *Blabbing with Bjarnisdóttirs* was enough to find out what men thought about women. If one thing was going to continue endlessly, incessant attempts at producing more children were it. Women's only hope was that men would find something else to – she shuddered at the memory – hump.

Future Frigg told Odin that she would lie to him. That, too, could have been a lie. Current and Past Friggs might have lived sheltered lives, but they knew the general mechanics of child production. Women walked around, doing whatever it was that they were doing, when suddenly children fell out of their... Frigg instinctively covered the involved body part with her hands. No wonder there were no children in *Blabbing with Bjarnisdóttirs*. It would have ruined their rugs.

How did they avoid it, though? Was childproofing invented in the future?

What Frigg got out of Loki's excited confessions, confirmed by Odin's reluctant nods, was that people hardly did anything but make weapons and reproduce. Frigg's imagination obligingly presented her with lands covered with a thick layer of screaming children falling out of helpless women. No wonder Future Frigg refused to have any. Odin really should have thought about "people" a bit longer.

Or that *other* All-Father. The one who must have created horses. Odin might have lied only by omission, but still, Frigg had spiders, Freya had a horse. What... what else hid in Vanaheim?

Frigg gasped. Her confidence, which was already feeling faint and in need of some water, faltered, then dramatically passed out. If there was another, horse-producing fake All-Father in Vanaheim, there might have also been a fake All-Mother. An immaculately dressed one, surrounded by very well behaved godlings, who worshipped her for having popped them out. Two maids, respectful on their knees, were removing a new one from underneath the fake All-Mother's gown's frills. The child looked like Freya, complete with miniskirt, just smaller.

The vision was so realistic that Frigg nearly screamed. The fake All-Mother might have started before Frigg was even created. Scandalous! Frigg would never be out-childrened!

Seething at the audacity of the fake All-Mother, Frigg suddenly found herself boarding the opposite train of thought. Perhaps, while the fake All-Mother greedily stored her children all for herself, Frigg would be generous and kind. She'd hand her children to others... or kiss their foreheads, muddy from falling out at inconvenient moments... or give them candy... or...? Her frustration was so palpable she could serve slices of it on the good china. If she were not allowed to visit her future selves and her remaining divine abilities consisted of doing as yet unknown things related to children, Frigg felt...pointless. She wanted agency, not a cave to sit in –

She inhaled sharply. If Future Frigg knew there would be no children, she *must* have checked.

She will have checked.

She will check.

It was important, very, very important to know about one's potential All-Motherhood. It was practically Frigg's *duty* to find out all about it. Since she was going to be visiting the non-capital-f future already, what harm could there be in taking a little look at...fashion? The Future Frigg had said the same thing Skuld had mentioned – once she saw something happening in the future, it would *have* to happen. Such as Future Frigg knowing (or lying) about never having children. Getting a hall all of her own, with windows, walls, and slam-mable doors. And – what was it that Emma and Lilith Bjarnisdóttir wore? Gowns. Opulent, extravagant gowns and dresses.

This time, thought Current Frigg, very pleased with

her own cunning, she'd go further and further. Beyond Emma's and Tinna's wildest dreams. She'd grab a steam train and ride it through the future and back. Unlike Odin's, Frigg's visual memory was as good as her drawing abilities were... oh. That's why she had to learn how to spin wool and make her own clothes before she could teach the maids how to do it. It wasn't about vanity at all. It was about education. The All-Mother, All-Designer, All-Tailor... All-Supermodel. Freya would *plead* for her hand-me-downs and Frigg would pout, but in a generous way, then, of course, magnanimously hand them down. Once her many maids had gotten bored with them.

Skuld's warning was also a hint. Witnessing Future Frigg owning a hall of her own ensured a cosy future for the Current Frigg. What would happen later, though? Future Frigg had said that she had foreseen it. Current Frigg would go further and find out. And then further, and further, ensuring a life of peace and elegance.

What else had Future Frigg said? The cheating Odin would have children with others, but not with her. Frigg intended to become a fully liberated woman. Who said her yet to-be-confirmed offspring had to overlap with Odin's? If he could create children with other women, nothing stopped Frigg from having her cheese and spinach lasagne and eating it too.

Odin asked Future Frigg about the size of his army, which meant a war, which could only mean removal of the fake All-Father and All-Mother. Freya, Frigg decided, amazed by her own generosity, could stay. As the lowest of Frigg's maids, her life devoted to cleaning sneakers. Little Frigglets would slowly take over the worlds, spreading happiness and last season's fashion. Oh, the future was so bright!

Maybe.

The plan was crystallising. One long trip with many stops, at which she'd already be expecting herself.

"On this very day, for the rest of my life," Frigg uttered, then paused. She had no idea which very day it was. She knew it was summer, because Odin had told her. According to his words, there were only summers and winters, and both of them were very long. There wasn't the slightest chance of Future Friggs regularly knitting pink sweaters in preparation for Current Frigg's regular visits. Time had to be measured in some sort of units.

Once Frigg returned from the future, equipped with the ability to tell a solstice from an equinox, and – while she was at it – a few new recipes, someone was already awaiting her.

"Hello," said Skuld in a resigned voice. "It will be I, your—"

"Hello, Humble Dream," said Frigg. "My apologies. I wasn't thinking. Would you like a cappuc – oh no, I completely forgot about coffee! I'll be right back…"

"No!" cried Skuld. "You will have to stop this insanity! The tapestry of time will look like one huge mess now and my sisters will insist that it is my fault! Okay, *fine*, Urðr will have watched you, she will know it wasn't my fault. She will still complain, of course, that representation of the Past will need a hobby. Verðandi, though? She won't shut up about how she'll have to untangle the Strings!"

"What strings? I'm sorry, Humble Dream, but you must speak a bit more clearly."

"The points in the future that you investigate will become fixed," hissed Skuld. "But nothing in between will. My job will not be to simply ensure that the tapestry of time will be smooth, now I will have to figure out how the Universe will get from one of those fixed points to the next! Then I will be the one who will be tasked with forcing it to become possible and you think it's frivolous!"

"I wouldn't say frivolous," said Frigg, rather delighted at the idea of apple pie, despite the fact that all she had at her disposal so far were raw apples. "Sumptuous! Can the tapestry of time possibly be more lush than burgundy red velvet with golden embroideries? I bet not."

"You will swear that you will stop doing this," Skuld hissed, using every available sibilant and at least one vowel.

"Why would I promise things to Humble Dreams? I am *the* Goddess of the future. And you are a—"

"I will have withheld my true identity from you for your own good," Skuld interrupted. "I will, in actual fact, not have been but a humble dream. I will be that Future. Capital 'F', if you please. It will be indecent of you to look at me this way."

"I haven't been looking at anything related to you, I'm not some sort of pervert! I have only investigated *my* personal life, which has nothing to do with you."

"Everything will have to do with *time*!" Skuld's many skin colours were now all tinted with an angry flush. "Everything will have a future, whether it will be interesting or not. This rock will have a future, and if someone will move it to the side, it will have a different future. Someone will be able to trip over it now – or not trip over it, as they will have had the opportunity to do. A grain of sand, a mountain, Mr Donnie, all of them will have futures that will affect everyone and everything else's futures. Will you understand?"

Frigg nodded. She couldn't care less about Skuld's lecture. While she could neither taste nor smell apple pie in the future, she was or would be or even will be, to this book's editor's despair, metaphorically salivating at its very sight.

"Your 'personal' life will not be only yours," Skuld said. "It will have other people in it, ones near you who will have other people near them. Ones who will no longer need to learn to spin wool, because you will have given it to them."

"That's because I'm a very generous and giving Goddess," agreed Frigg.

"You will not have invented the winter equinox. All you will do is witness a celebration of it. There will be people present. They will see you. You will see them. They will go home, or to taverns, or back to their ships. They will tell the others—"

"Taverns? Ships?"

Skuld actually growled. "I will have to keep them alive until they will join that celebration, ensure that the others around them will be there to listen, and all that will be your fault. The tapestry of time will look like it will have been shrunk in the wash!"

Frigg pursed her lips and tapped her foot. The only interesting thing she'd heard so far was that garments might shrink in the wash.

"You will stop," said Skuld softly. "Please. There will be many, many futures in which you will have stopped. None of them will come to pass, because you will not have stopped yourself just now. But you will be the Goddess of future. You, and you alone, will have the power to..." She hesitated. "Once you will witness one, none of the other futures or events that would have been able to lead towards them will happen. There might still be a future in which you will get to be the all-powerful All-Mother celebrated by every person in the Nine Worlds, but if you look too far, fix too many points, that future will stop being a possibility."

"All-Mother of the Nine Worlds," repeated Frigg dreamily. Finally, a confirmation.

"That is what you will be risking."

"Ah, but you don't know that, do you? Since the actual future is not set in stone. Until I go and make myself the All-Mother."

Skuld's lips were set in a line so white it illuminated the cave. "You will not be able to *make* yourself anything. It will not be your decision. It will be something that will, or rather might, take thousands of people hundreds of summers and winters..."

"And they will be celebrating *me*," Frigg breathed. This was getting better and better. She had predicted the future before she had looked into it, that's how good she was at Goddessing. "The all-powerful *me*. Thousands of people. I would very much like to see that."

"Then you will have to stop ruining your own chances."

"Good-*bye*, Humble Dream. It's been a pleasure."

Skuld let out a little cry before disappearing, replaced by Odin.

"Frigg, my love," he started.

"What is it?"

"I can't bring the sheep-shearers and the maids in

here. I put protective magic around the Tree, so that they can't come over." He paused. "Is there anything to eat?"

She needed the future to happen faster.

FOLLOWING FRIGG'S INSTRUCTIONS, Odin created a direct connection between Ásgard and Midgard. He named it the Rainbow Bridge, because it was just as tangible as a rainbow, and its beginning and end equally easy to reach. It was neither a rainbow nor a bridge, to confuse any potential adversaries, but it was a place not entirely unlike the Tree, present in both worlds at once.

The sentinel of Ásgard, Heimdall, had to be the strongest of men equipped with the sharpest of rocks, an owner of devastating eyelashes, golden skin, and a great horn to use in case of danger. All those specifications, Frigg explained, were dictated by the future. Even the fact that Heimdall would be a great kisser. It just had to be, she said, spreading her hands helplessly. It was what the future demanded.

"How do I know I'm a great kisser?" were Heimdall's first words.

Frigg winked at him, making him wince, which made Odin scowl.

The point of Heimdall, she explained, trying not to blush, would be letting just enough people in... and out.

"But why?" Odin squealed.

"Because soon we will live surrounded by luxury, opulence, and splendour," Frigg said. "Before then, though, we'll need something temporary. Does 'Valhalla' sound good to you? Yes, I just predicted it does. Now, you two go and bring me some construction workers and carpenters, while I draw up the architectural plans."

"What are con—" Odin started.

Frigg's glare shut him up. "Take your donkey along," she said. "Half of your diagram is gone by now, I don't want him ruining my plans."

Operation Future was progressing smoothly so far. As smoothly as the skin on Heimdall's muscular arms.

Valhalla was easy to draw – a rectangle somewhat bigger than the cave. All the construction workers needed to build was one room with doors and windows. Using it as an example, Odin would proceed to improve and expand it until Valhalla was as close to a hall as a donkey was to a horse. Fensalir, her own hall, had to wait until the pink sweater future came to pass. That reminded Frigg of two more important things: a ladies' powder room and a wood-burning pizza oven.

When the construction workers arrived, Frigg realised two things. First, Odin – as always – had gotten her instructions, admittedly brief, *almost* right. Second, men were her least favourite gender, and not just because of the grunting and the sweating.

"Ma'am," said one, interrupting Frigg as she was preparing lunch for everyone present – a simple Quattro Stagioni pizza. "There's a problem with the doors and windows."

Frigg looked up and smiled. "I'm happy to explain."

"Where can I find Mr Odin? The pizza smells lovely, ma'am."

"Why do you need him? He knows nothing about doors and windows."

"That's not how it works," the man explained. He was

clearly trying to stare at her from above despite the fact that Frigg was taller. "You see, he is a *man*."

Frigg's left eyebrow moved upwards.

"Women simply don't get these things."

Frigg's right eyebrow joined her left as her smile disappeared. "Pray tell, what things *do* women get?"

"Cooking," said the man, thoughtfully. "And they are good at sex. Then they give us sons. I mean, children."

"Really. They give you sons, you mean, children."

"You're smart for a woman, ma'am," the man said, looking at her approvingly. "Where is your husband?"

"I am here," said Odin, approaching, then embracing Frigg from behind. "What's the matter?"

"He needs to talk about doors and windows," cooed Frigg.

Odin frowned. "What does that have to do with me?"

The man stood on his toes, trying to look above Frigg's shoulder. "As a man…"

"As a man, what? My wife will explain everything to you."

"But she is a *woman*," the man said. His facial expression suggested that he'd imagined Gods to be smarter.

"All I know about windows is that you look through them and regarding doors… Frigg, my love? What was it that doors do?"

"Slam," Frigg said, observing another man, who joined the first one. His gaze was firmly glued to Frigg's chest.

"I'm glad it's all settled," Odin said and turned away.

"Well, actually, no, sir! We have questions!"

"Here," Frigg snapped. "You, on the left. My eyes are here. You, on the right. Do you know who I am?"

"Well, actually, yes. The wife of Mr Odin." The man

stood on his tiptoes again, helplessly watching Odin depart. "Sir? Sir?!"

"I am the All-Mother," Frigg said, which momentarily distracted her. "*The* All-Mother," she repeated, just to hear the glorious words again. "I am also the Goddess that can tell your future."

"Oh yeah?"

"I predict that in the very near future you will be in pain," she said solemnly.

The man smirked, his arms crossed over his chest, legs spread wide to take up more space than necessary. When Frigg's knee struck his crotch, the cry he let out was pitched much higher than his words.

"Ma'am, he – I mean, we meant nothing wrong, we just – your husb—" The other man's eyes, currently doing their utmost not to meet Frigg's chest, were filled with fear, uncertain admiration, and irritation. "We *do* need to learn more about doors and windows."

"I am here to teach you all about them."

"Well, actually…"

"Have I mentioned that I can read the future?"

His eyes widened as his hands covered his delicate bits. The other man continued groaning, still unable to lift himself from the ground.

"In the future," Frigg said slowly, "men who use the words 'well, actually' when speaking to women, will become incels. Do you know what that means?"

He shook his head slowly.

"It means that you will never have sex again."

He grinned. "I have a woman of my own."

"No, you don't. I now have a new maid and my maids are only allowed to have sex when I let them." Frigg admired her dirty, bitten fingernails in a way not dissimilar to how she saw Freya admire her own a while ago. "Well, actually, I simply won't allow them to settle beneath their position."

"What's beneath their position?"

"You two. Would you like me to explain doors and windows to you now?"

If flat caps had been invented, the man would have ruined his by now. "Yes, ma'am. Please, ma'am."

"I'm sorry, ma'am," said the other one, finally up on his feet. "But I think the pizza is burning."

FRIGG EXAMINED THEIR NEW HALL.

The walls were made of rocks big and small, held together by magic and moss to keep them from falling apart. The wooden chairs and tables were neither smooth, nor stable, nor shiny, but they were definitely wooden. Despite her explanations, either the construction workers or Frigg herself had gotten something wrong with the doors. Replacing them after every slam wasn't too much of a problem, as long as one did not confuse the pile of pre-slammed doors with the used ones. The real reason why Frigg wanted them was so that she could shut one of them quietly when she was ready to complete Operation Future.

"You were worth it," sighed Odin, as he placed himself on the furs of their new bedroom. Fire crackled in the fireplace, filling the room with heat and smoke, which caused the magical windows made of ice to melt. The smoke mostly escaped and the temperature inside the room became just right. Specifically, just right to be naked. "You are the only Goddess I would ever dream of."

"Doubtful," Frigg muttered under her breath.

"So... seeing as we are married and everything... and we have a bed now... Would you like to make sweet, sweet love?"

"Huh?"

"Have sex," Odin explained. "This," he said, pointing to his peeing dispenser, "goes into this," he said, pointing at a spot that Frigg honestly preferred not to think about. "Like this," he demonstrated with his fingers.

"I *know* what sex is. It's something men do before their sons fall out."

"...out?"

This time Frigg pointed at the spot. "We, the women, carry your children inside our bellies, and then at some point they fall out."

Odin's face turned a bit green. "That's... that's not how it works. There would be lots of women with – no. It feels good."

"Oh, really? How do you know that?"

Odin had no good answer to that.

"Okay, fine," sighed Frigg. "But this better feel good for me as well, not just you."

And then he did, and then he did it again but differently, and then Frigg discovered that she was a great fan of making sweet, sweet love until Odin pleaded for mercy and for a bit of sleep.

As he snored, Frigg lay next to him. She was finally experiencing some sort of pleasant not non-attachment to Odin. It wasn't too bad to have him around. True, she was his wife, but on the plus side he was also her husband.

"Yes," she whispered to herself, "it is I, the All-Mother." She cleared her throat. "You have been searching for the All-Mother," she whispered in a more divine tone. "It is I." Frigg tsk-tsked. "The All-Mother, the All-Fortune-Teller. Mrs All-Father. It is I, Goddess Frigg…"

"Can you be quiet," mumbled Odin. "Some of us are trying to sleep."

Offended, the All-Mother turned her back towards him, closed her eyes, and tried to dream of Heimdall. What she saw instead was Loki, still absent, the one part of Operation Future that she couldn't predict before Operation Future started.

As if he could read her mind, Loki redeemed himself the very next morning.

"A horse," gasped Odin.

"A horse," gasped Frigg in agreement.

"Neeeigh," Loki confirmed.

Loki's trips to Vanaheim and his schmoozing with Freya and Freyr were immediately forgiven. Now that Odin saw a real(istic-looking) horse, all Frigg had to do was decide on the exterior. A white one, she demanded. Whiter than anything that had ever been white. With a shiny mane and tail to put all other horses to shame. Or at least the two she had seen so far. Unprompted, Odin added a black one. They looked nice. Yet, somehow, not as nice as Loki.

"I've got some presents, too," said Loki, returning to his regular shape.

"They better be good," muttered Frigg.

"Fragrant oils, for hair," he said slowly. "And a hairbrush."

Frigg stopped breathing.

"Because you'll need to keep the horse's mane clean... I'm just joking! Ow! You'll break the hairbrush!"

"A golden one for Heimdall, husband, if you please," Frigg said. "Horse. Not hairbrush."

"Who's Heimdall?" asked Loki.

"Ah, he's a bit like a traffic policeman," said Frigg.

Both Odin and Loki gawked at her, their wide eyes and open mouths making them look like brothers.

"Uh. That must be something I picked up in the future. A...watcher of peace. Making sure nothing goes wrong. Order! That's it. Heimdall ensures order."

"I love him already," Loki muttered.

"Do you have any, say, fabric samples for me?"

"...pardon me?"

A brief idea flashed in Frigg's mind – she could ask Loki to "borrow" Freya's miniskirt. Clearly, though, his loyalties lay simultaneously with both sides and with neither. If Freya found out Frigg had *asked* him to steal something, she'd become a moral winner by default, and Frigg was not going to let some floozy put the word "moral" next to her name.

If only she could describe what it was that Freya wore...! There was simply nothing similar around that she could point to. The miniskirt was made of *something* and it looked as if the only way to figure it out was to keep trying.

Her sigh swept leaves off the ground.

It was time to start spinning wool and training the maids, and neither of those tasks could be delegated.

UNDER NEWLY CLEANED and combed Frigg's directions ("this is what the future demands") and with the maids practically hovering over Odin's head, he created a loom. This allowed them to make a new discovery. It wasn't until he'd gotten it right that he could name it. This was *a loom* – the previous attempts were nothing but nameless-not-quite-looms.

"What next?" Odin asked. A group of naked women, a man clad in a cow-skin, and Frigg with her rabbit skins stared at each other. Loki, standing at a certain distance, managed to simultaneously remain naked and give the impression of someone so impeccably dressed that no All-Father could hold a candle to him.

Ah, Frigg remembered, candles were not around yet. She'd take a look at them during Operation Future.

"What next?"

"You can put strings between those strings," Loki suggested, approaching.

"And then what?"

"Then move this thing up, use the comb to tighten the string between the strings... let me show you. Now you put it back down and put the string between the strings again. Then..."

"How do you know all that?" Odin interrupted before Frigg could interrupt his interruption.

"Oh no," Loki said, as too easily predicted. "I just remembered something very important. I'll be right back!"

"Oooh," said Odin. "That time he was a swallow. I hadn't seen one before. Let me quickly create..."

"Goodness me," snapped Frigg. "Write 'swallows' somewhere with your silly runes and loom me some red velvet with gold embroideries. Oh no, not that blank stare again. Uh... silk? Not silk, I guess. Polyester/nylon mix? Fetish rubber? This is hopeless."

"Leaves," suggested one of the maids. "My bestie, Eve…"

Once the maids were thoroughly removed from Valhalla's backyard, Frigg pointed at Loki's work. "This is fabric. I want more of it. Not more strips, but – uhm… bigger. And wider. And without all the holes."

"Hey presto," said Odin triumphantly. "This is wool."

Frigg's eyes nearly popped out in shock. The wool was brown, thick, coarse, and did not look like the string that Future Frigg had woven… will have woven from shorn sheep. It was neither soft nor nice to touch, it wasn't similar to Freya's miniskirt or Freyr's entendre cover, but it was actual fabric. One you could use to make clothes from. If you didn't mind itching and scratching.

Her muscles slowly relaxed as she recalled Future Frigg's wool. It was nothing like this and not just because it was pink. While Then-Current-Now-Past Frigg hadn't been able to touch it, that must have been some other sort of wool. Probably made from very old sheep that had never seen shampoo or a comb. Good ol' reliable Odin would never get things exactly right without the All-Mother, Fortune-Teller, soon-to-be Fashion-Teller. "Softer," she said. "Make it feel nicer." *Velvet*, she prayed to herself, the wisest and most modest Goddess she had ever met.

Hemp was, indeed, softer than wool. Frigg assessed it as something that would cause marginally less suffering, mostly limited to the most delicate body parts.

What was it that Freya's miniskirt was made of…?

"Softer," Frigg repeated helplessly. "Thinner and softer…" She sighed. "Sort of… silvery…"

"Thinner and softer," Odin muttered, scratching his chin in thought. "Thinner and softer..."

Frigg screamed. "Get it off me! Get them all off me!"

"It's thin and soft," Odin said.

"Get it off me *right now* or you will never make sweet, sweet love to anything but a hedgehog!"

A blink later, naked Frigg dropped down on the grass, breathing heavily.

"Spiderwebs are very thin," Odin said, "and very light, and soft..."

"They are also *spiderwebs*, you..." Frigg paused. "You *man*! They have spiders in them!"

"Yes, yes, but don't you think it would be lovely? Nobody could ever dress like – okay, fine, fine, I apologise!"

If fashion was all about things others couldn't wear, Frigg felt very generous about spiderwebs. Everyone could have them. She'd make herself special by owning absolutely none. "I'll stick with hemp for the time being. Never, ever let a spider near me, or I'll make you eat a celery pizza. *Capisce?*"

"Excuse me?"

This must have been from *Blabbing with Bjarnisdóttirs*, Frigg realised. Or from *Dwarffather*. When she was asleep, Frigg couldn't stop all of the future from having access to her at once. It made her nights both interesting and confusing.

"I need a drink," she said weakly. "And we have to talk."

"It was nothing," Odin quickly said. "Just one night, not even a whole night. He never mattered to me. You are the only one..."

"Who, he? Vé? The other All-Father?"

Odin's mouth dropped open.

"That floozy Freya," Frigg continued. "She thinks she can come here from her stupid Vanaheim..."

"Excuse me?"

"...declaring someone called Vé to be the real All-Father! Obviously, I told her off..."

"*Excuse* me?" Frigg's words died out, such was the power of the italics. When they arose from the dead, they were noticeably quieter.

"There is someone called Vé who lives in Vanaheim," she said. "He insists that he is the All-Father. He sent emissaries here, a halfwit who humps trees and some tramp who... whose hair... I will not allow anybody else to..." Frigg realised she was beginning to hyperventilate. "And Loki knows them, or they know Loki. Where did you think he found the fragrant oils? Who do you think created the first horse?"

"FML," Odin muttered. "No wonder I drink water." He filled two cups, using a stone jug only he could lift without the help of three to four well-fed men. "Vé is, obviously, an impostor. A man without shame."

"That I can believe," Frigg snorted and took the cup back. "Don't you think we should show him how The Real All-Father and..."

"And?"

Now that she had a chance to say it out loud, Frigg hesitated. Could she really call herself the All-Mother if she hadn't plopped out even one child yet? "And me. But not like this, not yet. That Freya made me look like a scarecrow. They came on horses, dressed beautifully, acting rude, and talking about how Vé was the real All-Father." Frigg paused. "I just stood here, dirty and ugly. I can see the future, you know it. I didn't need to use my gifts. I felt as if the future came to visit me." Her shoulders drooped. "Loki brought us something from Vanaheim. He took nothing back, because we have nothing. Freya was right. Vé is the powerful one. We live in dust and..." Her voice died out.

Odin's smile looked like an axe could learn a lot about sharpness from him. "Oh, yes," he said, slowly, dreamily, cruelly. "They came on horses, you say, my love? Soft fabrics? And called Vé the *Real* All-Father?" He snapped his fingers and the wonky walls of Valhalla stood to attention. "Let's get to it."

THE RED FIRE of the sunset painted Baldr's white mane, putting fire in his black eyes. If dictionaries existed, Baldr's photo would be placed next to the word "stunning." He was a muscular, peaceful stallion, so impeccably white he seemed to glow. He was more gracious than any horse in the Universe (although that had to be confirmed once Frigg learned how to get on his back – still, she just had a feeling) and faster (which also had to be confirmed). When she kissed his muzzle and Baldr's eyes briefly closed with pleasure, Frigg didn't need to investigate the future to know.

She felt a certain fondness towards Odin. This? This was love.

"My baby," she whispered. "Our baby. Our first."

Odin looked at her weirdly and Frigg felt as if he'd dragged her out of a warm, fuzzy dream where everything was just right.

"All I mean, I mean... we've created him together, you and I. He's my baby. I mean, he's our... I love him so much!" She threw herself into Odin's surprised arms.

"And you, I mean – only you... mostly! Do tell, are you too tired for the sweet, sweet love?"

"I can only do 'sweet' tonight. The double-sweet-sweet... I need some rest," Odin muttered. "The horse is not involved, I hope?"

"It's a *horse*, my love, of course he isn't!" She would ride Baldr as soon as she could, Frigg decided, rubbing her cheek against the wonderfully soft dressing-gown. In very near future, after the first night spent in a hall that now had chambers for the maids, bathing rooms with warm water filling comfortable tubs, and multiple use doors with just the right level of slammability. Odin would spend the day surrounding Valhalla with a stone wall and a gate that couldn't be opened without his or Frigg's permission. The next time Freya and Freyr came here, Odin's soon-to-be-hired manservants would throw horse faeces at them, while Frigg's more delicate maids showered them with cold urine.

With Loki away and Heimdall guarding the Rainbow Bridge, she only had to wait for Odin to depart in search of his future manservants. Operation Future was nearly here.

AND THEN IT was entirely here.

"Goodbye, my love," said Frigg, kissing Odin's lips. "I foresee you finding the very best men. Ones that will put Vé's to shame. Hunkiest of hunks. I foresee you searching for a while."

Odin grunted something.

"I will be safe here with Heimdall," Frigg continued, perhaps a bit too dreamily.

Odin grunted something again.

"And with my maids," she quickly added. The maids would depart on holiday once Heimdall assured her Odin was far enough away. He'd know – Ásgard's sentinel could hear the grass grow, butterflies yelling at each other, cats' paws banging against soft grass, and Odin's stallion's hooves. And literally everything else that took place in Midgard or Ásgard. He complained about sensory overload a lot, blaming – rightly – Frigg. He still wouldn't oppose her, not once Frigg requested that nobody made it near Valhalla for nine days and nine nights. For Frigg possessed the secret knowledge – with emphasis on secret.

Now that Odin had finally stopped bumbling around with cow-skins, Heimdall no longer looked devastating. He looked positively ruinous. His eyes were blacker than night. His hair was black like his eyes, if eyes were made of hair, or the other way round. His skin, a delightful shade of gold, completed the picture. Heimdall was completely aware of the effect he had on people and deities – and how much better, or worse, it got when he dressed in white. Even Odin's breath became a bit faster as he passed by. Heimdall spent his days guarding the Rainbow Bridge, groaning both from boredom, as nobody ever tried to cross it without proper authorisation, and from the curse of hearing every word uttered by Ask and Embla. (It was better for Frigg not to know, Odin had said, and Heimdall confirmed. He looked breathtaking even when he scowled in pain. In fact, he might have looked *more* breathtaking.) His nights were spent in a shed he named Himinnbjorg Beta.

One night, when Frigg couldn't sleep, she quietly slipped out of bed to pay him an accidental and completely unplanned visit, the goal of which was...

was... to discuss... important things and stuff. Even though she knew he'd hear each luxuriously shiny hair on her head rubbing against the other, she tiptoed towards Himinnbjorg Beta. She needn't have bothered. As it turned out, Heimdall had broken his orders and let in someone who definitely did not belong in Ásgard. The sounds they produced did not suggest a late-night architectural meeting to discuss Himinnbjorg 1.0.

As Heimdall later explained, his cheeks turning from gold to rose gold, a red-bearded man with a whip was exactly what he needed to briefly recover from all the reality he couldn't stop hearing. It was very unlikely that he would ever find any woman to be relaxing, even if she found a way to glue a fake beard to her chin. He would also be very, very grateful if nobody, especially the Real All-Father, found out.

As good as Odin was at failing to do things right, Frigg had a feeling he'd played this game well. Obviously, she felt for the poor, long-suffering, stressed-out great kisser, whose abilities she'd never be able to test. Heimdall definitely deserved some relaxation every now and then. Just not during *those* nine days and nights.

He dispelled her worries about Loki as well. The shapeshifter was in Midgard, where he wasn't so much visiting Madame A as had moved in with her. No matter how, when, or in what shape he tried to interrupt Frigg's peace, Heimdall would ensure he'd fail.

It was time for Operation Future to turn into Operation Right Now.

FRIGG RAN through the plan one last time.

Skuld was a woman. Sort of. She would understand,

she had to. All Frigg needed was to see herself All-Mothering around, while people of all Nine Worlds (mostly Freya) dropped to their knees, celebrating her All-Motherhood. She needed to figure out the terms and conditions that would elevate her above "Your Grace," the best she so far managed to squeeze out of her not-quite-worshippers. Once she knew that, she'd immediately stop looking.

On the other hand, since this was going to be her very last journey into the future, Frigg might as well find out what haute couture was... and would be... forever. Why not? What was the worst that could happen, an even longer lecture from Skuld than the ones before? Frigg would nod, apologise, agree that she'd been a very naughty Goddess, then never need to worry about anything ever again. *Nothing* would ever surprise her. She would sail through life filled with inner peace and wrapped in the most elaborately designed clothes. (With pockets.)

It would have been handy to have something to take notes on, or to be in possession of an apparatus capable of capturing images that could later be admired by Frigg's regularly-updated-influential-image-collection followers. If Skuld got so worked up about wool, though, she'd never forgive *that*. Frigg would ignore the new inventions unrelated to fashion and All-Motherhood. She'd spit in their general direction, safe in the knowledge that due to being incorporeal she wasn't affecting anything. Skuld could never be angry about that. Frigg would make her a frappuccino, they'd both laugh like the best of friends about how silly Frigg had been...

Nothing could possibly go wrong.

Everything had been meticulously prepared.

Frigg, the Goddess of future, was simply taking what was hers.

Why, then, were her hands so sweaty?

Regarding the All-Motherhood... perhaps she just needed to produce one child more special than any other, like her sweet baby Baldr, lighter, stronger, gentler than any horse could ever be? Hopefully it wouldn't have to be a...regular occasion... One of the maids, so oddly rounded around her waist that Frigg worried about her diet, explained the process of child-birth. Once one made enough sweet, sweet love, nine moon-turns – the holy number – had to pass before the child was ready to go. It did not plop out at an inconvenient moment, the maid explained. As pain flashed on her face, she assured Frigg through clenched teeth that it didn't feel unpleasant at all and she couldn't wait to do it again.

She then groaned and asked if she could possibly have a little nap, because the already expelled twins kept her up all night.

Frigg allowed it and returned to wondering why the holy number was nine and not five or seventeen. Only now she understood. Nine was the holy number, because people decided it was. Even Frigg herself booked all of Valhalla for nine days and nights without thinking about it. She wouldn't be the All-Mother until people decided she was. What if they wouldn't and all the child-birthing was for nothing?

Frigg realised her breathing was fast and shallow, wiped sweat off her hands on the underskirt she was wearing, and inhaled deeply. "Ommmmmmm," she exhaled.

What if the birthing had to be some sort of regular occasion, like the equinoxes? What if she had to spend nine out of each twelve moon-turns being full of twins? Did that explain both the sweatpants and the naps during which she caught some of the Future Friggs...?

"I feel like I should pray to someone," Frigg said to the fire crackling in the hearth. "But who could it be? I have no mother. I have no father. There are no Goddesses above me. Especially not that stupid bint Freya." She swallowed. "But it's going to be alright. Fine. Better than fine. Outstanding."

The crackle of the fire had nothing reassuring to say.

"I am *the* All-Mother," Frigg muttered to herself. It didn't sound assertive or proud. Just...shaky. She looked back at the bed, then at the fire again.

She only had two choices. Procrastinate until it was too late and live with the knowledge she might have wasted her only chance, or do it.

Frigg shut her eyes.

TEN SUMMERS from now her hair looked stunning. So did Ásgard. Not a single person, including her maids, addressed her as "All-Mother," though.

Twenty summers changed little, apart from Valhalla's interior decoration and seemingly constant expansion. Nothing pointed towards the newly added chambers being filled with children.

Thirty summers...

Frigg had to allow time to move on quickly. She didn't know how much future there was to look at and she only had nine days.

She observed Ásgard growing more and more beautiful. Seeds that took a blink to turn into massive, proud trees. Other people, other Gods and Goddesses. A war that came and went so fast Frigg nearly missed it... She suddenly remembered that she wasn't supposed to pay any attention to anything but the All-Mothering. It was impossible, though, to miss the fact that Freya and Freyr had apparently moved in at some point. Ignoring them to the best of her ability, Frigg tried to pay attention only to herself. Her worshippers. Her husband.

Her children.

It's not my fault that you have never given me children. You never will either, you said so yourself.

There were many more men in the Worlds. She could organise reality shows and pick the best specimens to give children to, Frigg improvised, nauseous with anxiety despite being incorporeal.

Her own hall, Fensalir, would be smaller – unlike Odin, Frigg had nothing to prove... of course she was not interested in Freya's hall... probably some dumpster... did she just hear a young woman call Future Frigg "mother"?! She quickly rewound the future. Her body, clothes, hair, mood, occupation changed, but at no point did Frigg seem to carry the woman inside her belly. She just...appeared – full-sized, way too large to fit in Frigg's... *calm down*, Frigg told herself, *stop hyperventilating, and remember they're smaller when they plop out. Pay attention.*

She jumped forward to discover more young women, all of them happy, smiling, laughing even, joking amongst each other, addressing her as "mother." There had to be an explanation somewhere... sometime. How, when did they appear?

A Future Frigg was presiding at a table, having

organised a candlelit supper. Current Frigg, as much as she was not looking at all, she couldn't fail to notice that Odin was not invited. Come to think of it, Odin wasn't around much in her future, not that she was paying attention. He had – he – he had so many children – where Frigg –

There were big festivals organised for her. Offerings were given. Feasts. Drink. Nakedness. Lots of sweet, sweet love-making in the name of Mother Frigg and – Frigg frowned incorporeally – Freya. Women pleading for Frigg's blessing. Strangers. Some bringing their babies to show others that Frigg's blessing was all they needed. Some cursing her name when the babies wouldn't come. Midgard, Álfheim, Svartálfheim… None of the women and men were of Frigg's flesh and blood and delicate parts. They were – strangers. Kind, welcoming, warm, thankful, resentful, screaming, cursing, hateful, battling, kissing strangers.

But – but she was just going to – how –

She must have missed it, she must have, there was no other possibility. They had said "mother," yes, they had, they will, they will have said it.

Frigg went back and forth in time, paying as much attention as she could, promises and bargains she had made with herself forgotten. Slower, then faster and faster, everything blurring into greyness. Empty. Frigg no longer cared whether a hundred or a thousand summers had passed. She was only searching for one thing and the more she looked for it, the more it didn't happen. If she could, she would have cried. All of a sudden there was nothing she wanted more than to have children of her own. She would be called "Mother," but she would never be one. It didn't matter, all of a sudden, that "All-Mother" would never trend. Clothes didn't matter, Freya didn't matter, Odin, hair, sweatpants, *Blabbing with Bjarnisdóttirs*, nothing mattered. She had seen, will see, the happiness of young mothers thanking her for the gifts, but she would never share them. There would be cries of those accusing her of withholding the gift. Curses. Fury.

This couldn't –

Further, further, faster, slower, alone, still alone as castles fell, cities grew, nobody calling her name anymore, dust, blood, so many people and not one of them *hers* –

And then –

The end of everything. Not just Frigg and her childish dreams, but *everything*.

She slowed it down and watched, every detail etching itself in her mind, until there was nothing left to watch.

THE FIRE HAD GONE OUT. Frigg was so exhausted she couldn't even tell whether she was real; the past, current, future, futures all one now. Instead of powerlessly watching everything at once... she saw it all.

Betrayals, betrothals, bereavements.

Snow and snow and snow, and then –

– fire.

Nothing mattered and nothing ever would. She'd have it all except for what would make it enough. It was the most terrifying life she had ever seen, and it was hers, and it was everyone's, and then it wasn't anyone's at all.

Frigg had never felt more lonely, even though she was not alone.

"Skuld," she just said, her voice flat. Dead.

"I will have told you."

"I know."

"Will you be happy?"

"No."

"This will be what will come to pass," Skuld said. "Everything you will have seen must happen now. Until the very end."

"No!" A screech of panic strangled by tears. "It's not my fault! I didn't want this to happen!"

"It won't matter what you will have wanted, Frigg. You will have been warned. By me. More than once. You will have seen it *all*. Before you will have done it, the number of possible futures were infinite. Now there will only be one future and you will have seen all of it. You will have taken in an infinite number of futures and you will have narrowed it down to one. This, the one you will have seen, this will be it."

"No, no, no, I refuse, this can't – can't be – I will do… I will – I will avoid it. I will change…" Frigg's lips continued to move, but no sound came out anymore.

"There is little reason left for me to continue speaking in future tense. You can't change anything," Skuld said softly. "The tapestry of time will change from a tapestry into one thin thread now. Unless a singularity appears, and singularities are…" She paused. "Take a look at me."

Skuld's face, clothes, skin, hair no longer continued changing. There was only one woman, barely visible in the light of dawn, her face – pale, hair – short, black, messy, lips – thin. One Future for one future.

"A singularity is something unpredictable. Something that can change the tapestry of time, that can change me. Something neither you nor I can predict. But you are the Goddess of the future. You can predict everything. You have. Everything you have witnessed *must* come to pass.

"It doesn't matter how hard you try to change things, because they won't. If you have foreseen someone's death by drowning and you tell them to stay at home, they will find a way to drown in a drop of water." Skuld sighed. "None of what you have foreseen can be avoided. You can try to change it or not, make those around you happy or unhappy, fight, run, hide, and it will *still* come to pass."

"The... fire... too...?"

Skuld nodded. "Three times I have warned you and three times you have ignored me. What do you expect me to say? Lie? Forgive you? I am not angry with you. I am disappointed."

Frigg just sat with her hands in her lap, staring into the darkness. "What if I promise not to tell anyone? Punish me. Just me. The others are innocent."

"Oh," said Skuld, "you have already punished yourself. I can't leave it there, though, you know, I have a reputation to uphold... much good as it does to me now that you've done what you've done. You shall not speak to anyone about any of what you have seen. About the gowns, the feasts, the sacrifices, the battles. Not a single word. There will be no more 'pre-inventions' of any sort. The future will unfold at its own pace. Because you are not a singularity. You're nothing but a problem."

Frigg's lips moved again. She didn't know what to

say anyway with all the conflicting feelings battling inside her. All she could think of was "no" and "please."

"You shall not speak to anyone at all," said Skuld. "For a year and a day you shall not utter a single word. You shall spend this time thinking about what you have done and what you will do. Do you remember when I told you that moving even the smallest rock will change that rock's future, and potentially the entire Universe's future? It will never change anything anymore. You have foreseen whether it will be moved. You are not the Goddess of the future, you are not a fortune-teller. You are Fate and you are Mother. Everyone's fate and everyone's mother."

Tears ran down Frigg's face when Skuld left.

There would be a lot of other summers between the current one and the last. Many of them would be lovely. Many – not so much. But most would just be...average. Things would happen, then they wouldn't. Nothing would ever surprise Frigg and nothing would excite her. Freya would burn at a stake three times while protesting that she was just helping. So what? Frigg saw her own hall, her upcoming legendary soirées and candlelit dinners, the endless cakes and pies she would bake, as her many future selves smiled the smiles that never quite reached their eyes.

She had to leave Odin behind – she would have to – because he'd eventually realise. Frigg knew exactly what he would ask and when. How he would try to threaten her, hurt her while insisting she was hurting him, scream, plead, leave, return. Promise, hope, insist that he was the one to change what couldn't be changed. He would contribute to it exactly as much as a grain of sand would. The end would come exactly when it would come and it would look exactly as it would look. Nothing Odin would do could delay or change it. It would *cause* it.

Frigg's tears dried as she wrapped her arms around her knees, rocking back and forth. Skuld's punishment felt like mercy; pity, rather. Frigg had nothing to say to anyone. Oh, she would start talking eventually, in that new, slightly flatter voice of someone who had ruined their own surprise birthday parties, how else could she keep refusing Odin's pleas and threats?

With a soundless groan, Frigg lifted herself up. So much awaited her. Wool to be spun, then knitted. Pies to be baked, burnt, improved. Barren girls to surround herself with, girls happy to call her "mother" and occasionally cause her to feel something. All this so that she would be prepared for the day when the singularity, slightly salivating, would climb on a stool and ask if she could please have another muffin.

THE WELL OF WISE DOM

"**O**din! Odin! Odin! Odin! Oh," said Loki, his excited gallop turning into an irritated standstill. "Bugger me sideways with a celery stick if it isn't the self-appointed so-called Law and Order."

"I appointed him, based on Frigg's predictions, and we are busy. Come back later."

"If he misses any details, I'll be glad to fill them in. It was a memorable…performance to witness." Loki retreated a bit, glanced back, met Odin's gaze and wisely decided to continue retreating until he was out of earshot.

"So," Odin said slowly, as Heimdall's cheeks turned from gold into rose gold, "you are not here *entirely* of your own accord to help Ásgard's greatness and satisfy my greatest wish?"

"All those things are true," Heimdall carefully confirmed, "although I must admit that little sh – I mean Loki – catching… I mean witnessing the… act… formed a part of my… motivation."

"In other words, you wanted to give me your version of events first."

"It could be argued, I mean – agreed, that it's not an incorrect way of phrasing the—"

Odin crossed his arms. "I would have thought you incapable of wrongdoing."

"I haven't done anything wrong. I have been performing…research."

"With a man called Mímir."

"Y-yes."

"Who was not supposed to enter Ásgard."

"That's—"

"With a man called *Sir* Mímir."

"I could tell you what a certain *Madame* A is up to right now," said Heimdall. "I hear everything that is said or done in Midgard and Ásgard. I hear the grass grow, I hear ants reproduce – super awkward, by the way – I hear the fish breathe and mountains move. You have no idea how irritating all that can get."

"Fascinating," Odin assured him, scowling. "Are you blackmailing me?"

"Absolutely not, All-Father! We share an understanding of how important research is, don't we?"

"Importantly, you want to be able to research in peace without Loki interrupting," Odin nodded. "I grant my permission. I will speak with Loki. Can't guarantee he'll keep it secret, though."

"Is there a way I could convince you, All-Father?"

Odin shrugged. "It's not me who needs to be convinced."

"Perhaps I could convince you to convince him…"

"If you hear all our secrets, why shouldn't everyone hear yours? It seems fair to me."

Heimdall cleared his throat. "Sir Mímir guards a treasure worth more than gold and jewels."

"That's hardly difficult," Odin said. "Want some gold and jewels?"

"With his help, if he is so inclined, you could achieve your greatest dream."

"Oh? And what is it?"

"Sir Mímir guards the well of wisdom. If I can persuade him to let you drink from it, you might learn many...wise things. You might even find out what Lady Frigg is thinking. Probably," Heimdall quickly added.

Odin gulped. Indeed. That was the thing he desired the most. So far, he had figured out only one reason why women would stop speaking to men – the dark magic was unleashed by the words "well, actually," which also deprived the aforementioned men of sweet, sweet love. It took a lot of convincing for those women to return to their previous state. Each of them required a different... something. Sometimes even someone. Odin would rather eat bacon than let the latter happen. He simply had to figure out what Frigg was thinking.

Simply.

Odin had tried everything he could think of. He had apologised for everything he had said and almost every-thing he had done. Then for things he hadn't said or done. His wife, though, remained silent. At night, she curled in her bed – not theirs anymore, hers. During the day she mostly sat on a stool and looked tortured as she did something that his mind identified as "spinning wool" using a "spindle." The only other times she went out of *her* chamber was to use the ladies' powder room, which, too, was a mystery, as she neither drank nor ate. She stared through him with unseeing eyes, failing to as much as wince when Odin tiptoed behind her back and screamed "boo!" There was absolutely no chance of making sweet, sweet love.

Also, which was completely unrelated to the previous thought, Madame A's schedule had become too full to fit *the* All-Father in.

"Do I, or we, have your promise, All-Father?"

"I will do my best," Odin muttered.

"Don't forget I will know whether Loki breaks the promise that you will, no doubt, persuade him to make to you. Obviously, I could, and most probably will, promise not to mention Madame A to Lady Frigg..." The Sentinel winked as the blush disappeared from his cheeks, relocating to Odin's. Somehow this conversation had turned from a confession into an irresistible offer – and his mumbling into something like a challenge to be challenged.

"I'll keep you posted," Odin muttered and dismissed Heimdall together with his smirk.

"Fine, fine," Loki said grumpily. "But I'm going to laugh at him."

"He can hear you."

"Quietly."

"He can hear you *right now*," Odin clarified.

"I'll promise to say nothing to anybody and that I'll still laugh at him. Maybe. What will I get out of it?"

"What do you want?"

"I want Angie to give up her day job."

"Oh yes, you were going to tell me who Angie is."

"I actually wasn't," said Loki, staring into space.

"Then I wasn't going to help you."

"Shouldn't it be beneath the All-Father to blackmail me so nastily?"

Odin studied his fingernails with great interest.

"You've met her," Loki muttered.

"Have I?"

"You know her as Madame A."

"Is... is this why Madame A's agenda has been filled to bursting recently?! Is it because of you?"

"Angie," said Loki, "is a hard-working lady."

"Oh yes," said Odin dreamily.

"Who makes a living out of her work."

"That's nice for her. What does it have to do with me?"

"How much do you pay her for her services?"

"Pay her?"

"Odin," Loki said, "this is way too much dialogue without any action. Let's at least start walking, so the readers don't notice we do nothing but talk."

Nervously glancing over at you, the All-Father sighed, grabbed Odin's Special Stick Which Was In Urgent Need Of Renaming and followed Loki towards nowhere in particular in the name of action. "You were saying?"

"The 'Madame' thing is what she does to earn her living. Her clients expect her to have an endless supply of those special mushrooms. Her work-tools cost a lot. Her clients pay for all that. You've never even returned the rope and the spear you 'borrowed' from her."

"I am the All-Father! It should be an honour for a mortal..."

Loki's silence did not encourage this line of defence.

"I'll give her two ropes and two spears."

Loki's silence rolled its eyes.

"She can't treat the All-Father like some commoner!"

"Well, actually," Loki said coldly, "right now she's not treating you at all."

Right there and then Odin understood why the words "well, actually" had the effect they did. "What does she want?!"

"Try jewels, or gold. You can just create those things," said Loki, snapping his fingers. "They cost you nothing and that's how she makes a living."

The idea of "making a living" puzzled Odin – living was something you just did, until you suddenly didn't. "I'll think about it," he said reluctantly. Conversations with Loki tended to feel a bit slippery. There was always something that... ah, he was going to create eels. "Are you saying Madame A's name is *Angie?*"

"Well, actually it's Angrboda, but that feels so official. So...motherly. She's my Angie. And" – Loki sighed – "others' Madame A. I have to go now. Should I pass on your greetings next time I bump into her?"

"Oh yes, absolutely."

"And promise her gold and jewels?"

"Definitely," Odin agreed. Had he already sipped from Sir Mímir's special horn, he would have noticed that Loki hadn't said he'd promise that Angrboda would get them from *Odin*. This was called a foreshadowing. Unfortunately, Odin didn't know about foreshadowings yet.

"Alright. Going to leave you to the All-Fathering. If someone steals Heimdall's horse, that wasn't me."

"Why would—" Odin started, but the owl was already in the air. Loki shifted depending on mood. An owl meant that he was feeling exceptionally smart.

· · ·

LEAVE YOU TO THE ALL-FATHERING.

Odin had a secret he would never reveal to anyone. He wished he could keep it secret even from himself. Namely, he didn't know what the All-Fathering should entail... Ah – he remembered and snapped his fingers, immediately scowling. Eels belonged in the water, not on sand roads. Odin promised himself he would never kill another living creature (except selected species of insects). Apparently, the alternative to killing the eel immediately was letting it suffer until it died on its own... aha! An epiphany struck and Odin created a small lake in the middle of the road. There. Problem solved.

It was not a particularly smart solution. Or useful. Or one he'd like anyone to witness. Certainly, nobody would guess that a small lake in the middle of the road, containing a lonely eel, had anything to do with All-Father being a bit of a failure. He had created Frigg, so that she would tell him what to do in the future. Now she didn't talk at all. Well, if he were entirely honest, he had also created her so that they could indulge in sweet, sweet love. This was another thing that wasn't happening.

In the name of – as Heimdall put it – research, he attempted to make sweet, sweet love to a jötunn woman, one Jörd, just a few days ago. Compared to Frigg's deep-fried ice-cream with sugar coating, the love he made to others (not that it happened often) ("often" was, luckily, a relative word) always had a whiff of a certain *je ne sais quoi* that Odin didn't want to *sais* at all.

Despite her beauty and his hopes, Jörd was at best a sweet potato, not that he'd ever say it to her face. It filled him with fibre, which was very important for digestion and contained slow-burning carbohydrates. Mainly, though, it filled him with dread that the dream that had visited him every night since could become true. In the dream, Jörd showed up nine – or, by now, eight-and-three-quarters-ish – months from now, carrying a red-haired, stubbly infant and yelling something that probably *would* get a reaction out of Frigg. Luckily, Odin couldn't predict the future. The recurring dream was, therefore, a coincidence. The All-Fathering would remain metaphorical...

The water in the small lake splashed, making Odin wince. He quickly departed the crime scene. If someone asked, he'd simply say this was done on purpose. Divinely mysterious purpose, so mysterious that even he had no clue what it was.

The three (currently down to two and a question mark) brothers must have existed for some reason. Odin had created a lot of creatures – so had Vé. He'd established a homestead – so had Vé. Odin wandered around Midgard, Jötunheim, sometimes the deserts of Svartálfheim if he felt his tan was fading. Worryingly, Vé probably did as well, and the more naive and stupid – so, most of them – people might think *he* was the real All-Father. Surely, in fact almost definitely, most probably, Vé was no wiser than Odin when it came to... everything, to be honest. Hope was Odin's only remaining option.

Oh!

Not at all!

There was one more thing he could always do.

Give up.

No.

Never.

Unless.

Dark, bitter thoughts descended upon Odin more and more often. He needed something. He couldn't explain what, though. It didn't matter how many times he repeated "I am the All-Father" or "FML!" There seemed to be a purpose-shaped gap inside him. He knew his mind would recognise a purpose once he saw one. Where did one search for purposes, though? Odin knew the runes and the charms. He should probably do something with them. What, though?

The thought that there was a Sir Daddy Mímir guarding a well of wisdom irritated him. Nothing could be wiser than the All-Father, since the All-Father must have created Sir Daddy. And the well. Unless... A shiver ran through him. No. Vé had *not* created them. Because that would mean Vé was wiser than the wise dom guarding a well of wisdom. Which would make Vé the All-Father and Odin – the well-meaning, but slightly embarrassing, All-Uncle.

In this mood Odin mounted Tyson, the Stallion of Fury. At a relaxed pace – Tyson was working through his anger issues and Odin couldn't have been more grateful – they headed for Midgard. Odin felt the need to do something big. Something that would disperse the feeling of being more or less ignored by Sir Daddies and Madames, and possibly many others. All others. Nobody cared that he had gone to Svartálfheim to create elephants – which he had done because he was bored, *but still*. Hamsters, ladybugs, giraffes? No compliments. Fibre and vitamins? Still no compliments. Not destroying all of obnoxious humanity? Not a single compliment!

No respect.

Aimlessly, he (or rather Tyson) galloped relaxedly towards absolutely not *Miss Angrboda*'s office. Odin was proud of how very much he wasn't wondering whether Loki had paid for her services, with what, and how much. He had no intention whatsoever of doubling her fees, and even less of tripling them–

Tyson swore nastily in Equinish as he nearly tripped over one of the way too many bunny rabbits in existence that shot out from under his hooves.

"The mantras! Remember the mantras!" cried Odin. The sudden movement was less shocking than the traumatic flashback of Tyson's Fury. The theory of Tyson was much more romantic than his existence.

Tyson expressed his opinion about the mantras, then silenced, breathing deeply. Odin didn't have to know Equinish to figure out that the neigh meant "FML!" only even more. To think he could have died, crushed under Tyson's massive body, because of a bunny rabbit aimlessly running around... not that Odin's journey had any particular aim. *Anyway*, bunny rabbits had something in common with people: there were way too many of both, while there was only one...

"Hail the All-Father!" someone yelled.

"Hail the All-Father!" multiple voices answered in unison.

...All-Father, the thought quickly finished.

Literature gasped at the plot convenience. Odin's mind quickly named it a "deus ex machina." [To think that it wasn't even foreshadowed! Too much! – Ed.] Odin parked Tyson by the nearest tree and jumped off, leaving the Stallion of Fury to his ruminations. He headed towards the mysterious gathering, as his self-confused mind puzzled over what deuses, exes, and machinas were.

Underneath something that looked like a straw canopy hanging on for dear life to a wooden construction, stood a group of people. In the middle, a man towered above the others, elevated on some sort of platform. The cowskin draped on him was completely white...except for the brown-red stains of dried blood. Odin didn't even have time to start feeling sick before the man bent to take something from his helper. The thing being handed over was noisy and terrified. It was a baby goat with its limbs tied together.

"Bless us, All-Father!" yelled the man.

"Bless us, All-Father!" answered the others.

"Urinate off!" snapped a man Odin elbowed in the ribs as he marched towards the platform.

"Here is the Holy Blade!"

Applause and the goat's protests welcomed a sharp, triangular rock.

"Here is our sacrifice, All-Fa- umpf!" yelled the man, ending on the note of someone inexplicably kicked in the ribs by a tied-up goat.

"Give me that," snapped Odin, climbing the platform with a little grunt. He snatched the rock away from the open-mouthed man and freed the goat, which sprinted away with a speed that would have made Loki jealous. "What do you think you're doing?"

This unpaused the white-cow-skinned man seemed to. "Give me back the Holy Blade! I am the All-Father's High Emissary! How dare you interrupt a High Mass?! Now you will be sacrificed in place of the goat!"

"You're all a high mess, I'll give you that. Lay down the mushrooms. What did that poor goat do to you?"

"What mushrooms?" asked a direct descendant of Ask and Embla. He was hushed quickly by the woman next to him, a direct descendant of someone with brain cells.

The High Emissary tried to push Odin away, with results similarly successful to pushing away a mountain. "Do you know what the All-Father does to sacrilegious fools like you?"

"What?" asked Odin curiously, before stiffening in what he'd never admit was fear. "Hold on, you mean Odin, I hope? The real All-Father? I mean, the only one, as there are no other All-Fathers?"

"You, you, and you," the High Emissary spat, pointing at a few unfortunate members of his congregation. "Come here and hold him down! Death and blood! Strength and courage!"

Both Odin and the High Emissary glared at the selected men as they approached the platform with all the vigour of the snail Odin had stepped on earlier in this book. Everyone ·else withdrew, leaving the three with plenty of space to look around helplessly. "Please?" one squealed.

"Leave this place," said Odin slowly, "and you may see the sun again. With emphasis on 'may'."

Two of them immediately bolted away. The third seemed unsure. His gaze kept moving between the High Emissary's narrowed eyes and Odin's narrowed eyes, as if trying to compare the narrowedness. Suddenly, the High Emissary snatched the Holy Blade from Odin.

"Hey," Odin said. "Not fair."

"Come back, cowards!" shrieked the High Emissary, raising the Holy Blade. "Witness the wrath of the All-Father!"

And they did.

THEY INTENDED TO KILL A GOAT. "SACRIFICE" it to the Odin. Someone, somehow, twisted his aversion to killing animals (except selected species of insects) into him *desiring* death and blood. Vé must have done it, using the High, Low, and all other sizes of Emissaries. All of them had to be…let go.

Relieved of their duties.

Fired, Odin thought, looking at the pile of ash that used to be the High Emissary. The choice of words didn't matter. They had to be killed. To save lives.

Odin shook his head helplessly. This made no sense. You couldn't kill to save lives. That wasn't how lives worked. That wasn't how killing worked. A memo warning Low- and Mid-Sized Emissaries, together with the smouldering remains of the canopy, should do it.

He picked up a piece of wood that had survived the All-Father's Wrath Demonstration and a still smouldering stick. "ODINN WUS H" he wrote with the tip of his tongue stuck out in concentration, before FML-ing and throwing the wood on the ground. He was the only one who knew the runes. The people wouldn't know they were being warned. That's what the One-Size-Fits-All Emissaries should be doing. Spreading the *right* message – about the runes and advantages of a vegetarian lifestyle. As of now they were unknowingly giving Odin dirty PR at Vé's command.

Madame A despised violence. No wonder she didn't want anything to do with him. That must have been it, not the "making a living" stuff. The latter would mean that Loki knew more than the All-Father. That he was…

was… Odin took a sharp intake of breath. What if Loki and Vé had already visited Mímir and learned Things and Stuff that made the egg whisker irrelevant and the feather duster – a commonplace item present in every household?! Could they have teamed up behind his back, laughing at the un-whiskered and un-dusted, hapless, *stupid* Odin not even knowing that gold and jewels were items women required for the services they performed to "make a living"? Not knowing that "making a living" was a thing at all?

Doubt rustled among his thoughts. Why would Frigg want gold and jewels? She had never shown interest in either. Not that Odin offered her any. She had no living to make. Or… was she stuck in bed due to lack of living that required jewels and gold to make? How did all her maids operate?

This probably *could* be resolved by giving Loki gold and jewels for Angie, so that Loki would promise to stay quiet about Heimdall and Sir Mímir, so that Heimdall would whisper a good word or two for Odin, so that Odin would be able to visit Mímir and his well of wisdom, and plead for–

No.

The All-Father didn't plead. The All-Father *ordered*. From now on, "Sir" "Daddy" "Mímir" would stay far away from Ásgard. Heimdall… Heimdall would be told to focus on the lives of ants, rather than Daddies and All-Fathers. Frigg and Madame A would squeal in enthusiasm at the sight of gold and jewels (although not at the same time). The dream about Jörd and a red-haired infant would go away. Loki would be tasked with spreading the news that Vé's wife was a hamster and Vé himself smelled of elderberries…

Odin sighed, leaning on Odin's Special Stick Which Was In Urgent Need Of Renaming, looking at the smouldering remains. He now had to explain to Tyson why the Stallion of Fury needed to focus on silent meditation, while his peaceful rider indulged in carnage and mass murder.

THE GOLD BRICK and a diamond the size of a fist indeed caused Frigg to react more animatedly than she had at any point in recent memory. Namely, she rolled her eyes real hard before turning away from her husband, who stood there with his gifts, feeling rather stupid. Apparently gold and jewels didn't work on all women. That might have only applied to Goddesses, though. Or only to Frigg. Or even only to Frigg at this time of this day and with this particular diamond cut.

How long would it take to visit a statistically significant sample of women, hand each of them those two things, and note their reactions?

"I should outsource that," Odin muttered, staring at what he was holding, feeling no wiser.

A stork sat on a windowsill and shifted into a grinning Loki, who stretched his arms and legs. He radiated that Angie's-doing-very-well afterglow Odin had not radiated for a while. "Outsource what?"

"Oh, it's just a thought. Memory. I'm the All-Father, not the All-Uh-Memorising-Something… er… Loki? If someone wanted to learn how to be wiser quickly, what would that someone do? Asking for a friend," Odin quickly added.

Both Odin and Loki knew Odin had no friends.

"Angie knows a wise woman," Loki said. "Who

knows a wiser woman, who knows an even wiser woman, who…"

"And at the end of all those many wise women is…?"

"I don't know," Loki admitted. "Probably someone very old. They say age brings wisdom."

So far, age had brought Odin nose hair and an awful lot of pointless work.

"How come there are not any wise men?"

Loki shrugged. "There might be. When I see Angie, we don't talk about other men. Not until I'm tied up, at least." His shoulders drooped a bit. "Shall we smoothly change the subject? How's Heimdall's gentleman friend doing? Has Mr. Neat-o introduced him to you yet?"

Odin immediately regretted having asked about wise men.

This entire conversation shouldn't be happening in the first place. Why would Odin need advice from a whole chain of progressively older and wiser women, and potentially a man here and there? All of them *should* know less. Odin was the oldest person in the Nine Worlds. He'd created them all, except for the ones that had been created by his brothers, which would suggest that his brothers might have been wiser than Odin, which also required switching trains of thought at the nearest station.

Unfortunately, it looked as if he'd gotten stuck in the Circle Line.

The Norns had given him runes. Frigg had explained how to make doors and windows, before she'd stopped explaining anything. People had come up with axes, knives, spears. Vili-Loki knew about "making a living." Vé had figured out how Odin felt about the thought that someone had cut a hole in Audhumla in order to wear her, so he'd spread misinformation that Odin craved blood and death. What had Odin done? Invented spiders when Frigg craved miniskirts. Maybe that was why she'd stopped talking to him, even when he'd tried to hand her gold and jewels... *surely* she hadn't found out about Jörd, or, much worse, Madame A?!

"Loki, my dear and greatly valued blood b-brother," said Odin, his voice nearly not trembling. "Why don't you go and visit Angie, ask her about all those wise women? I'll write you a note with my apologies. I mean, I'll write her a note and you'll deliver it. Uh, I'll teach you how to read runes very soon, but it will say that I apologise and will visit, um, at the earliest opportunity. And here's gold and the jewel. Is this right?"

"Smaller gold," Loki specified, staring at the brick. "Gold is valuable because there's so little of it. Gold, silver... you can get anything for gold and silver. This" – he nodded towards the brick – "would cause inflation and trust me, you don't want that."

Odin didn't know what inflation was and wouldn't until either he saw it, or Frigg explained it to him. Nevertheless, he nodded sagely. "And the diamond?"

"She wouldn't know what to do with it. Even I don't know what to do with it. Can you wear this on your finger?"

"Why would anyone wear that on their fingers? It's enormous."

"Exactly," Loki said. "Necklaces. Bracelets. Earrings. Rings. Any of those ring a bell?"

"...," Odin semi-nodded.

"Sigh," Loki semi-smirked. "We'll start small, so as not to overheat the economy."

"Oh yes," Odin nodded, "one must never overheat the economy." *It must be some sort of soup*, he thought.

"Anyway, it's important to approach women – even Angie – with smaller gifts first, or they won't be impressed by the bigger ones."

"How do you know all that?" Odin accidentally blurted out.

"I might not know what women think," Loki said, "the mysterious creatures that they are. I know what they desire, though."

"And what is that?"

"Me. I mean, jewellery and someone who nods every now and then when they talk. Have you ever tried being quiet when you're with Frigg?"

"Oooh," said Odin.

In ashamed silence he created jewellery under the instructions of Loki, nodding every now and then as Loki talked. The results were rather crude. His mind confirmed each of them was what it was meant to be. A ring, a necklace, a pair of earrings, and a pink diamond tiara.

"Thanks for these," Loki said without any warning, put the tiara on his head, grabbed the rest and departed. Odin barely managed to squeeze in another silent nod before the door quietly shut after him.

Oh no, he thought, he had forgotten about the note. It didn't matter, since Loki would definitely put in a good word for him. He would definitely pass along Odin's greetings and apologies. Even though he'd wanted to keep Angie from seeing other men. One of whom was Odin. Surely, Loki wouldn't neglect to mention that the gold and the jewels had come from someone else. Otherwise it would mean that Loki had tricked Odin. That Odin had blindly trusted his undead brother, who had proven repeatedly that his relationship with truth and honesty was more of passing acquaintance than everlasting love. Which was...

"FML!"

...unwise.

The All-Father gave up.

"TELL ME ABOUT, uh... the... gentleman friend of yours."

"Sir Mímir?" Heimdall checked.

Rather flushed, Odin nodded wordlessly, wondering how Heimdall's secret had somehow become his.

"Old-school leatherman," said the Sentinel, slightly salivating. "Hotter than Müspelheim. Bearded, hairy-chested..."

"Not that," Odin interrupted, his cheeks burning. "You told me he knows...wise things. Loki said there was a wise woman somewhere, and another, even wiser, and another, and so on. Would S – Mímir be able to direct me to the wisest one?"

"Even better, All-Father. I hear – literally – that Sir Mímir is the wisest of all creatures big and small."

Odin pondered over that for a bit. "How small?" he finally asked.

"Ah," said Heimdall, "not very. Quite large, actually. Sizeable. Huge."

"TMI!" Odin cried.

"I mean his size! No, no, I mean... his *height*. He's very tall. He is one of the ancient – I mean, your age – I mean, uh, old – I mean..."

"Stop *meaning*."

"He is a jötunn," Heimdall muttered. "An actual giant."

"A hairy, giant leatherman is the wisest of all women?"

"I know that sounds strange. I don't understand it either. One sip from his horn would change that, but he says I'm not ready..."

"..."

"Okay, technically it's my horn I'd have to sip from..."

"...!?"

"Sir Daddy Mímir holds it for, um, safekeeping. Only those he deems worthy can sip from the well of wis—"

"What do you mean?" the All-Father groaned. "How does he keep your...*horn* for...*safekeeping?*" The imagery-caused ellipses kept getting stuck in his throat. He needed a drink, badly, to swallow them all... a drink of water, his thoughts interrupted for clarity... water that came from...*other* sources... not from Heimdall's horn... the very presence of which threatened to turn this book into adult entertainment.

"He likes one-of-a-kind gifts," Heimdall said. "There's no other horn quite like mine, but I assure you he's worth it. Both Sir Mímir and the well he is guarding, completely filled with wis—"

"I can't take any more double entendres!"

"What? Those are not double entendres. It's a well. With special water in it. Which he drinks from my Gjallarhorn. The one that makes enough noise to wake everyone in the Nine Worlds. Sir is very pleased with it." Heimdall's eyes saddened. "I don't know why I can't sip from my own horn. He says it would be unfair towards me. I'm not wise enough to understand why."

"You gave Gjallarhorn to Sir" – Odin spat as quickly as possible, but it was too late, the word had already escaped his mouth and now heckled him openly – "Daddy..."

"You must gain Sir Mímir's favour before you can call him Daddy. Then..."

"I, the All-Father, must gain his favour to call him Daddy?!"

Heimdall swallowed and said nothing.

"That swallow was a double entendre," said Odin accusingly. "I could see. Do I look like a fool?"

"Listen, All-Father," Heimdall hissed, "do you want to drink from his well or not?"

ODIN REPEATED the instructions in his mind. He had to head under the roots of the Tree, in the direction of Jötunheim, turn left at the sign saying "MIMIR'S WELL," and look for a bearded, hairy-chested, giant leatherman. The rest was rather unclear. Heimdall insisted that he'd know what to do, though. Odin pushed aside two nagging thoughts. The first reminded him that the last time he'd followed his intuition he'd ended up with a spear in his side. The other one pointed out that Heimdall didn't specify which "he" would know. The thoughts had proven to be very aside-pushable, though. Because the Sentinel of Ásgard, the Mightiest of Kissers, the Golden-Skinned White-Clad Hottie McSizzling seemed to salivate a bit every time he uttered the word "leatherman," as if it came from a very moist language.

Odin completely, definitely, and utterly had no interest whatsoever at all in whatever caused the extra-

neous production of bodily fluids. Totally. It was just
that when he mentioned a feather duster for no particular reason, Heimdall's eyes slightly glazed. With
boredom.

Odin felt a bit warm and somewhat tingly. There was
research to be done. Once he acquired the wisdom,
whether by means of research or not, he'd find ways to:

1) keep Loki quiet by allowing Angie to retire from
the making a living;

2) unmute Frigg by... to be confirmed;

3) Heimdall's eyes narrowed slightly at Odin's
cunning stunt as the All-Father listed the third purpose
as "...and everything else." The holy number *was* three,
though. Nobody, not even a leatherman, could refute
that.

Odin's mind and other bits couldn't wait to find out
what a "leatherman" was.

It was a truth universally acknowledged that a man
in possession of leather was a leatherman. Heimdall kept
insisting, though, that there was an additional *je ne sais
quoi* that invisibly fit between those two words. Odin
knew men, but didn't know leather. Heimdall's explanations were of the "you know it when you see it" variety.
That was already Odin's mind's modus operandi. Once
it turned out that leather made the most saliva-worthy
boots, another reason for the trip had been found. Frigg
might have been secretly lusting after leather boots. The
longer he thought about it, the clearer it was becoming
that he was actually heading towards the well of wisdom
solely to make Frigg, Loki, and Heimdall happy. Odin's
selflessness was second only to his modesty.

Okay, fine, there was one more purpose. Mímir
needed a lesson. The All-Father would not call him

"Daddy" regardless of how wise and leathery Mímir was. In order to provide that lesson, Odin needed to drink from the well first. Mímir liked unique, handcrafted gifts, apparently. Odin had nothing but Odin's Special Stick Which Was In Urgent Need Of Renaming, and he'd rather poke his eye out than give it away, for safekeeping or not. It was irreplaceable.

Therefore, he could only rely on his masculine wiles.

In order to show "Daddy" how little he cared, Odin went through his entire wardrobe four times to pick some random old rags. A long, blue cloak with nothing underneath, which had the desired effect with some people he had previously researched, coupled with brown linen trousers, which were a bit on the tight side. (Mostly on the left.) Since underwear was not invented yet, the trousers also chafed a bit in the spots that should never be chafed. It was good to remove them as quickly as possible for health reasons. Not that he intended to do that. Titillating, yet aloof, until he got what he wanted in the first place, which would allow to figure him out what he wanted in the places that followed.

The All-Father was painfully aware that he had no chance to outshine golden-skinned Heimdall clad in white. Nevertheless, the All-Father was *the* All-Father, while Heimdall was his...employee. The trousers and the cloak, effortless and casual, if a bit tight (mostly on the left). And Odin's divine (literally) powers of persuasion.

With his head filled with fuzzy thoughts of what sort of present Sir Mímir would consider one-of-a-kind-enough and if a vase would do, Odin opened the door and came face to face with Frigg. She didn't even look like she had been about to knock. It was uncanny – as if she could predict what he intended to do.

"Ah, ahaha, FML, good morning," Odin said nervously, pulling his cloak to cover as much of himself as possible. "I mean, good afternoon. Good all day in general. How are you doing, my beloved?"

Silence.

"I'm just going for a walk."

Frigg slowly shook her head.

"Well," said Odin, wishing he'd only allowed his wife to know select parts of the future. Selected by him. "It's more of a research trip. For scientific reasons... like... like leather boots. For you. And, and wisdom. For the good of the Universe. Everyone wins."

Frigg slowly raised her hand and covered one eye.

"You are weird!" Odin erupted. "You are too weird! You freak me out! You don't talk, you – you do whatever that is, how am I supposed to understand? I have a Sir Daddy waiting for me to sip some wisdom from his horn, and I am doing it all for you, so we can make sweet, sweet love as you squeal with happiness!"

Frigg spread her hands and let out a soundless sigh before departing, still shaking her head.

"You know what?" Odin yelled after her. "I'm not talking to you either! I'm gravely offended! Now I told her," he muttered to himself when Frigg failed to react. "Now she will understand who is in charge here."

The answer was Sir Daddy Mímir, of course.

"Good day," Odin said. "Is this the – the Sir..."

The man turned abruptly towards Odin. "Who are you?" Mímir looked exactly how Heimdall described him, only worse, as in better. Because now Odin knew what a leatherman was.

"I," said Odin, seductively showing one tightly clad leg, "am *the* All-Father."

"Ah, that one," Mímir said, clearly losing interest. "My boy warned you might want to pester me. Leave me alone, Odin."

"It's the All-Father to you! What boy?!"

"Heimdall. Who else? I know about everything that happens in Ásgard and Midgard."

"That gossip," Odin gasped.

"About everything important," Mímir specified, dropping what seemed to be a small ball with two straps on the sides, probably useful for some sort of game. "My life's too busy for unnecessary detail."

"Isn't all you do guarding this alleged well of wisdom?"

"Oh," said Mímir, smiling to himself, "absolutely not. Didn't Heimdall tell you you'll be dealing with a wise dom?"

"Wise dom?! I thought he was saying 'wisdom' with strange accent!"

The man shrugged.

"You *are* Mímir?" Odin checked, in case there were multiple wells, guarded by crowds of bearded, hairy-chested leathermen... was that a piercing?!

"Sir Mímir, to you."

Odin withdrew his leg, which had begun to tingle. It was time to drop the masculine wiles and move to masculine threats. "If you don't give me the respect I deserve, you'll be called Sir A-Bloody-Stain a blink from now."

"I live in constant terror of that happening," said

Mímir. "Look at me shaking in fear. We both know I've got what you need, and you are a little spoiled brat who's gagging to get it."

"…," Odin answered.

Mímir sighed. "You're entirely not my type. I have standards, All-Father. And I don't like the sort of attitude you're giving me. What have you brought me? Is that a vase? Do I look like someone who needs a vase?"

"…?"

"Heimdall brought me Gjallarhorn," Mímir demonstrated. "He only gets to touch it now when I allow it. There is no other horn like his in the Universe. You claim to be more important than Heimdall. Why would I let you get away with a vase? It doesn't even have flowers or water in it."

"…water," Odin remembered, waking up from a trance. He just figured out what game the ball with the straps was for. "Yes. That." He pointed at the well. "As an All-Father I deserve to drink it. I, uh, created it."

Mímir shrugged. "Then create some more."

Odin hadn't created water of any sort. Vili had. Odin also definitely hadn't created wells. He could have, however, and Mímir couldn't prove that he hadn't, unless… unless Mímir had created wells. All Odin got out of this lie was a guilty conscience and yet more proof that he needed to drink some water of wisdom. He'd painted himself into a corner, forgetting to create paint before doing so.

Since Odin was already feeling very sorry for himself, he might as well try pity. "I'm so very old, as old as the Universe itself. And frail," he said, leaning heavily on Odin's Special Stick Which Was In Urgent Need Of Renaming. "And thirsty. Could I just have a bit to drink before I go on my way to continue All-Fathering? I won't bother you again."

Mímir looked at him curiously. "I drank this water."

This was most probably supposed to explain something.

"You didn't."

"Very good observation," Odin accidentally said.

"Therefore it doesn't matter what you do. You can't outwit me. You can't seduce me. You can kill me, I don't deny it, then deal with the consequences of knowing absolutely anybody will be able to drink from this well. Including your enemies."

"I could... I could... tie you up for just a while..."

Mímir flashed his teeth in a smile. "I do the tying up around here. From now on, finish every sentence with 'Sir' if you want me to answer. Don't forget who's the boy and who's the dom."

"Eh... what is a dom, s-s-sir?"

"Would you like me to demonstrate or explain, boy?"

For some reason, Odin's tight trousers became even tighter, although only on the left. It was getting a bit painful.

"I'm bored," Mímir said, sitting on a tree trunk, not offering a seat to Odin. "You're not my type. You've got a bratty attitude. You haven't brought me anything interesting. Come back when..."

"Oh no, you won't," barked Odin. "I am the Creator. The All-Father. I probably created you, although now I wish I hadn't. I'm completely not interested in your black leather. Or that ball with the straps. Or..." His words died out when Mímir reached for another item and gently slapped his own leg with it. "...," Odin finished, deciding to have the left side of his trousers altered as soon as possible, ideally right now. Madame A would have killed, although probably only a mosquito and even that lovingly, to see that... professional-looking item. "I – I – I'd just like some water, maybe, yes, please, sir. Then I'll leave you in peace, sir."

Mímir's eyebrows wandered up his forehead. "Well, well, if this isn't the All-Father calling me sir after all."

Odin's knees did that thing knees always did in books, namely turned into jelly, at the thought of how hard Heimdall had to be laughing right now.

"Nobody can hear us," Mímir said, as if guessing the Mostly-All-Father's thoughts. "This place is both in none of the Nine Worlds and in all of them at once. I like your attitude adjustment, boy. Now, what can you offer me that I don't already have?"

"Ehhh... my cloak?"

"Do I look like I need a cloak?"

"I don't have anything with me... I could bring you something? What do you need?"

Sir Daddy stretched comfortably and faked a yawn. "I have everything I need."

"Why do you want me to give you things then?!"

"Sir," Mímir said. "Why do you want me to give you things then, sir. Because I can. I like surprise gifts the most. The more unique and valuable – to you – the gift, the more you can expect from me."

Odin moved his gaze from the thigh-slappy leather item to the tight leather of Mímir's trousers, then to his hairy chest emerging from the opening of his leather jacket, then to Mímir's coolly blue eyes, shaded by the leather Village People style hat, but lit with curiosity and something more. Odin had seen that expression before, on Heimdall's face. The challenge to be challenged.

Mímir had a good point when it came to Odin's enemies, also known as brothers, drinking from this well if it were unguarded. If someone was going to get tied up here, it *had* to be Odin. Otherwise, Mímir wouldn't be strong enough to guard the well, and if it truly was a well of wisdom, the wise dom knew that. Leaving now would mean that the All-Father failed to get what he wanted from a "Sir Daddy." Was it wiser, from the PR point of view, to give Mímir that something, or to not give him anything? Which of those made the All-Father look like a winner of the not-quite-duel? Odin wouldn't know until it was over. Mímir did, though.

What *was* there to do? In order to re-create the water of wise dom, he would first need to try it to know what it was. Alternatively, he could become an even wiser dom... What made a dom a dom, though? It wasn't the beard, the silly hat, not even the thigh-slappy thingy. Sir Mímir knew – and he knew that he knew. He was surrounded by something like self-assured serenity. He didn't need to be arrogant, bark orders, threaten. Mímir truly didn't need anything. Even if Heimdall were willing to talk about what he and the wise dom...*performed* together, even if Odin attempted to practise the practice, he could still only clumsily attempt to learn something at which Mímir was, somehow, a master.

Perhaps that was it. A dom was someone who was a dom. A master was someone who was a master. The All-Father was someone who was desperate. An attempt to steal the well would cause the water to spill out. Producing a... a very long, short pipe that he could use at night to suck out some water without making noise would probably give Mímir a good laugh. It wasn't realistic. It just wasn't realistic. Mímir spoke the truth – he couldn't be outwitted.

"How bad do you want it?" asked Mímir slowly.

Defeated, Odin just sat on the ground. "Very bad."

"How very bad?"

Odin spread his arms as wide as he could. "This very bad."

"Hum," Mímir said. "That looks very bad indeed. You are the All-Father, who can create anything and everything. Give me something you can't create."

Odin's first thought was "the water of wise dom" which was further evidence that he needed some of it.

"When you drink this water, you will see everything. You will know and understand everything and everyone."

"Even my wife? A-asking for a friend."

Mímir rolled his eyes. "Everyone. You will be able to look at someone, like I am looking at you now, and know what they want and how badly. You'll be able to manipulate, cheat, steal anything from anyone. Do you think I couldn't tell what you were thinking about when you were glancing at that well? Or at my trousers?"

Odin had, indeed, thought so.

"I don't sleep," Mímir said shortly. "I know too much to sleep. That will be your fate as well. You don't understand this right now, but the reason why I haven't granted Heimdall a drop of this water is that I care for him more than anyone in the Nine. It's the sort of pain I wouldn't inflict on my worst enemies. I took his horn from him so that he doesn't use it too soon or too often."

"For sipping?"

Mímir rolled his eyes. "You can't undo this. Once you

have the wisdom, you can never stop having it. If you allow yourself to stop and think about it, it will crush you. You must constantly keep yourself distracted."

Odin puffed up. "Nothing can crush me. I am *the* All-Father."

"And how do we finish that sentence if we want it to be heard?"

"Uh. Sorry, sir. I am *the* All-Father, sir."

"Do I really have to keep explaining what I mean?"

"Not at all. Just tell me what you want for some of this water, sir." Odin was salivating now, imagining what wisdom would taste like. Kombucha? Probably kombucha.

"Give me something you can't create," Mímir said. "Let me know when you've finished thinking. Or give up. I advise the latter."

"I can create everything. That's the point of being an All-Father. Sometimes I don't know what that something is, but once I do, I can create it. So I only can't create things I don't know I can create... or don't understand. If you could give me a bit of your water, perhaps..."

"Can you create yourself?"

Odin huffed. "Of course not. Then there would be two and I won't have that." Suddenly, he stiffened in a way that did not affect the seams of his trousers. "Have you met someone named Vé... or Loki?"

Mímir grinned. "No, I haven't. Should I?"

"No, never, not even once, absolutely. They are not to be trusted. Liars, thieves, killers..."

"Exactly like you, then," Mímir summarised. "Give me something so valuable to you that they can't outbid you."

Odin stared into space, thinking so hard his forehead began to heat up. Loki was a question mark. If Odin could create something, though, Vé could make it bigger and more impressive. The only thing that Odin owned that Vé couldn't was...

...Odin's body.

If Odin could sacrifice all of himself to himself two stories ago, he could just as well give Mímir *one* body part to avoid doing that sort of stupid thing again.

Something else has to volunteer this time, the lung said. *Not my turn.*

Dumbo, the liver huffed. *He can't get you out from inside his rib cage anyway. Same as me. I say a hand.*

Odin looked at his hands. Both of them were quite useful. Very, in fact. He could even call them handy, he thought. He was at least already wise enough to know not to try to impress a wise dom with that failure of a joke. Feet were very useful for doing things such as walking. Nothing that hid inside All-Father's trousers was up for negotiation.

There were really only two things that Odin could spare. Ears and eyes. Ears were definitely more useful, especially when he put on hats. Without an ear, the hat would slide off, which would look ridiculous. "An eye," he said. "I will give you an eye."

Mímir actually gasped. "You can't be serious."

"I have two of those," Odin shrugged.

"You will give me your *eye* to get the water?"

"Well," Odin said, "this better be really good water. Will it teach me how to be a dom?"

"I can teach you..." Mímir's small, shaky voice belied his dom-ness. Strangely, he seemed to have shrunk inside his shiny jacket. "Doing this will only cause you twice as much pain. I – I can't agree. It's way too much. This water isn't worth it, trust me. You can always come to me. I'll answer any question. For free." He licked his lips nervously and for some reason Odin thought of Madame A explaining how she never wanted to actually *hurt* anyone.

"Ah," he said, ignoring the thought. "This was a lie. You gave me a riddle, I found an answer, now you're backpedalling. This water is fake news, isn't it?"

"It's as real as it gets," Mímir, who didn't seem like much of a sir now, muttered.

"Maybe it never gets very real," Odin said, as if to himself. "All there is to wise domming is a hairy chest and the thigh-slappy thing, and this here Mímir is a liar…"

"I am not a liar!"

"…who might as well die, since this water is worthless, therefore there is no need to guard it."

"I am not a liar," Mímir repeated through clenched teeth. "I am not cruel either. You're testing my patience, though."

Odin snorted. "An All-Father's eye seems to be worth more than some rank water that hasn't even been independently assessed. I think that I should drink some of it *first*, then consider whether…"

Mímir crossed his arms on his chest. Somehow, even though he was sitting, he towered over the standing Odin.

"So, since you've said the water alone is not worth it, I want more for my eye. Swear me an oath that you will never, ever give a single drop to either of my brothers."

"Vé and Loki, I assume."

"How do you know?"

"Do you remember what you said about two pages ago?"

"Oh. That. Yes. Uhh... if you could also maybe not tell Loki that he is my brother... so that would be three things. Water for me, no water for them, and no brothers for Loki."

Mímir sighed. "All-Father. Let me try one more time. I don't guard this well so that nobody else can obtain wisdom, I guard it so that nobody else has to live with it. I'm not guarding the well from you, but protecting you from the water..."

"I might not be wise, but I'm not stupid," Odin spoke. Clouds covered the sky and a cold wind blew leaves in Mímir's face. Covering his eyes with his arm, the man – after all, nothing more than that – let out a small sound. The whole thing had been an act, Odin thought, amused. Being a dom meant being good at theatrics. "I can see you don't want to share it," he rumbled further. "You asked for a gift I can't create; I am offering one. Your alternative is death. As much as I care for Heimdall, there's only ever going to be one Daddy. I mean, All-Father. Water for me, no water for them, no brothers for Loki – or no Mímir. Choose. Wisely." A thunderclap punctuated each sentence. The entire speech ended with a queer natural phenomenon, the aural expression of which was best described as a "ba-dum-tss."

As the wind calmed down and the clouds in the sky slowly dispersed, Mímir's arm dropped, revealing a face that looked as if it was chiselled in irate stone. "I will swear an oath," he said. "I will guard the water from your brothers with my own body until the day I die. You may drink as much as you want, you may bathe in it for all I care. As for Loki, he's an orphan, completely devoid of family members including cousins twice removed. Good enough?" There were no thunderclaps to replace his punctuation marks. Just the sort of fury that would make Tyson squeal and hide in the nearest literal rabbit hole. "What do I swear on? Just" – he gestured – "generally?"

Odin FML-ed in the general direction of the Norns. This would have been so much easier if future happened first. "You must swear on a – a – Odin's Special Stick."

That took Mímir aback. "Is that an offer or a challenge?"

Odin presented the inconspicuous piece of wood he leaned on even when the text insisted both of his hands were busy with something else. He'd sleep with it if that didn't seem offensive to Frigg. It was easier for him to offer an eye – he had a spare one – than to offer up Odin's Special Stick, Despite It Being In Urgent Need Of Renaming. It was a branch that fell off Yggdrasil, one he picked a long, long time ago in Midgard as he was running away... relocating from Ask and Embla. Odin's Special Stick had seen the creation. It might have even seen what had happened before it. Odin had put some of his strongest magic into reinforcing it, so that it could never be broken. Nor could any oath be sworn on it.

Very proud of himself, as he came up with all that at a moment's notice, he repeated it to Mímir.

"I'm not swearing an oath on 'Odin's Special Stick'. Even Heimdall's Big Horn has a real name, Gjallarhorn."

"Staff," Odin corrected himself. "It's not a 'stick', it's a 'staff'. For more gravitas. Do you know what that is? Oh, you do," he quickly said, assessing Mímir's grimace, feeling the nervousness return. "Haha, silly me. Okay.

Let's make sure I am not silly anymore. Left or right?
No, the oath first. On Odin's Staff."

Mímir took off his leather hat and massaged his
temples. "I'm only doing this because you're an asshole,"
he said. "In return for your eye, I shall never share this
water with your brothers, Vé and Loki. I shall never tell
Loki he is your brother. And you can drink a full horn"
– he produced one, a truly imposing object, the size of
which ensured that Odin would have more than enough
– "of the water from my well. Any time you like."

"That's nice!"

"It isn't. You will not want to. It's an easy oath for me
to make. So, this is my oath. And I am making it. Freely.
As in, not forced. On your staff, imaginatively named
'Odin's Staff' for more gravitas. Is that enough for you?"

"Why, yes, more than." Odin knew he was being
mocked. Odin's Staff was No Longer In Urgent Need Of
Renaming, though, and that was what mattered. Oh, and
the oath, too. "Cheers, thanks a lot. Left or right?"

"You pick," said Mímir, handing Odin an item.

Odin examined the thing curiously. It was shiny. A
large part of it was a handle, ending with something
vaguely ovoid, only flatter. It looked as if it was made for
carrying eggs, in case one suffered from egg phobia and
didn't want to touch them with their hands. "What is
this?"

"It's a spoon," said Mímir.

"It's very pretty."

"Thank you. Now take your eye out with it."

"Ah, of course," said Odin.

"Indeed, indeed," said Odin.

"I say," said Odin.

"What an ingenious invention," said Odin.

Mímir said nothing.

Goodbye, Odin thought to his left eye. Its reaction was unexpectedly robust, as it rolled itself so hard that Odin saw his brain. *Well, I suppose you're the one that's going,* Odin thought to his right eye. It decided to defend itself by itching and producing tears. That one was the stupider eye, Odin decided. What kind of defence was that?

Nevertheless...

In a blink, more or less literally, he would be drinking from the well of wisdom. A stupid eye would wisen. The sight of his own brain was something Odin never wanted to experience again. The left eye was dangerous. It had to go.

It felt rude, though. The eye was born inside Odin's skull, spent its entire life in its warmth and relative safety.

Or maybe Odin was just stalling a bit.

The hand holding the spoon dropped and both his eyes sighed in relieved unison.

"So you have seen the light after all," said Mímir. He looked relieved. "Two thirds of my oath stands. Firstly, your brothers won't get any of the water either. I couldn't live with myself if I knew I did that to someone. Seco—"

Odin attacked the left eye before it had a chance to act. As the right one shuddered in horror, Odin nearly attempted to pat it on the back. *Don't worry,* he thought, *I need you twice as much now, you're safe...* "I still see out of it! I see an ant! It's crawling on me! I mean, on my eye!"

Mímir's face was green as he fanned himself with a leather handkerchief. "You didn't just do that. Tell me my eyes are deceiving me."

"It's here!" Odin cried. "In the sand! With ants!" Picking it up between his fingers sent a wave of horrid pain through All-Father's skull, and trying to shake the sand off gave him a bouncy headache. "What do you want to do with it?"

"Nothing!" Mímir cried. "You weren't supposed to do it! You were supposed to chicken out at the last moment! Why? Why did you do that?"

"You asked!"

"How stupid was that?!"

"Very," said Odin. The eye was looking at the place where it used to dwell. It was not at all pleased with the sudden expulsion. "Clearly, I need some wise water... Aha!" Before Mímir had a chance to move, Odin threw the eye inside the well. It headed towards the bottom that didn't seem to exist, now surrounded by darkness and coolness. Both the eye and Odin's head were now free from their aches.

"I'm not drinking that water ever again," Mímir croaked.

"So it's all mine? Excellent. Will you be a darling and pass me that horn, sir?"

Gjallarhorn, filled with the water, was heavy. Odin ignored Mímir's weak pleas interspersed with retching. What? So there was a bit of blood. He'd wash it off with the water of wisdom. Once he drank some. He could *bathe* in it. It was so hard to decide what to do with all those possibilities. With his right eye, Odin admired Gjallarhorn. It was true – Heimdall's horn was thick and huge. No wonder Mímir liked holding on to it for safe-keeping...

Or maybe Odin was just stalling a bit.

He let the first drops roll over his tongue, savouring

the taste. The water of wisdom tasted of water and Odin scowled. If Sir Daddy had cheated him, he'd lose much more than an eye. Nevertheless, Odin actually was thirsty, so he swallowed greedily and was about to gulp more, when–

The horn fell to the ground, water spilling all over Odin's feet.

"That was dumb," Odin said in disbelief.

"You don't say. Now I'll be surrounded by the wisest ants and grass in the Nine... Sit down, All-Father. Do you need...something?"

Odin just shook his head. A droplet of blood landed on Mímir's face, making Sir Daddy shudder. Odin's right eye registered the sight without much interest. There would be more blood.

Wisdom was the most horrible thing Odin had ever experienced and that was including the time he once accidentally ate a bit of celery. Which, he now understood, was alive. Same as grass. Veganism was murder too, only quieter. The number one cause of death was life.

"There will be death," Odin said flatly. "So much death. Battles, wars, bigger wars."

Mímir just nodded.

"What have we done...?"

"You created greed," said Mímir. "Greed never ends..."

"...until everything ends," Odin finished for him, hiding his face in his hands, barely avoiding hiding his index finger in his eye socket. "It's not just greed. Pride, lust, anger, envy, gluttony, sloth. Oh, that reminds me to create sloths."

"What's the point?" Mímir asked. "They'll end, too."

"If I stop doing things, I'll have to – to think. I have to do *something*. What have I done... how do you live with this?"

"Do you know what is the first thing I do when Heimdall comes here? I put wax in his ears. Because I may not know what it feels like to constantly hear everything, but I can imagine it. So can you, now. Helping him distracts me, in turn. When none of my boys are around... trust me, one night every moon turn is not enough... I work on new ideas."

"I don't want to be a wise dom," Odin mumbled. His head was so full it was about to explode. He wished it would. "I don't want to be a wise anything. I don't want to understand. I should have listened to you."

"Do you understand Frigg now?"

"She knows, too." Odin's shoulders dropped. He felt older and older. Every single blink brought him closer to his own death... he gasped. "She knows what, when, where, and how. She knew I'd lose my eye. Mímir... Who are you – or what? You are not just a muscled jötunn who happened to walk into this spot and have a drink of...this."

"I don't know what I am. One day, a long time ago, I just began to exist. I sat up, naked, as if waking up from a dream that wasn't."

Odin's throat tightened.

"I walked around a bit, created a few things..."

Odin's throat began to list the benefits of self-asphyxiation.

"The well was already here. I didn't know what or why it was, I still don't. It had water in it, I was thirsty, so I drank from it. The understanding came slowly, as I watched you and your brothers. Everything you've done, created, destroyed had consequences, and those consequences will have consequences. Those ants," Mímir pointed at the insects indistinctly chattering between each other about algebra and calculus, "will have consequences."

"I knew that. I thought I knew that. But I thought if you made a list long enough, a diagram big enough… you could prevent it."

"You could have, until you created people. And cats," Mímir added after a brief pause, "but cats don't organise themselves to kill other cats because of pride, lust, greed. People will never stop until there's nothing left. Until everything has ended."

Both of them fell silent.

"No," Odin suddenly said. "I won't let this happen."

"You can't not let it happen. It's happening as we speak. The end is nigh. We just don't know how nigh."

"I'll fix it. I'll find a way. I'll start small and move up, or I'll start high and move down. I'll spend days and nights…" Odin's hair was slowly turning white, skin – pale. "It's better to know than to not know. Now I can change it. I will. I must."

"Nothing is worse than wisdom," said Mímir softly. "Nothing. No suffering, because you are wise enough to know the longer you live, the more you will suffer. And the end will come when your suffering is so great you can no longer withstand it."

"I disagree," Odin said. "I am the All-Father. I am the wisest, except perhaps for you and those ants. I caused all this. I will find a way to revert it."

"All-Father, there is no way."

"My wife, Frigg, can foretell the future. Once she tells me, I'll find a way to avoid it."

"What if she doesn't tell you? Heimdall tells me she doesn't speak."

"Heimdall should stick his nose in… whatever you call this thing. I'll ask again and again and again. I have all of the time in the Universe, literally. She will break, eventually."

"You want to 'break' your own wife?"

"I'll break anything and anyone," Odin said slowly, "to prove you wrong."

"You and what army?"

"Army of the dead. If Loki can make it back, so can others, and I'll pick the ones I need. Once they're dead, they can't die any further, can they?"

"All-Father…"

Odin smirked, the wrinkles around his lips deepening. "I was too stupid to know that I was right. You need to start wars to end them. Sacrifice lives to save them."

"This isn't…"

"Frigg will tell me what I need to know," Odin said coldly. The knuckles of his bony hand, gripping the staff firmly, whitened. "The only way to stop a great army is to have an even greater army. I will know what and when to expect. I will be there."

"All-Father…"

"The most powerful will die, so later they can save the living."

"That can't happen!" Mímir erupted. "When you stir wars, they'll lead to bigger wars. The more deadly weapons one side uses, the worse the other will invent."

"Exactly," Odin nodded. "I'll lead the leaders. I'll outwit the wittiest. And I'll always have the best, the strongest, the hardest."

"Why?"

"Because otherwise everything will end," Odin hissed. "Haven't we established that? If you have no faith in happy endings, you end up like Frigg, lie down and say nothing, wait for the inevitable. What I'm saying is that there is no such thing as inevitable when you have control."

"You can never control greed...!"

Odin snorted. "You can offer more and feed bigger greed. My army won't be burdened by limits. I don't need you or Madame A in it, because you have scruples. My army won't have scruples. I like you, but if I decide you need to die, you'll die."

"That's honest," said Mímir weakly.

"Look at me."

Mímir inhaled sharply. In the line of wiser and older women, and sometimes leathermen, Odin took his place. His hair and beard were no longer silver, but grey. The bloodied hole where his eye used to be disappeared, hidden in darkness of shadow no light could penetrate. The other eye shone red, reflecting fire that wasn't there. Odin's face was lined and creased, forehead and eyebrows wrinkled in calculating concentration. He no longer needed to prove anything. The All-Father was the wisest and the eldest now, as things were always meant to be, restoring balance in the Universe.

Suddenly, the All-Father's white teeth flashed in a grin. "Honesty is a weakness, Mímir. If there's a better disguise than that of a man too old and frail to walk, I don't know it. FML! No wonder you need something to take your mind off this stuff. This is why I'll drink. Eating is a weakness."

Mímir's eyes opened wide.

"FML doesn't really mean 'Frigg, My Love,' does it,"

Odin continued, the grin fading. "Because love, too, is a weakness."

"That isn't funny," Mímir said.

"Was it ever meant to be?"

"This *book* was meant to be funny."

Odin shrugged. "There will be a sequel or two. More, if I deem them necessary. Once I'm done with the author, his words will live on as another one takes his place to hone them further. I'll hand the sharpest pens to the greediest writers. They'll compete, cheat, stab each other in the back, fuelled by self-doubt. Friends will betray friends, brothers kill their fathers, with pen, sword, lies. Honour, honesty, generosity? Weaknesses. There *will* be a happy ever after."

"How can it be happy if it has no love in it? No kindness, no honour? What do you intend to rule over, a pile of smug ashes?"

"You're not listening, Mímir. My army will ensure the pile of ashes never happens. Ásgard will never fall. I will never fall."

"You'll sit on your throne surrounded by the dead," said Mímir. "Indeed. No wonder you'll drink. Er. What? This water?"

"Frigg will tell me," Odin said. "How do you find out what women think? You ask and listen. If she doesn't answer, I'll ask and listen again. And again. And again. She'll even know exactly when she'll give in."

"This is no life, if you ask me," Mímir muttered, picking up the horn and shaking out ants together with what they were busy with.

"I won't," Odin assured him. "What – what is this? Were they...making something?"

Mímir knelt, then bent to take a close look.

The largest of the ants stood in a tight formation. Each of them held either a grain of sand or a dark shard they'd managed to chip off the inside of the horn. A bit further, a small group wearing green jackets directed other ants towards the drops of water that still shone on the grass. Odin watched Mímir's hand extending to shake them off...

The largest, red ant raised its shard and the entire formation, as one, turned to throw their chips and grains of sand into Mímir's eye.

And just like that, the first season of the Universe ended with Mímir's "FML!"

I hope you enjoyed the book. I would be very grateful for a short comment or rating on Goodreads or any other website of your choice.

Subscribe to my newsletter at www.bjornlarssen.com/newsletter and/or follow at www.ko-fi.com/bjornlarssen for advance information, notifications about promotional events and discounts, freebies of various sorts, and anything else I can possibly come up with.

Feel free to contact me any time at bjorn@bjornlarssen.com

www.bjornlarssen.com
www.twitter.com/bjornlarssen
www.facebook.com/bjornlarssenwriter
www.ko-fi.com/bjornlarssen

ACKNOWLEDGMENTS

First and foremost, I would like to thank Odin for not having struck me dead (yet). Ragrfisk did such a great job with the cover that I was tempted to just publish the cover with nothing inside it, BECAUSE I MEAN LOOK AT IT, but I didn't think I'd get away with that. Therefore I begrudgingly produced 65,738 words, which my wonderful editor, Megan Dickman-Renard, helped turn into actual sentences.

Thank you: Lyra Wolf for telling me that the boring philosophical bits were actually the most interesting; Marian L Thorpe for being a beta reader and a wonderful friend; PL Stuart and Penni Ellington for never ending encouragement and support; and all of my ko-fi supporters for showing me that you enjoy what I do and would like more of it.

ABOUT THE AUTHOR

Bjørn Larssen is a Norse heathen made in Poland, but mostly located in a Dutch suburb, except for his heart which he lost in Iceland. Born in 1977, he self-published his first graphic novel at the age of seven in a limited edition of one, following this achievement several decades later with his first book containing multiple sentences and winning awards he didn't design himself. His writing is described as 'dark' and 'literary', but he remains incapable of taking anything seriously for more than 60 seconds.

Bjørn has a degree in mathematics and has worked as a graphic designer, a model, a bartender, and a blacksmith (not all at the same time). His hobbies include sitting by open fires, dressing like an extra from Vikings, installing operating systems, and dreaming about living in a log cabin in the north of Iceland. He owns one (1) husband and is owned by one (1) neighbourhood cat.

Made in the USA
Monee, IL
20 July 2022

10040271R00152